GW01454514

The Seven

Erin Curran

The Seven

© 2024, Erin Curran

No portion of this publication may be reproduced or transmitted without the express permission of the copyright holder.

This is a work of fiction. All characters and events portrayed in this story are products of the author's imagination. Any resemblance to actual persons, events, or locales are entirely coincidental.

No content within was produced using Artificial Intelligence.

All rights reserved.

ISBN: 978-1-3999-8461-4

Front cover image by Maria Spada

Book formatted by Nicole Hayes

Contents

Foreword

If all goes well, this book will be released on April 18th, marking the fifth anniversary of the publication of *The Seven*. A lot has happened in that time. Some of it good, and some of it bad. I'm a different person to the girl who submitted her work in 2019. For one thing, I'm now independent. Self-publication has been a saving grace for me, without it we may have lost The Seven forever.

This wooden edition, named as such for the material related to fifth anniversaries, is to tidy up some loose ends in the original script. I was young when I authored the original book, and quite naive in many respects. The story is still the same, with all the characters and plots from the original. I have simply fixed it up. A few grammar errors here, a punctuation mistake there…The changing of a title that I didn't realise sounded as bad as it did until after publication. (Readers of the original text might have an idea of what I'm talking about here.)

This is by no means a perfect version of The Seven. Nothing is ever going to be perfect, nor is any writer going to be perfect. But The Seven was my debut novel, and I will always love it regardless of its imperfections. This is just a tidier version than what was originally published. I hope you love it just as much as I do.

Finally, thank you to everyone who read the original The Seven. Without your support, I wouldn't be here today. And to the new readers who find my work through the remaster, I hope you enjoy the insanity of The Seven. I'm honoured that you have taken the time to even consider reading my book. You're all the reason I'm still a writer.

Thank you, and keep creating,
Erin

CHAPTER ONE

IT WAS SUNDAY.

There wasn't a calendar in Thursday's cell. What would the insane need one for? It was clear the doctors at the Asylum didn't believe that their patients would wish to stare at fluffy kittens hanging from branches with the month laid out below. They were probably right. Thursday wouldn't have needed a calendar, but it still would have been nice to have been asked.

Thursday couldn't tell what day it was spontaneously. She was able to sense when it was, unsurprisingly, a Thursday. From that, she would then work out the day from when she last sensed it was her namesake. She only did it sometimes, for she didn't care for the day of the week. Just a name slapped to a day so humans could keep track of things. Most of the names were derived from silly things, like how the months of the year were born of leaders and Gods and feasts. Humans were always so quick to slap labels onto things…

Thursday tapped the padded walls of her cell with her pointer finger. If she cared enough, she could blow the entire wall down. It would be awfully rude, especially since Moren Maldova was most likely sleeping next door, muttering about the future and the inevitable doom of the planet. That was the burden of being a real psychic, not one of those cheap frauds you see on television. When you're the real deal, you end up here. The back end of nowhere in a madhouse.

It was rather insulting, Thursday thought, that all residents of United Arms Asylum were branded as criminally insane. Thursday wasn't *criminal*. Well, not entirely anyway. What she had done had been fully justified, just not in the eyes of the law. Who wrote the law anyway?

Thursday threw her dark hair over her shoulder and crawled to her feet. Her cell wasn't soundproof, and it was clear that it was never intended to be so if the barred hole in the door was anything to go by. She could hear the deranged yelling of every captive on her floor. Declarations that 'the bitch deserved it!' and 'someday you'll all regret not having listened to me!' constantly filled the air around her. Thursday rolled her eyes, toeing her discarded strait jacket out of her path as she sauntered over to her cell door. The threats of the crazy were usually empty.

Pushing up onto her tiptoes, she peered out through the barred hole. The corridor was empty, as it usually would be at this time of day. Sometimes Thursday didn't even need her power to know what day it was. The wardens usually forgot to feed them on Sundays, most likely because there was a match on that just *demanded* their attention. The psychotic were viewed as … well …*psychotic*. Who would believe them if they tried to make a claim against the Asylum on grounds of undernourishment? Besides, they were 'criminals.' They'd all committed a crime of some sort. Who on the outside would care if the lawbreakers missed a meal?

Thursday pressed her face against the bars in her door. There was a rumbling outside, down the corridor and beyond the iron-wrought door that locked them all in twice. Thursday felt a warm ball grow in her stomach, and she narrowed her eyes.

No. Why now? What could they possibly want? She thought they were finally leaving her alone once and for all!

With a scowl, Thursday stepped back.

As soon as her face disappeared from the bars, an explosion ripped the iron door to pieces. An alarm so loud it could wake the dead punched gigantic holes into Thursday's eardrums, and her entire cell was drenched in dark red. The rest of the patients' yells had turned to screams, desperate pleas to be freed as whoever it was that had blown the door open passed their cells.

Thursday knew who they were coming for.

A shadow stopped in front of her door, and she heard the lock getting picked. It seemed to have been taking whoever it was too long, for someone else stepped in and seemed to blast it. The blast caused the lock to explode, and Thursday felt the ruptures of the action in her bones as the vibrations travelled through the pads on the floor.

Her cell door swung open, and the red light vanished, flooding the room in the same boring washed-out colour again. Two people were on the threshold. One on their knees and the other standing. Thursday flushed with rage, instant recognition confirming her earlier suspicions.

"What do you want?!" Thursday barked at them.

When what had to be the most beautiful woman Thursday had ever seen entered the room, her orange hair flowing down her back in a waterfall of fiery curls, Thursday almost lost her train of thought. It took the woman to be inches away from her face; porcelain skin unblemished with a cute smattering of freckles along her nose, for Thursday to remember how perplexing this situation was. Even then she was still a bit dazed.

"Thursday," the woman said, her voice not her own. "This is important. We need you to come with us."

"Oh?" Thursday said mildly, the impulse to kiss this beautiful woman strong within her gut. She felt like a spell had been cast over her head and she was in a daze. A daze that was a mixture of frilly; lustful; and confusing.

The woman nodded, her right eye suddenly flushing bright green while the left remained blue. Her skin rippled and horror washed over Thursday as she realised who it was. The next two words that came from the lips of what had once been the beautiful being chilled Thursday to her very bone.

"It's Sunday."

Twenty-four hours previous

"You know how the rhyme goes," Thursday said aloud.

She wasn't speaking to anyone in particular, as the only person in her cell was herself and she wasn't entirely sure if she had neighbours or not. There were cells flanking her own, of course, but whether they were occupied or not was another question entirely.

Thursday knew that her voice travelled and therefore hoped that maybe some of the other criminals on the wing would hear her thoughts. It wasn't like there was anything else to listen to besides the screams of the damned, so at least focusing on her conversation would give them something productive to do. Thursday was a remarkably interesting person, she had people who could confirm this, so it would be unwise of them not to grasp the opportunity to listen to her commentary.

"Monday's child is fair of face; Tuesday's child is full of grace; Wednesday's child is full of woe; Thursday's child has far to go." Thursday sighed, picking at her fingernail to unseat the grime that had gathered there from simply sitting in this abhorrent excuse for a holding cell. "Friday's child is loving and giving; Saturday's child works hard for a living; and the child born on the seventh day is fair and wise and good in every way…

"Well, it's not a rhyme. It's fact. Based on my pals and I." Thursday cringed. "I call them pals. Some of them are. We used to fight crime. Kind of like those heroes in the comics except less… ethical about our means of doing so. I was never into the good deeds nonsense, I always enjoyed chaos much more. Kind of why I ended up here, to be honest. Couldn't control that desire to ruin."

Thursday rolled to her feet, jumping a little in the process, and continued her monologue to whoever was listening. "There were seven of us, for the seven days. We're all gifted in one way or another. Not in the swotty protégée way, in the we-have-mad-supernatural-skills way. You may have heard of us, actually. Or at the very least me. I'm sure my villainous escapades are the talk of everyone around these parts"-Thursday paused for confirmation and tsked when nothing was returned but the foolish screams of the helpless cons surrounding her. "What do you idiots know anyway? I'm sure there are plenty of people who've heard of me outside of here."

It was utterly ridiculous that no one had heard of Thursday. This was an asylum for the criminally insane, this should have been heaven for her! Well, it would be heaven if there was a more interesting conversation flying around. The one-sided conversation was fun for a while-Thursday could run her mouth to the moon and back-but one would like to get a satisfactory response from the audience, who would no doubt be wowed by the fascinating stories she had to tell. If their minds hadn't run away to limbo, that was.

"Now, you may ask!" Thursday declared, sticking her finger into the air, and spinning in a circle on her heel. "'Thursday, if you're part of this amazing, gifted gang, why don't you use your ability to escape from this hellhole?' Well, the answer is easy: Why should I? I have a comfy-ish cell; the pads serve as excellent mattresses. On a good day, I get three meals a day, too. More than I got outside of here."

"Some may call me mad but…" Thursday wandered over to the door of her cell and looked out the tiny, barred window at the top. She couldn't see much outside other than the pathway that cut through the walls of cells. It would have been nice to have gotten a scenic view but, oh well. Thursday sighed, looking down at the padded cushions beneath her feet. "That's not exactly an oddity around here."

Her door was suddenly thrown open without warning, the force sending Thursday stumbling backwards. Two wardens wandered into her cell. They wore masks of metal that obscured their faces to avoid any injury that a crazed patient could cause to them.

"Are you ready to talk?" The one on the right asked.

"Oooh, about what? Are we going to exchange stories? I have plenty. One time I was out on a bender in the Blinders when this ten-year-old sold me a lollipop laced with LSD"-Thursday's head snapped to the side as the warden on the left slapped her across the face. It was a pathetic hit but enough to cause an annoying sting.

"You know what we're talking about."

Thursday hadn't been thrown into the asylum via confession. She had been arrested on suspicion and was considered unstable during the court hearing. Humans were so easy to manipulate. If Thursday had so wished, she could have seemed as sane as the next person but playing up the complete and utter madness act was so much more fun. Besides, asylums were more accommodating than prisons. Here you don't have to share your cell and you get free cushions built into the walls.

"Were you listening to my monologue?" Thursday asked, intrigued. "These lunatics clearly can't appreciate the never-ending roller-coaster that is my life. Pull up a pew and I'll tell you all about it."

"Look, you crazy bitch," the right warden barked. "We don't have time for your games. Just give us the information we're looking for." He snapped out his baton, clearly trying to look intimidating.

Thursday raised her eyebrows, eyes tracing the line of the weapon as casually as one would scan a dessert menu. "Ahhh, oh, um …If you wear those masks constantly, you're going to get some terrible acne?"

The warden without the baton sighed heavily, clearly not cut out for dealing with crazies regularly. The armed warden lifted his baton and attempted a swing on Thursday, but he was so slow it was almost laughable.

She grabbed the end of the weapon and twisted it, so the warden was thrown forward with it. Thursday wretched the baton out of his hands and used the momentum to swing herself around onto his back. Laughing like a maniac, Thursday grabbed both ends of the baton and pulled it up hard against the warden's neck; effectively choking him. She didn't need her ability to escape, if she had the energy to, she'd be perfectly capable of it on her own.

The warden yelled angrily and tried to fight her off, swinging wildly from side to side and throwing himself repeatedly against the wall behind him. Thursday choked on her laughter each time he smashed her against the wall, the pain of the impact travelling up her spine and causing her head to spin a little.

The other warden fumbled for his taser, which-when eventually found-he jammed into Thursday's back like a knife. She screamed, the electricity pumping through her system and causing her hands to shine purple, her Glow burning into both ends of the baton and singing the metal. They faded again as she released the warden and fell to the floor with a loud thud. She twitched on the ground, unable to hide the pain as her face crumpled a bit to combat the agony. The grin never left her face.

Sadly, having mad supernatural skills did not make one immune to pain.

"I don't know why they don't just charge the psycho," the attacked man commented, rubbing his abused neck while the other collected the burned baton. "Bitch is clearly unstable."

"She'll need a strait jacket," the other man sighed. "In case she tries to hurt herself."

"Herself? I'd think more in case she tries to hurt me again!"

"Don't worry," Thursday chuckled, rolling around on the ground as the aftermath of the taser pulsed through her body. "I don't hit the same weaklings twice!"

The man she attacked growled, clearly not up for Thursday's attitude. It made her wonder why he worked in an asylum at all. Either he desperately needed the money or in some way, he enjoyed beating the shit out of the criminally insane. Kind of ironic, since his partner had to save his ass in the end.

Her talking back was rewarded with a kick to the gut. One which didn't help Thursday's speed of recovery. Where was Finn when you needed him? He could make the pain go away so fast a man with a hole in his head would be fully recovered within a day. A slight exaggeration, but it got the point across well enough.

"We'll be back later with a strait jacket for you," the calmer of the two wardens informed her. "Then you'll be escorted to Dr. Weeks for questioning."

"Ha, questioning!" Thursday cackled at that description. One question, a gazillion shocks, and then a second question. Questioning was just a thin veil of deceit for Dr. Weeks' torture. "Maybe someone will finally listen to my incredible life story!"

The wardens laughed as if the possibility of listening to someone like Thursday was the most hilarious thing they'd heard all day. One of them planted their boot into Thursday's back, kicking her so she rolled out of the way of the door. Thursday flushed angrily, nostrils flaring as she looked up and watched the wardens leave. Assholes. Thursday wondered if they would still kick her around if they knew she could blast them out of the sky if the mood took her.

When the door to her cell shut, the mechanical whirring that Thursday heard regularly confirming that it was once again locked, Thursday staggered to her feet and threw herself against the door. She dug her fingers into the bars of the small window and shouted after the wardens,

"So, what will the excuse be this time for those bruises on your neck? Can't let all the big burly blokes you hang around with know you got your ass beat by a woman!"

The exterior door slammed, showing that they weren't amused with her jabs. Thursday grinned, sliding to the floor, and sitting against the door. She let her eyes fall shut, a tired sigh escaping her lips. "Weeks," she murmured, her stomach beginning to complain with each breath she took. A stupid grin grew on Thursday's face, and she chuckled. "How ironic."

~T~

Dr. Weeks peered at Thursday from across the table, the glasses perched on her birdlike nose balancing almost comically, in danger of falling right off. Thursday contemplated blowing a little, just for the sake of seeing if it would knock them off her face. The doctor was wearing all black, an outward representation of the soul Thursday believed lay inside of the woman's system. If there was any soul at all, that was.

"All of the signs point to you," Dr. Weeks said firmly, her finger dancing around the blue button on the remote control on the table. "All you need to do is confess."

Thursday cocked her head innocently. The movement made her neck feel like it was about to snap off her body due to the sheer weight of the headpiece on her head. Her skin pinched where the probes were attached, and it felt like the pinchers were trying to rip her head open and expose her skull. Maybe that was Dr. Weeks' true goal in life. She wanted to see her patients' skulls and maybe, if she got lucky, their brains.

"What signs?" Thursday asked. She had heard these 'signs' hundreds of times since she had been committed to the asylum but if Dr. Weeks didn't conduct her questioning correctly, which included answering all questions Thursday posed, anything the session provided would not stand up in a court of law. So, Thursday always asked the same questions each time. An experiment, if you will, to see if Dr. Weeks would lose her mind having to repeat the same stuff over and over again.

"You know what signs," Dr. Weeks growled. She slammed her finger down onto the blue button, holding it longer than necessary so the pulse of electricity that surged through Thursday's brain was as prolonged as possible.

Thursday ground her teeth together as the pulse frazzled her brain, shocking every nerve in her body into wakefulness. She refused to scream for Dr. Weeks. It was the sort of thing the woman got off on. She wasn't a doctor for the means of medicine, she was a doctor for the means of having control over patients. Why else did she cherish the shock button like one would cherish a child?

"The electricity has clouded my brain, Weeks," Thursday shouted through the agony, her fingers digging into the arms of the chair to elevate the pain. "I can't recall what you're talking about!"

Dr. Weeks released the button and Thursday gasped with relief. She slumped in her seat, the crisp smell of burning flesh consuming the room. Thursday was sure her hair had been singed. Hopefully not a great lot. She quite liked her hair.

"The murder and dismemberment of Francis Hyden and his lover Yvette Coolie has your paw prints written all over it," Dr. Weeks snarled. "The cruel and unmerciful means of death being the number one giveaway. Nobody murders as brutally as you, Trish."

"Well, for one, my name is actually Thursday," Thursday replied. "Please do at least get my name right, and another"-

Dr. Weeks pressed the button, sending a short pulse into Thursday to remind her of her place. Thursday tried not to glare, deciding that being the bigger person would be a very amusing outcome since she was allegedly the criminal here.

"*And another thing*," Thursday said pointedly when the burn of the shock passed, "if nobody murders as brutally as I, how come I haven't been captured until now?"

"That is irrelevant, everyone knows the Galvan High murder was orchestrated by you!" Dr. Weeks snapped. "There was just no conclusive evidence to put you away."

Ah, the Galvan High murder. Now that took Thursday back. One of her exes had been sitting her A-levels in Galvan High when she had been attacked one night during a football match and killed. Thursday had considered this quite rude since she should have been the one who murdered the girl for having the gall to dump her in the first place, so she set off to discover who it was that murdered her first.

It turned out to be the Principal of the school, who had a long string of student murders following in his wake. Thursday exacted her revenge thusly, breaking into the building late at night while he was still there and slitting his throat where he sat. Just to make sure the authorities knew why; she stapled the evidence of his bloody past onto the back of the educator's jacket. For some bizarre reason, they were all too focused on the man's murder instead of his history of murdering young girls. Justice was lost on some people.

"No conclusive evidence," Thursday repeated. "Normally that means the person didn't do it."

"Your fingerprints were found all over the crime scene!"

"My fingerprints had been stolen by the janitor to frame me, this was proven," Thursday threw back.

A quick trick she had implemented to frame the janitor who, in her own way, was also guilty. During her investigation of the school, Thursday had caught the janitor luring young boys into the broom closet, probably with promises of test answers stolen from educator's desks. So, it hadn't been that much of a loss.

Dr. Weeks tutted before reaching out and pressing the button again, simply for the sake of pushing it. Thursday had ground her teeth together so tight her jaw felt like it was going to snap, but she still refused to let Dr. Weeks have the pleasure of hearing her scream. Besides, she'd endured worse on a Friday evening trying to figure out why the electricity tripped in her house.

Dr. Weeks narrowed her eyes and stood up. Thursday watched the Doctor wearily as she wandered to the back of the room and retrieved a file from the top shelf. "We know you are part of them, so you might as well give yourself up," she said.

"Part of who?" Thursday asked, continuing to feign her innocence.

"The Seven." Dr. Weeks slapped the file onto the table so hard that it whipped up a wind, blowing Thursday's dark hair right off her shoulders.

Thursday stared at the boring brown file with disinterest. It had the word 'Seven' stamped onto the front in big, bold, red letters. "Now, if you people had taken the time to listen to me, you probably would have gathered this yourself," she said.

"So, you admit it?" Dr. Weeks snapped.

Thursday snorted. "Well, *duh*. My name is Thursday, for the love of Pete. It's rather baffling that it has taken you this long to figure it out in the first place."

Dr. Weeks looked slightly taken aback. She didn't even think to press the button on her shock remote to fill the time. Thursday waited for the information to process in the woman's brain. When it did, the woman reacted as expected.

The doctor slammed her hand down onto the table, right on top of the file, and yelled, "You'll tell us everything we want to know about the Seven or else"-

"What? You'll lock me up?" Thursday asked. "Haven't you already done that?"

Dr Weeks' nostrils flared angrily. "We will track down every one of your pals and sling them into a cell like yours."

"I thought that's what you wanted of us in the first place?" Thursday demanded. "You humans are afraid of us, you always were. Despite the things we've done to save your hides you can't look past the supernatural element, the superiority we possess! You want to lock us all up because you're terrified of what we're capable of."

"You people are a threat to society!" Dr. Weeks hit back. "We can't risk having people wandering around with *powers*, it's too dangerous!"

"We were on this planet long before idiots like you were even born," Thursday hissed. "If we were a threat to society, then it would have fallen apart long ago!"

Dr. Weeks growled and slammed her entire fist down on the button. The sudden pulse caused Thursday to yelp, but she refused to make another sound. "Tell me where the others are hiding," she shouted.

"I don't know, I'm not their mother!" Thursday answered. "We don't run around stuck to each other's hips you know!"

"You have an idea of where they may be, though."

Thursday rolled her eyes, fed up with this woman's idiocy. "Look, we're not the big group you think we are. Not anymore. I left years ago and everyone else just sort of drifted apart. If you look at your data records, you'd know there hasn't been a Seven sighting in almost a decade. We haven't been any bother. You just want to cage the freaks!"

Dr. Weeks folded her arms, her lips pulled tight. "I want to examine your genetic makeup. See what makes you what you are."

"Oh, I'm sorry, I'll correct myself then, you just want someone to *experiment* on!"

Dr Weeks admitted to nothing, but it was clear on her face that Thursday had hit the nail on the head. It was so easy to see through her. Once a criminal was admitted to United Arms, they were pretty much stripped of their rights. People don't care about the rights of criminals, and since the admitted are insane, they don't have the capacity to complain. If Thursday gave away where the rest were located-not that she knew anyway because she genuinely didn't-then Dr. Weeks could have them admitted from their actions in the past.

Then ...Well, then she had full reign and right to do as she wished.

Dr. Weeks straightened up, her posture stiff and her expression stern. "Tomorrow morning you'll be prepped for experimentation. One out of seven isn't bad, from a start-off perspective," she said.

"Ooooh, I'm positively trembling," Thursday said sarcastically.

Dr. Weeks did not rise to Thursday's attitude this time. She shook her head, as if genuinely saddened by her patient's behaviour, and dropped the 'Seven' file on top of the shock button. As Thursday's body seized up once more, a guttural gasp of surprise bursting past her lips, the doctor headed to the door and said one thing before leaving.

"You should be."

CHAPTER TWO

Present

MATTHEW RAN HIS TONGUE ALONG THE INSIDE OF HIS BOTTOM LIP AND WIGGLED HIS EYEBROWS AT THURSDAY, SEEMING INCREDIBLY PLEASED WITH HIMSELF FOR TRICKING HER INTO THINKING HE WAS SOMEONE ELSE. His amusement was short-lived, however, when Thursday pulled her fist back and punched him right in the face. There was a satisfying crunch, and Matthew reared backwards. He nearly bumped into Whitney, who had risen from her knees during their interaction, but she pushed him back towards Thursday before he could.

"Whoa, what sort of welcome is that?" Matthew hooted. His hand fell to his side; his face unblemished, almost as if he hadn't been punched at all. "I come to save you, and this is how you welcome me?"

"Was there a need to shift into a woman?" Thursday snapped back.

Matthew shrugged, feeling his nose even though he knew there would be no damage at all. "Sometimes I can't control it," he shrugged. He wasn't even trying to lie properly; he knew that Thursday could spot his bullshit from miles away.

"Lies," Thursday scoffed. It was true that Matthew had the self-control of a monkey in heat, but he had the same amount of control over his power as the rest of them. He was just full of it. He thought he was hilarious.

Thursday marched past Matthew and Whitney, out into the corridor of the asylum. The entrance door was blown wide open, the hinges blasted to molten rock. Thursday looked at her door and saw the hinges in a similar state. Whitney's handiwork, no doubt.

"Where's everyone else?" she asked.

"You should be honoured; we came to get you first!" Matthew sauntered out of Thursday's cell, the three of them standing at the threshold like work colleagues gathered at the water cooler. Like they weren't in dire danger of being captured.

Whitney looked around the corridor with displeasure, her nose turned up like she was permanently smelling something bad. "What did you do to end up in a hole like this one?" she asked, her voice borderline monotone.

Thursday rolled her neck on her shoulders. "This and that."

"I wouldn't call the torture and dismemberment of your lover this and that," Matthew snorted. He moved to Moren Maldova's room and peered in through the barred window. All the cons were screaming to be freed also, but Thursday knew that Matthew and Whitney were here to get her and her only. Thursday herself would have enjoyed the chaos such a thing as releasing everyone in her ward would ensue, but the other two didn't know how to have any fun at all.

"*Ex*-lover," Thursday corrected. "He thought the blonde across the road was more aesthetically pleasing." Matthew looked over his shoulder and quirked an eyebrow. Thursday smirked. "She wasn't once I was finished with her."

Matthew must have caught Moren's eye because the shifter grinned and waved in through the barred window. Odds were the psychic would ignore him. Moren Maldova stopped noticing people long ago, sometime after the twenty-fifth shock therapy session. When it was clear that Moren wasn't going to take part in Matthew's foolish behaviour-proving he was wise for a crazy psychic-Matthew stepped back from the cell door and turned to face the girls again.

"You said 'It's Sunday'," said Thursday, folding her arms against an invisible chill. "What did you mean by that?"

Matthew's unique eyes glistened under the harsh white spotlights above them. "You know what I meant," he said.

"I know what day it is," Thursday replied, even though she knew that this wasn't being questioned.

"It's not about the day. It's about Sunda-Sawyer. It's about Sawyer."

Even the name sent a chill through Thursday's being. She hadn't seen Sawyer in years, not since he was first to break away from the group. His reasoning hadn't been all that different from Thursday's when she eventually left the group as well, but she had never gone through with half the things she claimed she would. Sawyer was… Well, Sawyer was a psychopath. Plain and simple.

Thursday took pride in the fact that when Sawyer left, everything reverted to normal eventually. When *she* left, everyone drifted apart. She was the glue or sticky tape or some sort of adhesive product that kept everyone together.

"Can we get out of here?" Whitney snapped. "There will be time for a pow-wow later, I feel itchy just standing here."

Thursday laughed. "We may be criminally insane, but we do get a bath from time to time." This was a lie. The last bath Thursday had gotten had been before she had even been arrested, unless the hosing down she got on her first day counted. But there had been no candles or bath salts, so Thursday did not count it.

"Whatever, let's just get out of here!"

"What's the plan to get out, then?" asked Thursday.

Matthew spun around on his heels. "I figured you'd use your"-He waved his hands around in a manner that caused him to resemble an intoxicated gorilla- "to blast us out."

Thursday rolled her eyes. "Make me do all the work, why not?" she scoffed.

"Excuse you, we busted in here to get you out!" Matthew replied, placing his hand on his chest, and acting offended.

"Whatever," Thursday smirked. She took the lead, Matthew and Whitney following in step behind her. "We need to get to the roof. I'm not blasting through steel ceilings. Not only will it hurt like hell, but I am not getting tetanus from unnecessary cuts."

"Don't you have your shots?" Whitney frowned. It was hard to joke when Whitney was around. She poked holes in everything.

"No, I don't have my shots," Thursday answered in a high-pitched voice, mocking the other woman.

Matthew overtook them, jogging to the doorway and peering out. "The wardens will be waking up soon," he said, turning back around to face them. "They all had different tastes, so I could only stun them temporarily."

"Being a Black and White Asian who is tall and short at the same time was his limit," Whitney muttered as if this was ridiculous, and Matthew just hadn't tried hard enough.

The image of Matthew trying to shift to match the tastes of all the wardens who were trying to stop them was amusing. His ability was meant to stun the receiver, their senses overwhelmed by the perfection they were laying their eyes on. Except everyone had a different idea of what perfection was. Thursday had once seen Matthew shift into a half man half woman because of the different preferences of the men in their way. *That* was an image she wasn't going to be able to remove any time soon...

Thursday took the lead again, the three of them pouring out of the wing and heading for the stairs, leaving the desperate cries of the insane behind them. They tried to be as soundless as possible, as not to attract the attention of any wardens who had not been stunned yet, but the metal grating floors were designed specifically to rattle and clamour when walked upon.

"Why don't we just take the lift?!" Matthew exclaimed when Thursday jumped up the first three stairs.

"When you tripped the alarms, the elevators switched off," Thursday answered. "Duh!"

She turned and lurched up the first flight of stairs. She kept forgetting to check if Matthew and Whitney were keeping pace but the only thing in her head now was the possibility of escape. She would have been perfectly happy causing havoc in the asylum for the rest of her days but now that freedom was so close, she decided that she didn't care for her dank old cell.

They piled in through the door at the top of the stairs and were immediately met by a shower of bullets. Thursday cursed and reversed, throwing herself back out the door and onto the staircase. She grabbed the back of Matthew's shirt and dragged him with her, while Whitney rolled to the side of the interior wall.

Seconds later, the shooters were met with a wall of fire, their screams pouring out through the doorway in a symphony of agony. Thursday cringed, fighting a sick smirk as she could practically hear their blood crackling and boiling. Those wardens took pleasure in torturing her over the weeks, so she wasn't going to lose sleep over their painful deaths. They earned them.

Whitney's hands fell to her sides, the only sign of the carnage she had created being the bubbling bodies on the floor ahead and the small singe marks on the middle of her palms. She looked over her shoulder at Thursday and Matthew, both hunched over at the top of the stairs and narrowed her eyes. "What are you doing?" she asked as if they hadn't just been target practice for the wardens on that floor. "You know what, never mind, just get up! We need to keep moving!"

Thursday stumbled to her feet, taking off again down the corridor in pursuit of the next staircase. She jumped over the dead bodies, able to feel the heat on the soles of her feet that radiated from their burned corpses through the floor. A lot could be said about Whitney, but at least she got the job done fast.

"Behind all those doors, are there more wings?" Matthew asked as they ran up the next flight of stairs.

He was referring to the many doors that lined the corridors. Thursday barely noticed them; she had been here so long now they were just ... well, doors. "Yeah," she answered. "A fresh wing behind each one."

"That is a lot of insane to contain," Matthew commented.

Thursday blew a raspberry. "They've proved themselves to be very bad at the containing part don't you think?"

As soon as that last word left her mouth, a bullet ricocheted off the wall by her head. Thursday and Whitney simultaneously threw themselves at the closest bannister, looking over the edge to find more wardens pouring up the stairs after them.

"Time to just shut up and run!" Whitney exclaimed, giving Thursday a shove and slapping Matthew to get him moving too; not that either of them needed the incentive. If they were cartoons, Thursday would have been a hole in the opposite wall by now.

Thursday was not a runner. Sometimes, when she was bored, she would enrol in high school for a year. She protested vehemently against Physical Education, though. She used to lie in the grass and shout encouragements to the other girls, using the vague sort of asthma diagnosis from when she was six as an excuse not to take part. Running *from* something was a completely different thing, though, and Thursday ran like the devil himself was on her heels. No way they were putting her back into that cell now that she had gotten a tiny drop of freedom placed on her tongue. She took the stairs three at a time, practically leaping like a frog up each flight of stairs. Anything to get ahead of their chasers.

More wardens were waiting for them on each floor, but they were quickly disposed of by Whitney, who blasted them all to dust before their fingers got a chance to squeeze their triggers. She also took up the rear when they were on the stairs, taking care of anyone who got too close.

It felt like they'd been going around in circles for ages. The United Arms Asylum was massive, and every floor was a replica of the one that preceded it. Thursday had been on the ninth floor, and they were now on floor thirty-eight. There were thirty-nine floors in the building (because the architects given the task to design the establishment were assholes who thought having an odd number was a fantastic idea) so they were nearly there.

At the very top of the building, there was a fire exit that led out onto the roof. Whitney was going to blast it open, but Matthew decided that he needed to exert his dominance as the male of the three by kicking the door inwards.

Immediately, another alarm began to blare, and the sprinklers switched on. Thursday hoped as they stumbled out onto the roof that this would cause enough of a distraction for them to escape. Although, she doubted it. The wardens were more likely to think that they had broken out through a fire escape, not that they had spontaneously combusted, setting the alarms off in the process.

Thursday took a moment as they jogged to the edge of the roof to consume the fresh air. It felt like it had been years since she had been outside instead of mere weeks. She closed her eyes and greedily sucked in the foggy night air, despite the smoke and dirt that lingered like a cloud of smog above their heads. When she opened her eyes again, she could just make out the tiny dots of yellow that were the stars, a much more interesting view than the cockroach that crawled over the pads in the ceiling of her cell. Much kinder, too.

"One of you get on my back," Thursday instructed when they reached the edge. The view was nothing to be desired, just a lot of grey smog hiding anything worth looking at in a cloak of thick fog. The United Arms Asylum was high on a hill above the city of Castlebrooke, where Thursday herself hailed from. The city itself was somewhere beneath the layer of pollution that always seeped out during the nighttime. "Preferably, Matthew."

"Aww, Thursday, I didn't know you felt that way," Matthew said.

"Oh, shut up, you dingus, it's because Whitney is lighter than you and can hold onto my shoulder without pulling it out of its socket," Thursday replied.

Matthew tutted, acting offended. "I don't need you anyway. I've got people lining down the block begging for m"-

The remainder of the wardens that had been pursuing them on the stairs burst through the door, wielding their weapons, and raining another hail of bullets at them. Their aim sucked as the three of them were sitting ducks and instead of hitting them, all the bullets smattered the ground, kicking up the gravel on the ground beneath their feet. Thursday looked over her shoulder at them and spied the red bands around their arms. Ha! Only the rookies were left. No wonder they were missing their targets!

Adrenalin pulsing through her body, Thursday crouched over, a clear message for Matthew to stop his whinging and just do as she said. Since a bullet had grazed his shoe; the damage snapping a hole in his sneaker, Matthew didn't question Thursday's urgency. He jumped onto her back, his weight admittedly being a tad unbearable.

"What do you eat, steel rocks?" Thursday shouted, stumbling further to the edge of the roof as Whitney latched onto her shoulder.

"Shut up for Christ's sake!" Whitney screamed, her voice going up a notch as another rain of bullets showered upon them.

One of the rookies managed to hit the target this time, the bullet lodging itself in Whitney's ankle. The girl crumbled, roaring like a bear into Thursday's ear (understandably so, but Thursday still found it quite rude) and she probably would have fallen off the edge of the building if it weren't for her iron-clad grip on Thursday's shoulder.

The rookies' alarming pace of improvement was enough incentive for Thursday to quit dilly-dallying. She let herself fall forward, dropping bonelessly off the roof of the asylum.

Gravity grabbed them, believing it was going to claim another victim. Thursday allowed it to believe this for several moments. She had always enjoyed the way her stomach swooped up into her throat when she fell and how the ground plummeted towards her so quickly that if she mistimed herself even by a second, she could die.

"Thursday!" Matthew screamed; his voice hilariously high-pitched as they fell at rapid speed towards the forest-coated incline of the United Arms hill.

Thursday laughed, her true insanity slipping through the cracks in her demeanour momentarily as she basked in the control she had in this situation. If she so desired, she could kill all three of them right now. Her own life would need to be sacrificed for such a thrill but what's chaos without risk?

"Thursday, stop it!" Whitney barked over the wind that whistled in their ears and the blaring escape alarms coming from the asylum.

That's what they got for entrusting their lives to a mad woman.

Thursday's hands snapped outwards. Her Glow blew from the appendages like fire from an engine, the force throwing them back up into the air again. Thursday stretched her fingers out, so the light grew stronger and stronger, and the force continued to throw them up into the air. Her Glow caused them to sail upwards like a bird cutting through the sky and Thursday would probably have kept going until they broke the atmosphere if it weren't for the asylum search lights forcing her to dodge them by moving constantly in different directions.

"That was not funny!" Whitney growled.

"Oh yes, it was!" Thursday cackled, leaning forward and throwing her hands backwards so that they were propelled forward.

"I can't feel my lungs," Matthew muttered, his face nestled into Thursday's hair. She could feel his chest heaving against her back. He thought she would have killed them for the giggles of it.

"Can you normally feel your lungs?" asked Thursday. The shifter bit her shoulder, clearly not in the mood for joking anymore, but this only caused her to laugh even harder.

The alarm of the asylum began to fade into the distance the further away they got from the building. Soon they were flying through the smog, the lights of the city below almost discernible in the thick mist. Thursday sucked the air in again, the fact that they had successfully escaped causing her heart to pound with anticipation. What to do first? What mayhem to become responsible for? What-

Thursday remembered Matthew's entering words when he and Whitney rescued her.

It's Sunday.

It seemed like she would have to stick with them for the foreseeable future.

"Where do I go?" Thursday asked.

"I need medical attention," Whitney said with authority, making sure it was clear to be a statement, not a question.

Matthew lifted his head from Thursday's hair, and she could practically feel his grin burning into the back of her head before he had even spoken. "I know how we can get medical attention for Whitney and continue our quest of reunion!"

Thursday snorted, curling her fingers inwards just the slightest of bits so that they lowered closer to the city skyline. "Quest of reunion?"

"Oh yeah, we haven't gotten around to explaining everything yet. The short of it is this: we're bringing the band back together! Minus the obvious," Matthew explained.

"But why? Because of Sawyer?" Thursday asked. "There's so much he's done in the past, what could possibly be so bad that we have to"-

"I hate to be the person to interrupt but I am bleeding here," Whitney grunted, digging her fingers into Thursday's shoulders hard enough to draw blood of her own. "What's your plan, Matthew?"

When Matthew spoke, Thursday realised that he had probably been planning this since the moment Whitney was shot. Not for concern of her health, but for his own personal gain. In a way, Thursday was proud.

"Let's go get Friday."

CHAPTER THREE

FOR YOUR AVERAGE SUNDAY NIGHT, THE HOSPITAL GROUNDS WERE TERRIBLY BUSY. The lights that poured in from the building lit up the outside, the sterile environment almost seeming to seep out through the doors.

Thursday wondered as she sat on a bench in the walkway how every person who walked into the A&E section was injured. Accident? Mishap? Self-infliction? Murder? Suicide? Plumbing escapade gone wrong? Things like that had always fascinated Thursday, in the same way she liked people with scars because she liked hearing the stories behind them. Even if it was just a severe paper cut there was always the question of what book was being read.

Matthew was sitting beside Thursday, trying to act like the epitome of cool. It would damage his reputation if he came off as excited or giddy, but he was an idiot if he thought he could hide it from Thursday and Whitney. Matthew didn't get excited about a lot of things, not in this way anyway, and it certainly wasn't the prospect of healing Whitney that was putting him on edge so much.

"His shift should be over by now," Matthew yawned, his attempts at seeming nonchalant bordering on ridiculous.

"Stalker much?" Whitney ground out between gritted teeth. The effects of being shot in the ankle had decreased her mood so drastically that she could now cool her wound with her hands. Her ability was controlled by her emotions; one extreme equating fire, the other extreme equating ice.

"Excuse you, I call it being well-informed," Matthew threw back. "I did basic research on all the gang. Makes the quest easier."

Thursday shook her head, tying her hair back with an elastic she found on the ground. "What's my middle name then?" she asked.

Matthew squinted as if trying to read the answer from the look on Thursday's face. "Trish?" he guessed.

"Trish Trish?" Thursday didn't like her first name, hence why she went by her Soul Day instead. The only people who knew her by her real name were the old gang and they only called her Trish when they wanted to annoy her. A pretty weak guess on Matthew's part.

"Could all be!" Matthew declared, grinning smugly as if he had gotten the answer correct.

Thursday spotted a bronze-haired man exiting the hospital. Good, the very man they were looking for! She stood up, helping Whitney to her feet also and supporting the girl's weight so she could stand. Matthew was a bit late, staring at the girls instead of where he had previously been watching like a hawk. When he did finally notice, he was off like a shot.

Thursday watched with bemusement at the shifter's sudden ability to run like a cheetah.

Matthew ran up to Finn and threw his hands over the doctor's eyes. "Guess who?" he asked.

Finn paled considerably, having been forced to stop in his tracks by Matthew's embarrassment of an interception. "If this is who I think it is you have five seconds to get the hell away from me before I"- Anything else he may have wanted to say was cut short as Matthew pulled Finn's head back and silenced him with a kiss.

Thursday stood off to the side, feeling slightly left out. She watched the two men with a cocked head. People passing by didn't have the same level of interest, some even throwing a couple of dirty looks at the four of them. Thursday was amused by their disgust and was tempted to kiss Whitney just to add to their ignition. Except such an act would result in her head being blown off her body.

Thursday needed her head, so she decided against it.

Due to being Monday's child and the ability that gave him, the theory stated that Matthew should not have had the capacity to develop feelings. Sure, he could morph into whatever body he wanted and get practically anyone he so desired, but it was always supposed to be merely on a physical level and nothing else. Yet, against the odds, he developed feelings. Long ago, too, when the group was first starting. All because of the man Matthew currently wasn't allowing to breathe.

Matthew's ability meant that he changed his appearance a lot. The first time someone set eyes on him, he didn't have much control over the change but once he had changed to look like what they wanted, he had the power to change back to normal or even later choose to look that way again if he so wished. If someone changed the way they viewed beauty, then Matthew would be forced to change again when they next saw him. It was rather complex, and Thursday was glad that she didn't have to endure such an ability. She wouldn't have the patience for it.

Thursday didn't have much insight into how Matthew developed emotions that resembled sentient feelings for Finn, who was Friday's Child, and the healer of the old group. All she knew was what she had seen, which honestly wasn't a lot.

Matthew's ability meant that the first thing each of them saw when they first met Matthew was their dream partner. Thursday herself had helped Sybil rescue Matthew and introducing him to the others had been an arduous process indeed, especially since sometimes the wires got tangled and Matthew's ability wouldn't know what to change into first. They got past it, though, like they always did. Matthew trained himself under their leader's watchful eye to use his ability properly. Teaching himself to change back quickly so it was barely noticeable that his appearance had altered at all. Eventually, he could go out into public places without having to worry about being caught.

Finn was the last person to join the group. He had been discovered in a travelling circus. *The Man Who Can Heal Anything*! It was a torture house more than anything else. They were chopping off animal limbs just to show the audience how Finn could heal the limb back. They rescued him as soon as they could and brought him back to meet the group.

Thursday would never forget that day. Mainly because she'd never seen Matthew look so stunned before in the entire time, she'd known him. How Finn's hand had hung in the air painfully awaiting the shifter to shake it, not understanding why Matthew was staring at him with such intensity still made her giggle. The fact was, *Matthew didn't shift* when Finn had first looked at him. This had never happened. It was a concept that Thursday knew Matthew had never been introduced to before. Someone liked him as himself, not some fake body he didn't own and would be gone as soon as it arrived. He, Matthew, in his natural body, was viewed as beautiful.

It wasn't long before they were an item.

Their relationship was on and off. Their main problem was that their personalities conflicted, something Thursday had been forced to endure on many a Saturday night. Her room had been right next to theirs and, honestly, she had probably heard the entire progression of their relationship through the wall separating them.

It almost seemed like they were just going to stand there kissing forever. Thursday had always been fascinated by some people's ability just to go at it like machines and she tried to have sympathy for the fact that they hadn't seen each other in what had to be at least a decade now but the novelty of watching wears off when you aren't a participant.

"Yeah, okay, this is great and all, but Whitney here is bleeding o"- Thursday was interrupted by Finn suddenly pulling away from Matthew like he'd been physically dragged away by the front of his jacket.

The healer spun around and planted an almighty slap across the shifter's face, the crack so loud and satisfying it sent chills through Thursday's being. The baffled look on Matthew's face was both adorable and hilarious. Last Thursday checked, Finn was a pacifist, which just added to the humour of having witnessed him slap the sense clean out of Matthew.

"What was that for?" Matthew exclaimed.

"You can't just come waltzing back into my life like this!" Finn yelled back, sounding like an estranged mother who just found out that her insane brother was coming for Christmas tea.

"I said I'd come back," Matthew childishly muttered, rubbing his face despite the lack of marking on his skin. "I got held up."

"It's been ten years!"

"*Really* held up."

"You self-satisfied piece of sh"-

"Not that we're not in awe of your riveting domestic spat," Thursday reluctantly intercepted. If it weren't for the pool of blood that was slowly growing larger by Whitney's feet, Thursday probably would have let the men argue for hours. It was much more entertaining than watching them try to suck each other's brains out through their mouths. "But Whitney is bleeding over here."

Finn looked away from Matthew, seeming to notice for the first time that Thursday and Whitney were there at all. "Wednes-I mean, Whitney? What happened?" he asked.

"It's a quest of reunion," Matthew explained. "Except Thursday was in a bit of a pickle. Of course, by pickle, I mean big, fortified asylum."

Finn shook his head, confused. "Reunion? We separated for good reason. Sybil said herself that"-

"It's Sunday," Thursday took the liberty of explaining, to spare Finn the trouble of the confused stage. "As in Sawyer, not the day."

If Finn had looked pale at Matthew's appearance, the news of Sawyer being up to something drained any remaining colour from his face. He suddenly looked like a standing corpse. "Oh."

Matthew nodded, grinning like an idiot and eyes glistening like jewels, focused only on the man in front of him and nothing else. Ten years apart and Finn was still the apple of Matthew's eye. It was sickeningly sweet. Thursday couldn't stand it. "Yeah," the shifter said.

Finn had no choice but to take the three of them back to his place. Thursday had no qualms with staying at his place, even though in some cultures it was probably viewed as an intrusion. If the clingy ex-lover was allowed, then Thursday was not going to even bother with quibbling in her head about whether she was welcome or not.

Besides, Whitney certainly wasn't going to appreciate them dithering on Finn's lawn to debate mannerisms while she slowly bled out.

The house was very impressive. On the outskirts of the city, Finn's house wasn't extravagant, but it wasn't a shack either. It was your classic suburban home, almost as if it had been plucked from a cul-de-sac and deposited outside Castlebrooke. All pristine white with red doors and hanging baskets full of flowers. Kind of fruity, in Thursday's opinion, but if she had a house of her own the standard of upkeep would be a lot lower. The building alone probably cost all the apartments Thursday had ever lived in times five. Finn was a doctor, she supposed. It wasn't that large a stretch to assume that he could afford such a place.

Thursday laid Whitney down on the sofa in the front room. Finn didn't seem bothered by the blood getting all over his furniture, even though the red liquid had probably destroyed his shag rug completely. The healer had gone into hospital mode, rolling his sleeves up and even disappearing to the kitchen to wash his hands.

"Why does a healer need to wash his damn hands?" Whitney shouted. Her face was screwed up and she yelled with pain, clearly having been holding back up until now.

"It's a quirk, I can't help it," Finn called back.

Matthew plopped onto the floor, crossing his legs like a child about to hear a bedtime story. "Hasn't changed a bit," he grinned, shaking his head as if sharing a private joke with himself.

Thursday groaned. "Hey, Romeo, cut it out, we don't care," she said, dropping onto the floor beside Matthew.

"Thursday, you kick my bleeding heart," Matthew teased. He slapped a hand onto her knee and shook it, despite the scowl he earned from it.

"I'll show you what else I'll be kicking in a moment if you don't close your lamenting mouth."

Finn returned, drying his hands with a cloth. He walked around Matthew and Thursday, sitting on the arm of the sofa at the end by Whitney's feet. The healer looked down at the two people on the floor, his face turning a hilarious shade of pink as he realised, he had an audience. "Must you both stare at me like that?" he asked.

"Yes," Matthew and Thursday said at the same time.

Not amused, Finn focused his attention on Whitney. "I haven't done this in a while," he admitted, rubbing his hands together. Golden sparks flew from his fingers like tiny stars rebounding off him.

"Don't you do it at the hospital?" Thursday frowned.

"No, of course not," Finn replied. "If I did then nobody would die and that's messing with the forces of nature. Besides, imagine how overpopulated Castlebrooke would become if nobody died?"

Thursday shuddered. She hated people on an ordinary day, especially in crowds. In her opinion, there were already too many people in Castlebrooke. What they needed was another villainous attack to shave the numbers down again. Although, with Sawyer plotting again, that reality didn't seem all too farfetched.

Finn pulled his hands apart. A golden web stretching between his palms kept them connected. He gently touched Whitney's ankle, wrapping his fingers around the wound and placing his other hand over the top. Whitney didn't scream or yell with pain, the process was relatively painless. When her head rolled to the side, Thursday thought she looked rather mollified.

"I'm guessing this doesn't hurt her?" Thursday said, rather baffled at how content Whitney was. Thursday had been healed by Finn numerous times before when the group was whole but that had been a decade ago and she would be lucky if she could remember what hairstyle she had back then never mind what Finn's healing ability felt like.

"If anything, it feels fantastic," Matthew put forward.

Thursday snorted. "How do you know? You don't take damage."

Matthew shrugged. "I would stub my toe from time to time," he said. "I can still feel the pain of it, y'know."

Thursday stared at Matthew. "You got Finn to heal you when you stubbed your toe?" she asked slowly. "What else? When you burned your tongue on soup?"

Matthew flushed. "Shut up." The shifter heaved himself off the floor and laid a hand on Finn's shoulder. "This guy has healed me out of many a pickle."

Rolling his eyes, Finn removed a hand from Whitney's ankle and pushed Matthew backwards into the armchair by the sofa so that the shifter's hand was forcibly removed. Thursday's nose twitched, and what she liked to call 'the curse of the curious' (but was just flat-out nosiness) crept up on her. She ignored it though because she figured Finn wouldn't appreciate a twenty-question quiz on why he was being so cold to Matthew.

"Who did you plan to get next, since approaching Finn was a matter of Whitney's health?" Thursday asked Matthew, disbelief at her statement written all over her voice.

Matthew looked surprised by the question. He had lost sight of his mission since he had set foot into Finn's home. "Uh … Titus? Yes. Titus." He threaded his fingers together and stretched his legs out in front of him. "I was planning to go in order, but I figured Whitney's powers would be the most useful and you were, well, probably going to be the most challenging so getting you next seemed like the easiest option."

Finn placed his other hand back over Whitney's ankle, the effort it was taking to heal her taking it out of him. Sweat was breaking out across his furrowed brow, and he was grinding his teeth together to remain focused. Thursday could understand being out of practice. She didn't use her ability for six months once and when she tried to go again, she nearly blasted herself off a cliff.

"So basically, you were going to go in order but then didn't," Finn commented through clenched teeth.

Matthew blew a raspberry. "Pretty much, yeah," he admitted without shame.

"So, we're getting Titus next?" Thursday clarified just to be sure. Matthew nodded. "He hasn't put the weight back on, has he?"

Matthew snorted with amusement. "God, I hope not. He won't be any help then."

Thursday chuckled. "Your concern for our old friend's health is overwhelming Mattie," she said.

"Old friend? Titus hated me," Matthew answered. "Why should I care?"

Finn released Whitney's ankle, the golden glow fading from his hands instantly. Whitney seemed to have been lulled to sleep by the healing sensation. Thursday certainly wasn't going to wake her up. The girl's rotten mood was bad enough when she wasn't injured, let alone injured *and* tired. It was best to let her sleep for now and fully absorb the effects of the healing process.

"Yeah, he did hate you," Finn agreed. "It could have something to do with you morphing into his ex-wife at any opportunity."

Matthew grinned and shrugged. "As I say, sometimes I can't control it. It's not my fault the idiot got married so quickly and was then surprised when she left him for a Duke."

"You could have been more respectful."

"I seriously can't control it sometimes!"

Thursday rolled her eyes and jumped to her feet. "You two can sit and argue all you like; I'm going to take a nap. I had to fly across the skyline, and it has taken it out of me. Gives you both time to sort out…" Thursday waved her hands around in a confusing gesture that even she didn't understand. "Whatever it is you both need to sort out."

Finn shook his head, clearly not taking to this idea at all. "I'm going for a walk," he said. He didn't even grab a coat before he left.

Thursday jumped at the slam of the door. She looked at Matthew, who was rubbing the bridge of his nose with shut eyes. Very rarely did the shifter not have a smile on his face and it was rather odd for Thursday to see him … Not frowning, exactly, but he was not wearing the face of a happy man.

"Seriously," Thursday said, "what did you do to him?"

Matthew rubbed his hand over his face and shook his head. "He, ah, wanted me to stay with him when we all broke apart."

Thursday raised her eyebrows. "And you didn't want to?" she asked.

"I did, but I didn't think that"-Matthew stopped and frowned. "Why should I tell you this? It's not any of your business."

Raising her hands in surrender, Thursday spun on her heel and headed for the door. "Okay, okay, I'll not ask any more questions," she said. "Jeez, ask one thing and you get your head bitten off."

Thursday left the sitting room and headed for the spiral staircase. In a small way, she was relieved that Matthew didn't tell her. She didn't want to develop an opinion on this matter and get involved. The only relationship drama she wanted to deal with was her own and right now she didn't have any, which was how she wanted it to stay.

No idea where she was going, Thursday wandered down the hallway looking for a room to throw herself into. On one hand, she was happy for Finn. He was the only one out of the seven of them who attempted to make a decent life for himself. On the other hand, she was peeved. Imagine having the patience to study and get a good career while the rest of them were slumming it. Well, she said slumming it. Titus owned a dance studio, and she was quite sure Sybil and Whitney had stable enough jobs. Maybe Thursday was the only one slumming it, come to think of it...

After detouring to the bathroom and having a quick shower, Thursday eventually found a guest room. Or what she assumed was a guest room. All she could do in the matter of clothes was strategically tie her ripped strait jacket around her torso so that it covered all the parts that were considered inappropriate for public viewing.

The other room that was closer to the top of the stairs looked more lived in, which made her assume that it was Finn's room. She would have taken it, but if the two men patched things up (which Thursday really couldn't see happening anyway) then they'd want the double bed. Despite the unlikelihood of such a thing happening, Thursday wasn't going to risk unintentionally inserting herself into a spat. She did that way too often.

The urge to hoke around in Finn's drawers out of rabid curiosity was strong, but Thursday stayed her hand. She did fall to her knees beside the bed for a quick sweep underneath, though. There was nothing there but some dust bunnies and a folded-up blanket. Thursday wasn't sure what she had expected to find, but it would have been nice to find something to make Matthew giggle since he was suddenly in such an annoyingly foul mood. She kind of figured that Finn wouldn't leave terminally embarrassing objects around his spare room anyway but it would have been nice.

It had been worth a shot.

Thursday huffed and heaved herself up onto the bed. She didn't get underneath the covers and lay on top of them, staring at the ceiling. This entire situation was so strange. Thursday had always thought that if she escaped from United Arms, she'd wreak havoc in Castlebrooke. She had debts to collect; people who owed her for their acts against her in the past. Thursday may not have had the soundest of minds, but she remembered every person who had double-crossed her in the past shit storm of a year, and she intended to remind them exactly who they had betrayed. Starting with whoever had ratted her out to the authorities.

Now she had somehow gotten roped into Matthew's strange reunion quest. Thursday had always said that she would never return to the Seven, no matter what was said or done to try to convince her to do so. She had never considered the possibility of this happening. All Matthew had said was 'Sunday' and Thursday knew that she had no choice.

It had always just been the Seven of them, in all of existence. Their origin was unknown, as there had never been any explanation towards how they got their abilities. They just ...did.

The Seven of them had been born, obviously, on their Soul Day, in the same week. Back in 1801, Matthew was the first to be born since his Soul Day was Monday and was the technical oldest. Titus then followed on Tuesday, Whitney on Wednesday, Thursday on Thursday, Finn on Friday and Sybil on Saturday. Sawyer was the last to be born at the end of that week on the Sunday and was the technical youngest.

It took fifty-five years for the Seven of them to find one another, but once they did, they formed their group. They weren't interested in becoming heroes or anything, but they did use their abilities to solve their issues throughout the following centuries. Sybil kept them in line and made sure that none of them went too far. Endangering themselves meant endangering the entire group. There were rumours about them, especially when the twenty-first century hit, and the internet exploded into existence. The rhyme had already been written about them, which was dangerous enough in itself, but thankfully it only idealised the fact they were just fictional characters.

If any one of them were captured, then it could affect all seven of them.

Sawyer was the most unstable out of them all. Sure, they were all unhinged in one way or another (some more than others), but it had always been on a different level with Sawyer. He didn't know when to stop and would often go too far. The Seven's policy had always been to do what was necessary to get the job done. Whether that be having to mow through those who got in the way or something as simple as crossing the grass that had an obvious 'DON'T STEP ON THE GRASS' sign on it; they did it if it was necessary to their mission. If it wasn't necessary, they didn't bother. It would only attract unwanted attention, and attention was something they couldn't afford. They already got enough from doing what they had to do, Thursday couldn't imagine how much worse it would have gotten if they just did what they wanted when they wanted.

Sawyer, however …Sawyer preferred to do things just because he wanted to. Maybe he had a problem with Sybil's authority, Thursday wasn't sure, but sometimes it felt like he was going out of his way every single time to irritate the group's leader and go against her word. Thursday could understand such a desire, but she couldn't say she approved of Sawyer's behaviour. At first, Thursday and Sawyer had been terrors together, causing trouble around every corner, but when Sawyer began to act out against the Seven itself, Thursday began to grow away from him.

Thursday loved chaos, she really did, but not chaos against your own. Even the maddest of mares need a few friends to pull them back when they nearly veer off the edge of the peripheral cliff. Sawyer didn't have the same thinking as Thursday. It was rather odd since Sawyer was pretty much obsessed with the Seven and its members. He adored them all, and that wasn't an understatement. Maybe his obsession caused his behaviour to be irrational. Thursday had never been able to work it out. The insane don't tend to make sense often.

When it became clear that the Seven weren't going to support his behaviour, Sawyer left them and became a law on himself. It didn't help the matter that his Soul Day blessed him with good fortune. *'And the child that's born on the seventh day, is fair and wise and good in every way.'* Good, ha! Such a joke. Good at being an unhinged; psychotic; villainous fraud. But in every way? Definitely not.

However, Sawyer's Soul Day being Sunday meant that anything he wanted fell into his lap through means most would chalk down to coincidence. He knew how to manipulate luck and fate to work in his favour. Thursday despised this and couldn't understand how such a crazy freak could get such a desirable Soul Day ability. Sawyer was famously known for using his ability to excess and abusing it to ridiculous lengths. Where Finn would use his ability sparingly, for example, Sawyer just threw his out whenever he felt like it.

Sawyer had this …*theory* …that if they somehow figured out how to merge all the Seven's powers then they would become a force to be reckoned with. Almost like Gods. Sybil had always debunked this, with the backing of most of the Seven. The reason they were each given their isolated ability was because they knew how to control it. They knew how to use and refine their gifts. If someone suddenly had them all then they wouldn't know how to deal with it. It just wouldn't work. Like every madman, however, Sawyer had never budged in his belief that it would work. He would fight his point, and try to gain support from the others, but Thursday had always been firm in her belief that Sybil was the smartest out of them all and knew what was best.

Thursday liked a little spontaneity and if Sawyer's theory hadn't been so flawed maybe she would have been inclined to believe it. Sybil's reasoning had always made so much more sense. Thursday couldn't imagine Whitney having her ability to manipulate the elements through her emotions while also having Finn's power to heal. Such a thing was impossible because the abilities couldn't co-exist in the same body. Wednesday and Friday couldn't mix, nor could Tuesday and Saturday. Okay, sure, this wasn't known for definite, but why take the risk? The Seven were the only humans in recorded existence to have been given powers like this and there had never been anyone after them who had been born with a Soul Day, so why risk possible death in pursuit of a crazy theory that may or may not work?

Besides, it was obvious that Sawyer just wanted this to happen so that he could have all the abilities himself. That sort of power in the hands of Sawyer made Thursday shudder. It would be chaotic but not in a safe way. Some people just couldn't handle being insane and it was abundantly clear that Sawyer was one of those people. Having unimaginable power like that in his hands made even Thursday feel a bit ill.

The only plausible reason that Matthew could have for trying to reunite the group was that Sawyer was trying to fulfill his theory and the only way to stop him was to get everyone together before he got there first. It was good that Matthew got a hold of Whitney first. Her ability was the one that could cause the most devastation if placed in the wrong hands. Even if it hadn't been Matthew's thought process, at least he had done something semi-smart. Being clever wasn't exactly something that Matthew was known for. Neither was forward thinking.

Somewhere during her thoughts, Thursday drifted off to sleep. She rarely dreamed, or more so if she did, she didn't remember it when she woke up. When you spend so long staring at four padded walls you end up drifting in and out of consciousness without really noticing. Thursday had grown used to blank dreams, and it became less about getting from one day to another and more about losing and gaining consciousness as her body grew tired and needed to regain strength again.

She was awoken by a loud noise somewhere downstairs. Thursday's eyes snapped open, and she rolled onto her back. The room was cloaked in darkness, and she assumed that it was quite late. She waited. The sound came again, a lot louder and more aggressive this time around. That wasn't normal. Not unless Finn had a habit of staying up at ridiculous times and throwing pots and pans around in the kitchen.

Thursday jumped off the bed and wandered out into the hallway. She could look out over the bannister into the entrance hall below but, as soon as she set foot outside, the house fell into complete silence again. Thursday waited again, dragging her hand along the bannister as she walked down the hallway to the top of the stairs. Thankfully, Finn's top floor was carpeted, so her feet didn't make any noise as she moved. She passed one of the larger rooms and when she glanced through the crack in the door, she could see Finn still fast asleep, undisturbed.

There was another bang and Thursday jumped in surprise. She turned around and looked back over the bannister again. A figure wandered out from the living room and Thursday realised it was Whitney. She must have been left to sleep on the sofa. The blonde woman looked up and saw Thursday standing there. "What is that?" she asked, her voice hushed.

"I don't know," Thursday answered.

This was instantly followed by a much louder bang. Thursday realised that it was coming from the door. Whitney must have noticed, too, because she turned to look at the door also. "Are they trying to break the door down or something?"

"Maybe you should wake up Finn," Whitney replied. She moved to the door and placed her hand over the doorknob, freezing it so that it was harder to open. Thursday supposed that if Finn was as wealthy as he seemed, maybe people trying to break into the house was a common thing? No matter, they chose the wrong night to try to break in.

Thursday pushed open the door and entered Finn's room. It was just as dark as the spare room had been the floor-to-ceiling curtains were drawn closed to prevent any form of light from seeping in. She didn't feel like an intruder nor was she worried about entering the room uninvited. She skipped over to the bed and slapped the lump beneath the covers.

"Finn, someone is trying to break into your house," she said, speaking with the tone of a person informing someone that they'd left the kettle on.

"Huh?" There was a stir and the covers shifted. Tufts of blond hair peeked out from the top and a frown wormed onto Thursday's face.

"Finn?" Thursday threw the covers back completely and sighed heavily as she revealed Matthew lying on the mattress, rubbing his eyes tiredly. "Matthew, what the hell?!"

The shifter groaned and heaved himself up into a sitting position. He squinted in the darkness to try to make out Thursday standing over him. "Finn didn't come back," he said. "So, I figured I should just sleep here."

"In his bed?" Thursday finished.

Matthew rolled out of the bed onto the floor, sluggishly dragging himself to his feet. "Where else was I going to sleep?" he asked defensively.

"What if Finn came home?" Thursday exclaimed, muffling her laughter with her hand. She couldn't help being amused by the image of Finn coming home and finding Matthew snoring away in his bed, drooling on his pillow like the epitome of class that he was.

Matthew frowned. "Ahhh, he'd get a sexy surprise?" he guessed.

Thursday pushed her finger into the centre of Matthew's chest, pushing him back a little. "You're an idiot."

Matthew rolled his eyes. "Why are you here?"

"Someone is trying to break into Finn's house."

"Did it ever cross your mind it could be Finn himself?"

Thursday raised her eyebrows. "Does Finn tend to enter his house by pounding on his own door?"

As soon as the sentence was out of her mouth, there was a louder, much more prominent thud on the door. It sounded like something had broken through the wood. A second later, Whitney's loud curse confirmed this.

Thursday ran out of Finn's room and jumped over the hallway bannister, using her Glow to soften the fall. She heard Matthew hurrying down the stairs after her. When her feet touched the ground again, she immediately saw what was going on. Whitney must have switched the lights on, as it was much easier to see.

What looked like an axe was smashing through the door, again and again and again.

"Shit," Whitney cursed. "What the hell?! Where's Finn?"

"He didn't come back, apparently," Thursday answered.

"Who are you?!" Matthew shouted.

The axe wielders only started whacking the door harder, seeming invigorated by the fact that there were people inside.

"Good job, Matthew, now they know we're in here!" Whitney snapped.

"I think they knew anyway!" Matthew threw back. "They wouldn't have broken in if they hadn't known!"

"So, what? They were trying to get in to kidnap Finn?!" Whitney exclaimed sarcastically. "You're an idiot, they were probably coming in to steal something!"

"Who gives a shit, they're still breaking the door down!" Thursday shouted over them.

Suddenly the door was kicked in, clearly having been weakened by the axe. The three of them simultaneously took a step backwards.

A bunch of armed men stormed in; faces obscured by masks with visors.

It was instantaneous. Whitney jumped in front of them and threw her arms up, a wall of ice shooting up between them. The men rained bullets down on the ice, the flashes of bright yellow light visible through the thick, almost glass-like wall. The blurry forms of the men were only barely visible through the sheet of clear ice but judging by their urgent movements, they were already planning another way in.

"We need to find Finn," Matthew said.

"Agreed," said Whitney.

Thursday looked around before running into the kitchen to her right. She stumbled into the islet that sat in the middle of the room and shouted, "Is there a back door?"

There was a blur that rushed past her, ruffling Thursday's hair and clothes in the process. She realised a moment later that it was Matthew speeding by her to reach the back door. "It's here!" he answered. Realising that it was locked, the shifter cursed and spun around. "Where does Finn keep his keys?"

"Screw keys!" Thursday shouted, pushing Matthew out of the way.

Thursday threw her hands at the doorknob and thrust her fingers outwards, so swirls of purple sparked from the tips. As soon as the first spark touched the metal knob it exploded into shrapnel.

"Who are these guys?!" Whitney yelled over the continuous gunfire. "Is it Sawyer?"

They fell silent as they heard a window smash upstairs and footsteps overhead.

Thursday inwardly cursed. "This isn't Sawyer's style," she responded. She jammed her finger into the hole she'd created and pressed her free hand against the wall, trying to get it open.

It was true, it wasn't Sawyer's style at all. Sawyer may have been after them for whatever his reasoning was, but he wouldn't barge in all guns blazing. Sure, he would have people do the dirty work for him a great deal of the time, but he was more of a … knock on the door to see who answers kind of guy, not kick it down and start shooting whatever moved. Especially not against one of the Seven. Sawyer was mad, but he wasn't disloyal. His dedication to the protection of the Seven ran deep.

"Then who the hell could it be?" Whitney snapped.

"Now isn't exactly the time to start a debate on it," Thursday replied through gritted teeth. She gave the door a hard yank and it finally gave in, cracking open with a wooden groan.

The three of them practically jumped over one another to get out, Whitney overpowering both Thursday and Matthew to get out first. It was completely dark outside but as soon as Whitney ran out into the back garden a massive spotlight switched on, engulfing the area in blinding white light. It was less of a garden and more of a field. Thursday couldn't see where Finn's garden ended.

"Where's the fence?!" Thursday exclaimed as Matthew gave her a shove to keep moving. "There's always a fence to jump at the end of the yard to know where the property en-Christ!"

Thursday ducked as bullets showered down on them from above, out through the broken window. Whitney was off like a shot, running down the grass even though she didn't know where she was headed. At this point, anywhere if it was far from here seemed like a promising idea. Matthew did the same thing, vaulting over a deckchair and sprinting after her. Thursday cursed.

She hated running.

As they were running, there was a loud smash and Thursday didn't need to look back to know that they had broken through the ice wall. She was lagging Matthew and Whitney already; she didn't need to get any further behind. She couldn't even see them anymore.

Thursday shook her hands off, sweat pouring from her face like a running faucet, preparing to take off into the sky. Flying was the only way she'd be able to catch up.

Something exploded through her arm, the force knocking her straight to the ground. Thursday screamed as the bullet pierced straight through her, the burst of blood and flesh like a border in the corner of her vision. The shock of it sent her tumbling to her knees, rolling in the grass a couple of metres before stopping. She lay on her face, panting heavily and trying to stay still.

A boot connected with her hip barely a moment later, kicking her around onto her back. Thursday started shouting curses into the night air, clutching her bleeding arm tight to try to staunch the flow. A masked face came into view, looming over her intimidatingly and thrusting a gun into her face.

"I knew we should have put you in a straitjacket," a voice hissed. It was robotic, clearly put through a voice distorter of some sort, however, the content of the statement rang all too familiar.

"Are you from United Arms?!" Thursday exclaimed.

The masked man didn't answer and instead responded to her with the click of his gun getting cocked. Thursday growled and kicked the weapon out of the man's hand. Despite the amusement she got from hearing him curse profanity at her, the shouting from the other men grew louder as they approached curdling her stomach. She couldn't fight them all off single-handedly. Even if that single hand was charged with energy. All it would take would be one bullet to her head and she'd be unhealable, even to Finn.

With a loud grunt, Thursday rocked back onto her shoulder blades and flipped her lower body off the ground. Bending her knees, Thursday's feet thumped the ground and she swung herself off the grass. The masked man growled, and Thursday grinned back. She ducked beneath the man's arm as he took a swing at her and spun around behind him, planting her foot into his lower back and kicking him to the ground.

"Bitch," he cursed. He lunged at Thursday and she was barely able to scoot out of his way. She slipped out of his grasp and grabbed his visor, using the leverage to slam his head against the closest tree.

Thursday slammed his head against the tree repeatedly. She heard a crack but didn't worry whether it was just his helmet or his actual skull. Whacking him against the trunk one final time just to be sure, she tossed him to the ground, dead or alive. She needed to get away from here or else she was going to get captured again.

"If you know what's good for you, you'll stay down," Thursday snapped. "Bitch."

Thursday didn't wait around. As soon as the guy was sprawled onto the ground, she started running again. She didn't know what propelled her forward as her vision slowly began to fade out with pain, but she kept moving, nonetheless. Maybe it was her determination not to die, or just the rush of adrenalin almost dying had given her. Either way, Thursday wasn't going to question it.

Soon she was stumbling through the forest that Finn's garden seemed to fade into, the shouts of the United Arms wardens thankfully getting quieter. Thursday had no idea where Matthew and Whitney had run off to, but they had to be close by.

She was losing blood fast. Her vision was blacking out. Her heart was thrumming so hard it felt like it was outside her body. It didn't help that she couldn't see a damn well thing.

Thursday staggered into a tree. She cursed and looked around. It was so dark she couldn't see anything, just blackness. She couldn't hear the wardens at all anymore. Why hadn't they followed her? She slid to the ground, leaning heavily against the tree trunk as she plodded onto her butt on the forest floor. Something wasn't right. Something wasn't right at all. Why hadn't they followed her?

Her head was fuzzy like her brain had been hollowed out and stuffed with cotton balls. The only thing that seemed to have remained was the part that processed pain. Unable to control herself, Thursday's head thudded against the hard bark of the tree trunk and her eyes slid shut. She was so tired. Bleeding out really took it out of a girl.

Passing out was a detrimental release. One in which Thursday could not control.

~T~

It didn't feel like she had passed out at all. It was like Thursday had blinked. One minute she was leaning heavily against the tree, panting in the dark as her arm wept crimson, the next minute she was lying in the grass and her skin burning. Behind her scorching lids, she could see flashes of orange and red. For a moment, she contemplated that maybe she had died and gone to hell.

This idea was shattered as the voices began to slowly fade into her reality. They started muffled but the more Thursday lay there, they grew to be clearer. Matthew and Whitney. Confusion began to set in, and Thursday frowned in her black abyss. She tiredly forced her eyes open, having to flutter her lids to detangle her eyelashes.

Her vision slid into focus and Thursday found the source of the heat. A massive fire was blazing a short distance from where she lay. It was sideways due to her current position on the ground, but she didn't need to be sitting up to know that it was man-made. She flung her heavy body into a sitting position and looked at her arm. It was healed, the only sign that she had been shot at all being the blood that stained her clothes.

Due to her exhausted state, it took Thursday a moment to process what was going on. She looked around and spotted Matthew and Whitney. They were standing a couple of yards away from Thursday. Whitney was saying something in a hushed voice, but Matthew seemed more interested in the fire blazing in front of him. The flames reflected in his blue and green eyes, giving them a glazed-over quality.

Someone sat a couple of steps in front of the pair, legs crossed, and arms loosely wrapped around the knees. Thursday squinted, the shadows that flickered across the grass constantly crossing the figure, so she was unable to pinpoint their identity. When the light radiating from the fierce carnage grew larger, it bounced off their hair and Thursday recognised that it was Finn. She couldn't see his face fully, but his body looked so tense and straight, that Thursday instantly knew that something was wrong.

Then it finally clicked.

Thursday realised that she was sitting at the bottom of Finn's garden, just before where it broke into the forest. The fire was where Finn's house should have stood. The United Arms wardens must have set it on fire when Thursday escaped. Everything he had built up in the past ten years, dashed to nothing in a couple of hours.

Anger welled up in Thursday's chest. She stood up and walked along the tree line to where Whitney and Matthew stood. Whitney had fallen silent, having given up on trying to get Matthew's attention and instead staring at the inferno in shocked silence. Thursday stopped beside her and turned to face the fire, despite the burn that seared through her skin. The three of them stood there for a couple of minutes, simply gawking at the devastation in angered quiet, Finn sitting in the grass at their feet.

"It was United Arms," Thursday eventually said, breaking the silence. "They must have come looking for me. Looking for *us*."

"Looking for us?" Whitney repeated, her voice devoid of emotion.

"They want to study us. Find out why we are the way we are," Thursday explained.

This was the perfect example of why United Arms should never have become an established mental hospital. They didn't see their patients as people. They simply saw them as pawns; toys; insentient creatures that didn't feel due to their disabilities. The wardens broke into Finn's home on the pure assumption that he was Friday's Child and burned it to the ground when they escaped their clutches because it was nothing more than a reminder of their failure.

"Can't you stop the fire somehow?" Thursday asked Whitney.

Whitney shook her head. "It's too late. I could try to but when we got back here the fire had already been going for ages. Nothing would be saved either way."

Matthew cursed. Thursday and Whitney looked his way. The shifter's fists shook angrily, and he didn't break his stare at the fire, almost like he was locked in a staring contest with the destruction the wardens had caused. "I'll kill them. I'll kill them all."

Thursday's eyes fell on the back of Finn's head. The healer hadn't moved, not even a flinch, since she had awoken. "Where was he? When the wardens broke into the house?"

"He went out and fell asleep on a park bench," Matthew stopped his explanation abruptly, and Whitney took the liberty of finishing the story.

"He didn't want to come back to the house," she said.

Thursday tsked. If his house wasn't burning to the ground, she would have chastised Finn for letting personal drama get in the way of what they needed to do. This wasn't a time for that kind of rubbish. However, his house *was* burning to the ground and as it stood so far today Finn had been reunited with an ex he had never wanted to see again and had his house burned to the ground. As far as shitty days go, this one was up there with the worst.

Besides, by the looks of it, Thursday had been healed by Finn. Therefore, she was in his debt. Finn couldn't undo what he had done once he healed someone, however, if Thursday tried to tell him off right now, she could bet her ass that he would make sure that she got her wound back in one way or another.

"They won't expect us to come back here," Whitney said. "We should get some sleep before morning hits and head to Titus' studio tomorrow. I'll see what I can do about dampening the fire."

Whitney made her way up the garden, waving her hands around each other in continuous circles so that water began to bead on her skin. By the time she reached the blistering wreckage, streams of water were gushing from her palms freely, ready to try to put out the flames.

Thursday turned to Matthew but didn't get a chance to say anything. The shifter moved away from her and deposited himself on the ground beside Finn. He left a space between them so that the healer wasn't uncomfortable by his presence.

Thursday blew a strand of dark hair away from her eyes and sighed. She followed suit, moving around to the other side of Finn and sitting down on the grass. The three of them sat in silence, watching with stoic faces as Whitney put the fire out.

This was why the Seven broke apart.

Whenever they were together, nothing but devastation followed in their wake.

CHAPTER FOUR

NOW THAT THEY KNEW THAT UNITED ARMS WAS ACTIVELY SEEKING THE SEVEN, MATTHEW'S QUEST HAD BECOME SO MUCH MORE IMPORTANT. Not only were they trying to foil Sawyer, but they had to keep out of the way of Dr. Weeks' goons or else they'd all end up in a padded cell. Thursday knew for sure that this was the work of the crazy physician. The woman's warning when she had been interrogated Thursday was hard to misinterpret. She wanted the Seven to experiment on them, to cut them open and find out what made them the way they were. Now it seemed she was showing just how far she was willing to go to get what she wanted.

Thursday had known that the specialists who worked at United Arms weren't professional. The regular beatings and mistreatment made this abundantly clear. Thursday didn't think that they were burn-someone's-house-down unprofessional, though. Sure, there were lengths that they were willing to go to, but why do something unnecessary like that? It was clear that Dr. Weeks was trying to weed them all out. Thankfully, once Thursday and the others tracked down Titus, they would only have to find Sybil.

As much as she hated to admit it to herself, this did mean that they'd also have to locate Sawyer himself and attempt to warn him. Thursday wanted to let Weeks find him and do what she wanted to him. It would make their mission so much easier. That would be too dangerous, though. If United Arms captured Sawyer, they would experiment on him and maybe unlock secrets that the Seven needed to keep hidden. Even they didn't understand enough about their histories to know what would be discovered if they were cut open and studied. Which meant they couldn't afford the risk.

It was turning into a real shit storm, that was for sure.

Titus' studio was deep in Castlebrooke, meaning they'd have to hijack a vehicle.

They stood on the road outside the city, the sky a pale blue above their heads. The air was bitingly cold, a sign that it was still early morning. They had decided to get moving at six o'clock since they didn't know how long it would take them to find Titus, and now that they knew that United Arms was on their tail, it was preferred to find him today.

Finn was still in a foul mood. Understandably enough since they'd just left behind the remains of his house. Whitney was also her usual irritated self. The early start didn't help. Thursday felt the negativity sitting on top of her like an overbearing weight. She tried to be as positive as possible, even at the most insane of times, but it was hard to keep the charade going when no one was entertaining her whims.

"Hijack a car?" Matthew cracked his knuckles. "This is the sort of stuff I'm made for."

"One of your very few uses," Thursday added with a teasing grin.

Matthew mimed thrusting his hand through his chest and yanking out his heart in mocking. With a goofy grin, he broke from the group and headed to the curb. Since it was early morning, there weren't many cars leaving the city. Thursday watched as the shifter dithered on the edge of the pavement; hip cocked to rest most of his weight on one side.

Matthew's mannerisms were often a mixture between feminine and masculine; sassy and sensible; hard and soft. He was neither one nor the other and not in the usual 'humans aren't completely one-way' kind of sense. Sometimes his body language portrayed completely different people, sometimes all at once. Thursday assumed that centuries of changing his appearance to suit the whims of others eventually took its toll on Matthew's natural form. Such a thing must have been very confusing. Thursday had always been impressed by Matthew's ability not to lose himself in the flux of change that he endured regularly.

A car suddenly appeared exiting the city. Matthew straightened as the vehicle drew nearer to him. As soon as the driver spotted him standing there, he changed.

It was an instantaneous process. Blink and you miss it. Now standing on the curb at the side of the road was a slim, full-chested woman with short, red hair. The car meandered towards 'her' like God himself had appeared.

The driver pulled down their window and Matthew stuck his head in. Thursday approached as Matthew talked to the driver like they were lifelong pals. The car's owner was a short but muscular man who had more hair on his arms than Thursday had on her head. He climbed out of his car and began to walk away like this had been his intention all along.

Thursday moved around Matthew and examined the car. It was big; green seven-seater. It would be useful when they collected Titus and Sybil.

"What did you say to him?" she heard Whitney ask as she joined them on the side of the road.

Matthew, still in his redheaded form, shrugged. He was able to hold the appearance of an alter for more than a day after transforming if he so wished. If no one new looked at him, that was. "I told him if he walked to the next city over, I'd meet him there and I"-He paused- "promised things."

"*Things*?" Thursday teased, plopping into the passenger seat, and letting her legs sit out of the open door.

It was easy for Thursday, and the rest of the Seven, to talk to Matthew's alters without feeling like they were talking to a stranger. Matthew's persona shone through no matter what he looked like so even now, when he was a busty redhead with so many freckles on his face that his skin might as well have been blood red, it still felt like Matthew.

Finn finally joined them, having made a point out of taking his sweet time. Thursday didn't doubt that he wouldn't have come with them as easily if his house hadn't been burned down. With the tension between him and Matthew, it seemed that the healer did not want to be a part of any of their schemes, whether Sawyer was involved or not. He had always been that way; tried to steer as far away from trouble as possible. Sadly, being a part of the Seven meant that trouble couldn't be lost; simply detoured.

Now Finn had no home, and he had no choice but to follow them to stop whatever Sawyer was planning.

Matthew glanced at the healer. His guard must have been down because he instantly flickered back into his normal form as soon as their eyes met. Finn looked bored, his face completely placid and unaffected by Matthew's turning back to normal. He clearly did not care how it could be interpreted.

Thursday supposed it would take a while for Finn to get over the loss of his home. His entire life had been in there, near enough, so it certainly wasn't something he was going to get over in a day.

"You two better not turn this into a soap opera," Thursday warned.

Matthew gasped dramatically. "But what if I'm pregnant with Finn's illegitimate child?"

"Keep it to yourself," Whitney scowled.

"And I'm not paying child benefit," Finn surprised them by adding.

Matthew didn't turn back to look at Finn, but grinned nonetheless, despite the healer's tone having been as flat as a burnt pancake.

"Come on then, let's go!" Thursday flipped onto her knees and tried to climb into the driver's seat. She was stopped by a hand grabbing the back of her shirt and dragging her back out through the passenger's side. "What?!" she complained as Whitney deposited her on the grass.

"You are the last person anyone would trust to drive a vehicle," Whitney said.

"I can drive!" Thursday snapped. "I got my licence!"

"Where is it?" Matthew asked.

Thursday chewed on her lip. It was most likely at the bottom of the Heritage Pond outside Castlebrooke. How it got there was a long and rather boring story involving her driving instructor and the many times she disagreed with him during their lessons. In the end, she had gotten her licence, but she didn't like her instructor's attitude as he signed off the sheet. So, once she was given her licence, she found him behind the Instructor Centre and may or may not have driven his car into the Pond. His car, which he may or may not have been inside.

"Not here," Thursday opted to answer.

"Right. So that's a no," Whitney replied.

"Well, I don't see any of you idiots flashing your licences!" Thursday threw back.

"That's because we don't need it. We're lawbreakers, but we're not suicidal," Matthew answered.

Thursday clamoured to her feet, grumbling irritably. "You're both just trying to get back at me for the incident on the hill," she said.

"Maybe if you *hadn't* made us believe we were going to drop to our deaths then I'd be a lot more understanding now." Whitney moved to get into the driver's seat herself, but Thursday stuck her arm out angrily. If she wasn't going to be allowed to drive without a licence, then these two weren't either! Besides, last Thursday heard, Whitney couldn't drive anyway!

"Christ's sake, am I the only organized one here?" Finn yanked his wallet out of his back pocket and chucked it at Thursday, who caught it clumsily.

Thursday fiddled the wallet open while Finn made his way around the car to the driver's side. Whitney and Matthew huddled around her as she fished his driver's licence out of the plastic window. Whitney snatched it out of Thursday's hand as soon as it was free and held it up to the light like a shopkeeper making sure that the money they had been handed wasn't counterfeit.

"Let me guess, you drove a Jag?" Thursday snipped as she clamoured into the passenger seat.

Matthew and Whitney slotted themselves into the first row of backseats. Thursday turned in her seat and hugged the headrest as Finn pulled away from the curb and started driving back to Castlebrooke. "Put my licence back into its slot."

"Or what?" Matthew questioned, taking the piece of card

from Whitney and running his thumb over the picture of Finn on the front.

"Or it'll get damaged or, most likely since it's in your hands, *lost*. And if you lose my licence, Matthew, I'll brake this car when you're least expecting it and I know you haven't got your belt on right, if you even have it on at all." Finn reached behind his seat, letting his hand lie flat in waiting for Matthew to hand it over.

Out of badness, Matthew slipped the licence behind his ear and high-fived Finn instead. "Brake the car?" he snorted. "When I'm least expecting it? I'm ready for anything, my senses are always on high alert!"

"Stop being a dick, Mattie," Thursday groaned, flipping around to sit properly and kicking her feet up onto the dashboard. "Just hand over the damn licence."

"I am ready for anything, it's practically my second gift," Matthew pressed, ignoring Thursday completely. Whitney rolled her eyes and tried to snatch the licence back. If Finn got in any more of a slump, then they were going to be dragging him around by his ankles. "Just try me, I'm like a cat I'm on such high alert"-

Finn slammed his foot down on the brake with a growl of frustration. Whitney fell forward into the back of Thursday's chair, while Thursday's forehead smacked off her knees. The best reaction, however, was Matthew, who was silenced from his smug rant as his body flung forward and cracked off the window. He fell backwards and lay unconscious across the seat.

Whitney turned her nose up and pushed him off her body onto the floor. "Idiot," she muttered.

Thursday looked over her shoulder and snickered at Matthew's face, which was wedged between the two front seats. She shook her head and slid the licence out from behind his ear. She passed it back to Whitney, who took it and pushed it back into its respective slot in Finn's wallet.

"He has a mouth that never stops," Whitney muttered. "I hate him. Why did he have to get me first? My god, he just doesn't *shut up.*"

"He means well," Finn murmured.

"He could mean the best of the best, but unless he shuts his mouth, I don't care," Whitney answered.

Thursday liked Matthew; his personality just gelled so well with her own, but even she knew that he was hard to swallow. The word inappropriate, nor its meaning, ever seemed to process in his brain.

"Does anyone even really know what the true purpose of this quest is?" Finn asked. "How do you know that Matthew didn't just make this all up to stir shit?"

Thursday laughed. "Matthew isn't that bright!" she barked. "Besides, why now? It doesn't make sense! I mean, I'm an advocate for nonsense but I doubt Matthew would think that far ahead."

"You're applying logic to a man that doesn't have any," Whitney reminded them. "Matthew's an idiot but he's not a pretend-Sunday's-back idiot."

Finn was chewing on his bottom lip like it was a stick of gum. They were nearing Castlebrooke, the buildings growing larger the closer they got. Thursday despised the city and wished she could just tell Finn to turn around. What was the next city over? Opara City, wasn't it? A fresh start sounded amazing.

If only...

Thursday would have done it if the situation had been any different. She had a stupid obligation to these people. They'd saved her sorry ass a ridiculous number of times and she hated that. Even Matthew's 'quest' had saved her from torture in United Arms. She owed him for that and so here she was. Thursday had a track record of obligation. Most of the time she wouldn't care as much but Thursday had a soft spot for Matthew. Out of the six others, Matthew was the closest thing she had to a friend. Mainly because he wasn't too serious about everything, just like her.

"I don't know if I trust it or not," Finn muttered, almost to himself.

Thursday heard him.

"Well, riddle me this then: If Matthew was just doing this to stir the pot, why would he choose something that includes reuniting the seven of us? *Especially* since we are currently heading in the direction of the man who hates Matthew's very existence and will most likely attempt to murder him as soon as he lays eyes on him?" Thursday asked.

"That's an exaggeration," Finn said flatly.

Whitney kicked her feet up on the top of Thursday's chair and threw in, "Who cares either way? Whether Matthew is a liar or not, we now have those United Arms savages on our tails."

Thursday scratched her head. "Yeah, sorry about that. To be fair, though, I think Dr. Weeks had her suspicions about us. She had this file on us and everything. I mean, I didn't reveal your identity-I didn't reveal *anyone's* identity- yet she still knew to come to your house, Finn."

"The United Arms have offices the size of the Grand Canyon, filled with files on everyone in Castlebrooke." Finn released one hand from the steering wheel to anxiously rub the back of his neck. "If anyone were to notice unusual behaviour that could be related to the Seven, it would be them."

Thursday saw Whitney move in the rear-view mirror. She was grabbing the back of Matthew's shirt and dragging him backwards into his seat. The growing sunlight made something sparkle on her face. Thursday squinted and realised that it was a nose ring.

"If Matthew hadn't come up with this ridiculous reunion plot, I feel like we would have been forced together again anyway," Whitney admitted as she haphazardly buckled Matthew's seatbelt. He was immune to damage, but he wasn't immune to death, and for all, they knew a United Arms lackey could crash into the car at any moment. "In much less desirable circumstances."

"The United Arms cells are comfortable, I shall admit, but not desirable for a long-term stay," Thursday added.

Beside her, Finn shuddered. Thursday slouched down in her seat. Even he knew that some wounds couldn't be healed.

~T~

Titus' dance studio had expanded since Thursday had last seen it. Titus had been an avid member since the building opened in 1955 and he bought the joint over twenty years ago. Of course, he had to come and go every decade or so due to his inability to age to make sure he didn't arouse suspicion. Even back in the 50s, some people would have paid a pretty penny to get their hands on the seven magical beings that always seemed to leave some sort of supernatural mess in their wake.

Thursday supposed it made sense that the studio had renovated itself again in the last decade. Nothing stayed the same anymore, everything was constantly morphing and changing into something new. It was amazing how many buildings could rise and fall repeatedly in such a short space of time. Ten years was nothing to the Seven but to human beings, entire worlds could be built up and knocked down again in that space of time.

The four of them (Matthew woke up while the three of them were bickering about parking, thankfully having the sense not to complain about the braking incident) entered through the automatic doors and headed towards the reception desk.

The interior was very sterile, the only break in the plain white colouring seeming to be the black mirror flooring. Thursday liked the disorientating sensation that fluttered through her system as her mirrored counterpart walked right below her, in complete sync with every movement she made.

"I feel funny," Matthew commented as Finn spoke to the receptionist.

They stood a couple of feet away from the desk, trusting Finn to get the information they needed. He was the most diplomatic and sensible out of the four of them.

"When do you ever feel normal?" Whitney moodily replied, tossing her golden hair back over her shoulders to get it out of the way of her face.

"No, seriously, I think hitting my head has messed me up," Matthew insisted.

Thursday frowned at him. "In what way?"

The sentence was barely out of Thursday's mouth before the skin on Matthew's arm rippled like he was struggling to keep his appearance at bay.

"Well, damn," said Thursday.

"Is that all you have to say?" Matthew exclaimed. "If I don't sort this out now, I'm going to turn into Yvanna in front of Titus and he's going to kill me!"

Whitney snorted softly to herself, casting her gaze to the entrance of the studio. "Would that be all that bad?" she quietly muttered.

Ignoring Whitney, Thursday shrugged off Matthew's concerns. "We'll say you hit your head and you honestly can't control it," she said. "I mean, at least this time you're not lying, even Finn will back you up. It is his fault your head is messed up anyway."

"It doesn't help that it's a Monday!" Matthew hysterically answered. Thursday was irked by the fact that it seemed like he hadn't taken what she had said on board at all. "My powers are going off the charts! I'll be lucky if my eyes stay different!"

Already bored with Matthew's complaining, Thursday turned to Whitney. She looked like she was about to go to some sort of emo concert from the noughties; nearly in complete black save for her denim shorts. If it weren't for her bright blonde hair, she'd have melted into the background. Maybe that was her intention.

"When did you get your nose pierced?" Thursday demanded to know.

Whitney touched the silver hoop in her nose, eyebrows narrowed. "Years ago. Why?"

"Are you going for some sort of punk look? What with the leather jacket; the fishnets and the hoop in your nose?" Thursday asked.

Whitney scowled. "What does it matter to you?"

Thursday inhaled. "Jeez, alright, I won't ask any questions. Why is everyone so highly strung?" She blew a raspberry. "You know what they say, the bigger the hoop, the bigger the whor"-

"Can someone please help me here?!" Matthew exclaimed.

"What do you mean you can't tell me?" Finn's voice intercepted their conversation.

Thursday looked over her shoulder to where Finn had been left to converse with the receptionist.

He had an extremely perplexed expression on his face that hadn't been there before. "This is a dance studio, not Fort Knox!"

The bleach-blonde girl behind the reception desk's face was closed off and she was shaking her head. "I'm sorry, Mr Warhol specifically said"-

"Mr. *Who?*"

"Titus. He specifically said not to allow anyone to see him."

"But this is different."

"It doesn't matter."

"Trust me, it *does*."

Thursday sighed and crossed the short distance to where Finn stood, leaving Matthew to continue to complain to Whitney. She jumped the final few inches and landed feet first on top of the reception desk. Kicking the girl's book off the desk, Thursday crouched onto her haunches. "Look, Sharon"-

"It's Cate," the receptionist corrected.

"That's nice, Sharon," Thursday said. She waved her ripped jacket sleeve in Sharon's face, making sure that she could see the buckles. "What does this look like?"

Sharon looked confused. Like she knew perfectly well what was being presented before her, but she just couldn't bring herself to understand why Thursday would be in one. "A …a strait jacket?" she asked unsurely.

"Yes! Well done, the bleach didn't go to your head," Thursday beamed. "Why do you think it's been ripped?"

"I…I have no idea." Sharon's beady green eyes grew smaller as she tried to put two and two together. Judging by the slightly constipated expression on her face, it seemed to be giving her some severe trouble.

"Want to at least hazard a guess?" asked Thursday. She plopped onto her butt on the desk and crossed her legs. She heard Finn sigh heavily behind her. "I'll wait."

Sharon's throat bobbed as she took a slow step back from her desk. The realisation of where Thursday had come from seemed to have made her scared of moving too fast in case this sudden change of speed forced Thursday to suddenly attack her. "United Arms," Sharon stated. She didn't clarify further.

"Ex-*hey*!" Thursday yelped as Finn grabbed her shoulder and forcibly pulled her from the reception desk. He wasn't gentle but made sure she didn't land on her head. Thursday burst into hysterical laughter, suddenly amused as she realised that he probably didn't want her to hit her head so that she didn't act any crazier than she already did.

"Look, Cate, we're kind of in a hurry here so can we please just"- Finn was cut off as Sharon bolted away from the desk, disappearing into a back room without looking back. Thursday wasn't sure, but she could swear she heard a high-pitched shrill of a voice scream, "*Titus! There're psychos outside asking for you!*"

"Well done, Thursday," Whitney said flatly from the waiting area.

"It worked, didn't it?" Thursday responded, lying on her back on the floor and closing her eyes.

"Yeah, and now someone knows where you are," Finn said. "You don't think it's been all over the news that you escaped? Because it has!"

"*What?!*" Thursday bolted upright, her ripped strait jacket slipping down her arms and resting at her elbows. "Do you think they used my admission picture? I hate that picture! My hair was not on fair that day at all! I had just gotten my revenge on a wretched old man who was leering at a group of girls at a nightclub when I was jumped by those Arms clones. I didn't have time to fix myself, I was covered in blood and"-

"As riveting as this story is; really, I'm so hooked," Whitney muttered with no interest in her voice whatsoever, "I feel compelled to point out that Cate"-

"Sharon," Thursday corrected.

Whitney closed her eyes, nostrils flaring angrily as she muttered, "God, give me strength."

Matthew suddenly made a squeaking noise that resembled a mouse getting castrated. Three incredulous faces turned his way as he slapped a hand over his mouth. Thursday couldn't resist laughing at the girlish sound he'd made, the concern for whatever created the sound being the last thing on her mind.

The answer to the latter question was quickly answered when the back door Cate had disappeared through opened again to reveal Titus. Matthew instantly fell on his ass, unable to control the change and trying to hide from Titus' view.

Thursday had forgotten how lovely Yvanna had looked. Long, silky black hair always coupled well with pale, porcelain skin. The woman's beauty had never been powerful enough to hide the rot that ate away at her black heart. Thursday had had the woman pegged from the start, but Titus had been so blinded by her allure that he lost sight of rhyme or reason. He still mourned his marriage one hundred years later, even though Yvanna had been cheating on him with the Duke for an extraordinarily long time.

Matthew was a blur of black hair as he slipped beneath Whitney's chair to hide. Whitney rolled her eyes but didn't say anything. Thursday looked back to Titus, who didn't seem to notice what had happened since Matthew had fallen so quickly.

"What are you three doing here?" Titus asked angrily.

Titus had not changed at all. His dark skin was smooth and unblemished, and his dancer's body lithe but strong. His black t-shirt had '**VICE DANCE STUDIOS**' branded across the chest with the studio's signature lightning bolt slicing through the letters.

"We're getting the band back together!" Thursday declared, taking on Matthew's job as the enthusiast.

Titus stared at Thursday. "Last I heard, you'd been committed," he said.

"Yes, I'm sure you did," Thursday sniffed. She pulled her jacket sleeves up and clumsily staggered to her feet. "It was all a big misunderstanding." She beamed. "Besides, I'm needed for the cause."

Titus' golden eyes scanned Thursday with a look of distaste. He looked to Finn with a stern but kinder gaze. "Cause?" he asked.

Finn ran a hand through his bronze hair. "It's Sawyer. He's been active recently. You know how dangerous he is; we're concerned he might be trying to ..." He trailed off, deciding that he didn't need to finish the sentence.

Titus didn't move from where he stood, nor did he seem at all convinced that their mission was legitimate. Titus; Finn; and Sybil had always been the boring threesome. Ever since the beginning, they acted like parents. Constantly questioning everything and shepherding the remaining four around. However, if Finn was on board, Thursday knew that no matter how much he dragged his heels, Titus would be too. If Matthew; Whitney and Thursday had only shown up at the studio, Titus would have had no qualms with telling them to go away. Since Finn- one of the fellow boring; sceptical parents-was with them confirming the story, it made everything completely different.

"How can you be so sure?" Titus asked, nonetheless.

Finn opened his mouth, but no words came out. He turned to where Whitney was sitting and saw the state Matthew was in; clearly in no place to explain anything. He rotated back around and said, "Matthew knows the details, but he's indisposed right now."

"Indisposed how?"

"It's his Soul Day, Titus, you've got to be easy on him," Whitney grumbled with no further explanation.

"The fact of the matter is that you know how hard it becomes to control our abilities when it's our Soul Day," said Finn. "Matthew isn't suicidal either-he's stupid, but not that stupid-so whatever you see right now is not a product of malice"-

"He looks like my Yvanna right now, doesn't he?" Titus sighed, rubbing his eyes. He already looked tired, and he had barely been speaking to them for five minutes.

There was a pregnant pause. The only thing that could be heard was the soft clicking of Whitney picking at her fingernails. Thursday burst into a fit of giggles. She could never take long silences seriously and always tried to fill that thick gap of *nothing with something.*

Finally, a tiny voice piped up from beneath Whitney's chair. "Sorry," Matthew squeaked.

Titus moved around the receptionist's desk and looked beneath Whitney's chair with a bored expression. "Get out from under there, you fool," he said.

Matthew scrambled out from beneath the chair, skidding on the floor like a skater on ice. He waved his black hair back from his face. "I've got this completely under control," he quickly said to Titus, gesturing to his current appearance. "We were in a small accident"-

Thursday snorted. "Small accident," she muttered.

Matthew glared at her pointedly and continued, "We were in a small accident, and I hit my head so I'm not in complete control anymore." As if to further prove this statement, his arms and face rippled like the ocean, momentarily changing his face to normal before returning to the pointed face of Yvanna again. "But, ah, yeah. Where were we?"

"Tell Titus what you know about Sawyer," Thursday ordered. She threw herself onto the arm of Whitney's chair, despite the other woman's protests.

"Oh. That. Yeah." Matthew scratched his head and moved towards Titus, only to be stopped when the latter held their hand up in warning not to get too close. "Um, yes. You see, the thing is, I was out with this girl on a date the other week"-Titus sighed heavily and moved to leave- "It's important, I swear!"

"How are your romantic escapades important?"

"Listen to me for once, *God!*" Matthew exclaimed.

Thursday herself was quite interested in this story, as she hadn't heard the true reasoning behind Matthew's belief that Sawyer was active again yet.

"I was on a date with a girl the other week and we were passing Sawyer's building. You know the one, big-in-your-face-skyscraper? Yeah, I was passing there when I saw people from United Arms going in."

This captured Thursday's immediate attention. "What?"

Matthew nodded. "I told the girl to go on without me"-He suddenly looked to Finn with partial alarm and quickly added, "She was boring anyway! I didn't like her all that much," before continuing. "I told her to go on without me and I sat on a bench just out of sight. God, it was so boring waiting for something to happen. I honestly wanted to shoot myself…"

Matthew kept diverting from the main point of what the story was supposed to tell them. Thursday tried to remain focused, but her brain kept mindlessly wandering off while Matthew rambled. One minute her attention could be solely on the part of the story where Matthew got a date with a girl simply by winking at her while she passed him on the bench, and the next minute she would be wondering if it was the time of year where the birds flew south for the Winter yet.

"Hardly the main point here," said Whitney in a flat voice as Matthew began to detail the colour of the eyes this easily ensnared woman had.

"My attention span isn't all that admirable," Thursday added. She frowned. "Is it Wintertime yet?"

Despite this story having an extremely egotistical vibe to it, it was unmistakable how Matthew kept anxiously glancing at Finn to take in his reaction to what he was saying. From what Thursday could tell, either Finn didn't give a shit about any of Matthew's detailed conquests, or he had mastered the art of hiding his emotions to the point of extreme indifference.

"*Anyway*," Finn interrupted, "get to the point, Matthew."

"Right. Okay. I was waiting for at least three hours when the United Arms guys came out again. This time they were with *Sawyer*."

"What would Sawyer get from hanging around United Arms lackeys?" Titus frowned.

Thursday jumped to her feet. "Were they all lackeys?" she asked.

Matthew shrugged. "One of them looked like she could be a Doctor, I guess. She had a white lab coat on…"

"Was she blonde?" Thursday insisted. "Blonde with shit brown eyes? Blonde with shit brown eyes and a nose that you could hang your clothes out to dry on?"

"That sounds about right, yeah. Yes, that sounds *really* familiar. She was practically attached to Sawyer's side. They were huddled together like they didn't want the other guys to hear what they were talking about." Matthew's skin rippled, and he finally turned back to normal again. He took in Thursday's alarmed expression. "Why? Do you know her?"

"He's been talking to Dr. Weeks!" Thursday exclaimed.

"Doctor what?" asked Titus.

"*Weeks!* She was my assigned doctor at the asylum. No wonder she knew all about me, I bet Sawyer has told her everything about us! I bet that's how they knew where you lived as well, Finn!"

It sounded just like Dr. Weeks to stick her nose in where it wasn't wanted! But how did she know to go to Sawyer, of all people? Unless Dr. Weeks didn't come to him, and he went to her instead ...Oh. Oh dear.

"Was she carrying a big folder, Matthew?"

Matthew rubbed the bridge of his nose. "I don't know, Thursday, I can't remember everything!"

"It's important! She had this massive file with information on all of us in it! If Sawyer provided her with that information for whatever reason, then there probably isn't a lot she doesn't know. I bet that's why she wanted to interrogate me so suddenly with accusations about the seven of us! She *knows!*"

Titus made a noise at the back of his throat. He still didn't seem too convinced. "What would Sawyer get from exposing us? He'd be simultaneously exposing himself as well. It's counterproductive."

Thursday snorted. "To achieve his goals? Sawyer would do anything, whether it be counterproductive or not."

Finn rubbed his eyes with the heels of his hand. It looked like the conversation had toppled an extra fifty years to his face.

Titus noticed this and insisted, "It's nothing, surely. Just a couple of coincidental events that could be misinterpreted into something bigger than it really is. I wouldn't worry about it."

It was no secret that Finn was the most terrified of Sawyer. Not out of natural cowardice but out of fear of the unknown. Thursday had never been afraid of Sawyer, more out of familiarity than a disrespect of his insanity. Thursday was her brand of crazy, meaning that she knew how to recognise people who were off-the-wall insane like her. Sawyer was just like her, just in a subtler way. Finn, however, had a different viewpoint of the entire situation. Understandably so, too.

Sawyer had always said that if he were to combine the powers of all the seven into one body, the first person he would need would be Finn. It used to be in a funny 'tee-hee-well-that'll-never-happen' way but now it was different. If Sawyer somehow figured out a way to take Finn's healing ability for himself, there would be no stopping him at all. He would be able to heal himself from all damage, and the only way that he would be stopped would be a fatal gunshot wound to the head at point-blank range or decapitation.

The problem was that Finn *couldn't* heal himself. He could heal any and every wound in the world except anything that would instantly kill but he could never heal himself. It just didn't work. It was like Finn had a different body type from everyone else, a system immune to the healing ability he was blessed with.

Sawyer didn't see it that way, though. He believed that there was a way around it. He believed that if he had had enough time to play around with the idea and experiment a little, he'd discover a cure to this, as he had called it, 'minor setback'.

Time in which he had had plenty of since he left.

"Enough talk about Sawyer right now," Whitney barked irritably. Thursday couldn't help snickering. Whitney was always moody and irritable, but this was different. Thursday could decipher a tinge of panic.

The thing was, where Finn was number one on Sawyer's list, Whitney sat at number two.

"We need to find Sybil, don't we?" Whitney continued. "If this situation is going to get worse then we need to find her before United Arms or Sawyer get to her first."

"Where even is Sybil nowadays? Is she a recluse now? I never see her around," Matthew frowned, scratching his head in confusion. The fact that he never passed by Sybil in the past ten years seemed to be struggling to process correctly in his brain. It wasn't a common occurrence in his highly socialised life for him to not know where everyone was.

Finn and Titus exchanged a look. Thursday noticed it. "What?" she demanded. "Have the three of you been meeting up in secret or something?" She sneered. "The trio of *parents*."

Finn sighed. "Let's go. We need to go anyway before Cate"-

"You mean Shar"-

- "Calls United Arms."

"To be fair," Whitney pointed out, "she probably already has."

The five of them piled out of Titus' dance studio, Titus reluctantly following. They made their way to the car, four out of five of them looking slightly unseated and on edge. Thursday, however, felt like she was on top of the world, skipping down the path to the car like she was skipping through a field of daisies. What was the point of getting worked up about this? It would cloud their judgement. Staying calm and happy was the best way forward, it would make their decisions more rational.

Besides, Thursday had learned long ago that the United Arms lackeys were nothing more than a bunch of wimps hiding behind masks and authority.

"Where are we going now?" Matthew asked as he crammed himself into the first backseat with Whitney and Titus. Titus had been about to get into the front seat, but Thursday had intercepted him, nearly mowing him over in the process.

"The hospital," Finn answered as he pulled out from the pavement.

"The hospital?" Thursday snapped. "Can't your paycheque wait?"

Finn's nostrils flared, the dimple above his jaw that only appeared when he was frustrated standing prominently against his skin. "No," he eventually said. "We're collecting Sybil. She has an appointment with me today."

"At the hospital?" Whitney frowned.

"What's wrong with her?" Matthew chuckled. "Overworked?"

Thursday laughed. "Well, as they say, Saturday's child wo"-

"You don't know?" Titus interrupted.

"Obviously not!" Whitney shouted. "Just spit it out!"

Finn turned a corner so suddenly that the three in the back toppled to the left like collapsing dominos. "Sybil has an appointment with me because she is due for a scan." Thursday looked at him sharply. He ignored her cutting gaze. "She's four months pregnant."

CHAPTER FIVE

IT WASN'T POSSIBLE.

Right?

Thursday wasn't normally someone who could be taken off guard. She liked to think that she was always ready for any and every possibility. Not in the way Matthew had thought he had been, but more in a way that she was just always more prepared for sudden turns on a mental level rather than physical.

This, however, had come from left field and smacked her sideways.

They were barren and sterile. That was the point. None of the Seven were able to have children. They were the *only ones* of their kind in existence! How had Sybil managed to skirt around that? Had she even *meant* to skirt around it?

Did this mean that the baby would be like them? Would it have Sybil's ability or a new one? Would the pregnancy affect Sybil's *own* ability? Was it possible to have an eighth member of the Seven? So many questions! So many questions Finn wouldn't damn well answer! He refused to say any more as they drove to the hospital as he had already said too much.

Thursday and the others followed Finn through the winding corridors of the hospital, passing cases ranging from flu to Cancer to arthritis. At least if Sybil had had Cancer or arthritis, Finn would have had a chance of healing her. Finn couldn't heal a baby out of someone. Or as far as Thursday was aware, he couldn't.

As they approached Finn's office, Thursday could see Sybil sitting in the waiting area by the door. In a way, it was good that Finn had warned them that she was pregnant, or else Thursday would have just believed that Saturday's child had gotten really, *really* round in the belly area.

"Sybil!" Thursday exclaimed from the top of the corridor. "You've gotten fat!"

Sybil looked up from the book she was reading. Her face instantly melted into an expression that was a picture-perfect rendition of extreme horror. Thursday didn't know if it was the fat comment, or the fact that Thursday was there at all, or the fact that the five of them were there at all, but she couldn't help finding it amazingly hilarious that Sybil looked like she had just been told she was going to give birth to a sewer rat in five months.

"What is wrong with you?" Titus hissed at Thursday as Finn began to walk ahead of them, overtaking the group entirely.

"I don't know. I think my left nostril is bigger than the right," Thursday shrugged.

Her ears were also slightly misshapen and if she moved her thumb a certain way it dislocated itself. She had an idea that this wasn't what Titus meant but delving into the poor state of her mental health would take a year and a half and she didn't believe that Titus would be willing to listen to her for that length of time.

Sybil backed away from them. "You told me you wouldn't tell them!" she snapped at Finn.

"I didn't"-

"Yes, you did," Thursday frowned, standing herself beside the healer. A cheeky smile bloomed on her face. "Don't tell me you forgot already. We asked why we were going to the hospital, and you told us"-

"He told us out of necessity," Titus insisted.

Sybil looked extremely uncomfortable, her eyes bouncing from Thursday to Matthew to Whitney and back again. "Why are you together?" she asked. She straightened with realisation, concern washing over her face. "What's happened?"

"No one's dead," Finn assured.

"Tragically," Thursday added.

When they parted ways a decade ago, they agreed that the only time that they would reunite would be if one of them died. Thursday had anticipated such news and had had her eye on a fabulous black dress in the window of Marvellous May's Miraculous Maidens, but it had never come. Who knew, maybe all this would end in death. Maybe it would be hers! Then she could haunt Matthew for the rest of his life! Then when he bit the dust, they could haunt Titus!

The six of them crammed themselves into Finn's office. It was a spacious room lined with expensive-looking furniture. The view from the window wasn't great, but the window itself was quite big and the sky was at least visible. Either Finn was so respected in the hospital that he had been given the best office in the building, or he had worked his way up to deserving it himself. Thursday didn't know which to believe.

They explained the situation to Sybil. She sat and listened to Matthew's story of his escapades outside Sawyer's building, asking questions every so often and telling him to get on with it whenever he diverted from the main point. Thursday's patience was tested during this time. It was so *boring* listening to the same story rehashed over again.

"And United Arms have been tailing you ever since?" Sybil asked once caught up.

"They've been smoking us out," said Whitney.

"*Literally,*" Thursday muttered.

Whitney rolled her eyes. "Thanks for that clarification."

Thursday winked at Whitney and clicked her tongue. She stopped pacing. "Don't take this the wrong way but not one of you would last a week in United Arms. Once you're admitted, you have no rights." Her eyes fell on Sybil's belly. "Your little 'en would be taken from you."

Sybil drummed her fingers against Finn's desk. "I know. I've researched how the Arms deal with their patients. Of course, the website was a load of folly. It took a while to access the files of the staff but once I did, I uncovered a lot of skeletons."

"Why were you researching the Arms?" asked Thursday.

Sybil shrugged. "I heard you'd been admitted. I wanted to know what was going on."

Thursday grimaced. "Bleck. Why bother with a crazy biddy like me? You must have been run off your feet!"

"Aye, completely," Sybil said flatly. "You're not as hard to follow as you think you are. Spontaneous murders? Acts of arson? Assaults? It's always you. If you hadn't told me that it was United Arms that destroyed Finn's home, I would have thought it was you."

This news amused Thursday. "Oh, well, that's good! It's about time my handiwork was recognised!"

"Your trademark is recklessness, Thursday. Any one of us could recognise your work," Titus muttered.

Thursday placed her hand on her chest, a smile infecting her face. "Aw, thank you, Titus, I didn't think you liked me that much!"

Finn, who had been rummaging inside the drawers of his desk, finally appeared and slapped a bunch of files on top. "Come on, Sybil," he said, "we'll get your scan sorted and then we can talk more when it's done."

"While you are doing that, I'm going to take a nap." Thursday jumped onto Finn's desk, disturbing the papers and making the lamp shake. The wooden legs of the desk creaked in protest to the extra weight but didn't collapse. Finn didn't bother commenting and ushered Sybil out of the room.

Thursday waved them out and turned her back on the others to sleep on the desk. She had slept in more awkward spaces and the papers worked quite well as a thin mattress.

It felt like barely five minutes before she was woken up by Titus' voice. "Matthew, come here." His voice was right by Thursday's head. She hoped he moved soon or else she'd have to get up and make him move, which would mean disturbing her current sleeping position.

"What?" There was a shift as Matthew crossed to where Titus must have been standing.

"Is that the woman you were talking about?"

"What woman?"

"The woman from United Arms, Matthew."

"Who? The blonde one?"

Thursday's eyes shot open. She knocked the lamp off the desk as she jumped off, making both Matthew and Titus jump. "Dr Weeks?" she demanded, pushing past them and pressing her face against the window.

The view from Finn's office was abhorrent because the roof of the attached A&E ward obscured anything worth looking at. Thursday had just got there in time, however, to catch a wisp of blonde hair and a massive nose before said woman disappeared behind the roof.

"What could she be here for?" Matthew wondered aloud.

"I don't know Matthew, maybe she's dislocated her shoulder," Thursday sarcastically answered.

"How could she possibly know that we're here?" Matthew threw back.

Titus palmed his forehead tiredly. There was a sheen of sweat on his dark skin, giving the impression that he was glistening under the overhead lights. "Cate knows that Finn is a doctor. Maybe they came to my studio and asked where we went, and she made a guess."

"If Sharon knows Finn, then why didn't she let him pass through to see you?" Thursday frowned.

Titus shrugged. "I told her I didn't want to see anyone." A pause. "Who the heck is Sharon?"

Ignoring Titus' question, Thursday rotated on her heel, noticing that they were down one person. "Where is Whitney?"

"Sybil wanted some female company," Matthew shrugged. "And I didn't count, since I've been exerting some extreme self-control to resist turning into the wet dream of every doctor and patient in this joint."

"And she didn't ask for *me*?" Thursday demanded. "How rude. She's officially off my Christmas card list."

"If it makes you feel any better Whitney did not want to go at all and complained that they should have taken you instead," Titus answered.

Matthew snorted, weaving around the two of them and heading to the door of the office. "I doubt it was even Sybil's idea to have female company, it was probably Finn's. He's too sentimental that way."

"So, it was Finn who didn't want me then?" Thursday complained, following Matthew to the door with folded arms and a pout. "Then *he's* off my Christmas card list."

"Where are you going?" asked Titus.

"We can't stay here if Dr. Weeks is coming!"

"Where else are we going to go?!"

Thursday cracked her knuckles and didn't answer. She could sense a fight coming.

Matthew opened the door and poked his head out, trying to act like some sort of spy. Thursday planted her boot on his butt and kicked him out the door before exiting with Titus in reluctant tow. Thursday was tempted to ditch, but they needed to find Finn. It was all well and good for them to run off but if they didn't at the very least warn Finn and the others then there was no way they would be capable of escaping.

If Dr. Weeks captured those three, then not only would Sawyer have access to his experiment subjects one and two, but Sybil was also experiment subject number three.

Thursday was fairly sure she was experiment number four, but she wasn't worried about that.

She wasn't scared of Sawyer one bit.

"Where do they do baby scans? Is there a baby scan room?!" Thursday asked incredulously. The last time she had set foot inside a hospital had been when she had to finish off a job that had gone awry. A quick air bubble to an IV drip and she had been gone again.

"Follow me!" Matthew yelled.

"How do *you* know where it is?!" Titus exclaimed.

Despite being just as confused as Titus was, Thursday followed the shifter as he took off down a corridor. All hospitals looked the same. The same corridor repeated over and over again. An endless river of pale walls that had absorbed an astronomical amount of misery and death. Thursday could practically taste the salty tang of the tears that had been shed along these floors. If they weren't in such dire circumstances, she would probably have dropped to the ground and tasted it, just to make sure it wasn't all in her head.

Matthew led them down so many of those endlessly similar corridors, each one as morbidly boring and plain as the previous. Sometimes they passed patients and visitors. Thursday was tempted to try to knock someone unconscious and steal their clothes, so they could sneak out of the hospital in disguise, but one glance at Titus-who had a glare that could make a clock not just break, but spontaneously combust-meant that it was a no-go. Titus was a hard man to argue with and even she knew that they didn't have time to waste.

Thursday had become so focused on trying to make sure she didn't trip out of excitement that she rammed straight into someone, the force knocking her clean off her feet. Titus jumped onto a chair to avoid being pushed over by Thursday's body. The action had come to him so easily you would almost believe it had been his intention all along.

"Thanks for catching me, Thumbelina!" Thursday barked, rubbing the back of her head as she scrambled back to her feet. She looked at who she had banged into and grinned at the sight of Whitney lying on the ground, glowering like a beast. "There you are!"

Matthew was a short distance beyond, explaining to Finn and Sybil what was happening with a great deal of exaggerated hand gestures.

"We know, we saw them," Finn insisted.

"What do you mean *you* saw them?! They were coming in through the front!" Matthew exclaimed.

"No, we saw them coming through the smoking entrance," Sybil said calmly. "Sawyer and some of the United Arms workers"-

"*Sawyer*?! We saw Dr. Weeks!"

Thursday opened her mouth to offer her own stellar opinion on what was going on when she was jumped on from behind.

Everything erupted into chaos.

There was so much screaming Thursday couldn't tell if it was her own enraged yelling or the terrified screeches of the hospital dwellers as they ran away.

"Get the hell off me!" Thursday barked. She threw herself at the closest wall. She went into complete psycho mode, letting her body overtake her mind to get the freak off her back.

Something cool touched her throat. *Knife*. With a growl that could easily be mistaken for that of a wild animal, Thursday grabbed the hand clutching the weapon and used the leverage to toss them over her shoulder. She looked at her attacker and realised with a jolt that it was more of the United Arms men. They had caught up with them.

Finally, Thursday registered what was going on around her. They had been ambushed. With a curse, Thursday wretched the knife from her attacker and stamped down on their throat before jumping into the fray, wrestling someone off Finn and stabbing them in the neck.

In combat, Thursday always had the backs of the weakest in the group. She knew that it left her open for attack, but she couldn't help it. When you spend hundreds of years with the same people, a decade apart doesn't change much. Not many of the Seven were actual fighters. Heck, Thursday was barely a fighter herself. A lot of them were saved by their power, and that was it. Without it, they would be dead.

There was a chill in the air and Thursday ducked just in time to avoid getting speared with a long shard of ice. It went straight through one of the United Arms goons, the point going straight through their chest and attaching itself to the wall behind. Baffled, Thursday spun on her heel and saw an exploded water cooler down the corridor. Whitney's handiwork.

Whitney could always look after herself in a fight; her ability to control the elements was strong enough to make her almost impossible to attack successfully Or, at the very least, difficult to attack without coming out with severe injuries to the attacker.

Another lackey bolted straight for Thursday. Thursday, however, was ten steps ahead and used Whitney's frozen spear of water to swing on, utilising the momentum to kick the freak in the face.

The force sent them tumbling backwards in Titus' direction, but situations like these were an inconvenience at best for him. The graceful idiot leapt into the air as the lackey came towards him, putting one of his ridiculous dance spins to it to gather speed which he then used to kick the United Arms solider in the head. Just to be sure, Titus stamped down on the attacker's face.

"Can't we just visit the hospital in peace?!" Thursday exclaimed, throwing her knife into the air and catching it again before digging it into the back of a lackey heading in Finn's direction. It was clear they had orders to obtain experiment number one. "Matthew's bacterial infection is very serious! We need to get it sorted and being interrupted like this is extremely rude!"

Where the hell was Matthew anyway? Oh yes. He could be anyone right now. Perfect. What if she stabbed *him*?! What if she had already stabbed him?! Or worse, stamped on his throat and killed him?!

Thursday rotated on her heel a few times. There were so *many* of them! Where were they all coming from?!

The knife was suddenly wrenched from Thursday's hand, and she thought she had been attacked again in her moment of pause. "Hey!" She spun; her hand rigid as steel as she prepared to clock someone in the throat but stumbled when she was met by nothing. All the lackeys had lost their weapons, the instruments of destruction lying on the floor at the end of the corridor.

Sybil had mounted the highest point she could find (an overturned bin) and had her hand raised above her head in a claw-like shape. "Enough!" she yelled.

"I was just getting started!" Thursday protested.

The United Arms lackeys looked very confused at what had just happened. Thursday looked to the closest one and kicked them in the knee so that when they bent forward in pain, she could kick them in the face. She chuckled to herself as they fell to the ground, but when she looked up to Sybil, the leader didn't look impressed.

"What? They deserve it!"

"We're not animals!" Sybil exclaimed.

"Speak for yourself," Thursday huffed, folding her arms childishly.

To prevent Thursday from doing anything else to the United Arms lackeys, Sybil thrust her arm outwards and suddenly every single lackey smacked their head off a solid surface. All of them fell to the floor, unconscious.

"You are no fun," Thursday pouted.

"Is anyone hurt?" Finn lifted himself from the wall he had been leaning against. He seemed to be bleeding. The entire right side of his face was soaked in the crimson liquid. A long cut along his eyebrow was gushing blood right over his eye.

"I think the question is are *you* hurt?" Whitney cautiously asked. She slid underneath her frozen spear to join them on the other side. "You're bleeding a bit there."

Finn rubbed the cut with his tie and shrugged. "That doesn't matter right now. Does anyone need to be healed? We can't stick around here or else"-

"What? *I* might find you?"

Thursday had seen fear in numerous different forms, but never had she seen it so potently than when Finn's face melted at the sound of Sawyer's voice.

Sybil instinctively grabbed Finn and all but threw him on Thursday. She just about managed not to fall as he crashed against her.

A black-haired man came running out of a destroyed doorway to their left, also almost crashing into her as well. Thursday immediately knew it was Matthew from how he cursed and flailed to a stop.

Sawyer strolled down the corridor towards the six of them like he was taking a leisurely walk in the park. Titus jumped over Whitney's ice spear and Thursday made to follow but cursed at the sight of Dr. Weeks approaching from the other end. They were surrounded again. Not that Thursday didn't think that she couldn't take on Dr. Weeks. She just didn't trust that either of the psychos didn't have something up their sleeves.

"Hello, my dearest friends!" Sawyer declared, waving both hands as he finally reached them. "I trust you've all been well since I last seen you?"

Thursday took in their old friend with distaste. His dark hair had gotten longer, and he now had what looked like an electronic eye patch over his right eye. "What the hell happened your eye?" she sneered at him.

"Oh, this?" Sawyer tapped his electronic patch with a smirk. "This is just a piece of technology I designed myself. You didn't think I spent the time we've been apart sitting on my hands doing nothing? Of course not. I've been doing what I always do."

"Which is?" Finn asked apprehensively.

"Experimenting." The one eye that wasn't covered by some sort of ridiculous-looking patch was glinting with a sick pleasure Thursday recognised all too well from when the group used to be whole.

"What do you want?" Sybil demanded. Despite being pregnant, their leader jumped from the bin and took a protective stance in front of the group. "There's a reason you left and there's a reason I told you I didn't want to see your twisted face ever again."

"It's been too long, my friends," Sawyer said warmly, spreading his arms as if he was expecting a hug. "I have come to make you all part of a greater cause!"

"What cause?"

"*My* cause."

Thursday rolled her eyes. "Of course. You want us to donate to the loving charity of Sawyer."

Sybil was already shaking her head.

"Do you think we're stupid?" Titus demanded.

"No." Sawyer's grin had a way of settling on top of your soul like a cold mist. Thursday shuddered. "That's exactly why I'm asking." He looked at each of them, even Matthew, despite him being in a different body. "You know that my cause will benefit all of us in one way or another if you just cooperate."

"All of us? This only benefits you!" Matthew exclaimed. "You want to turn yourself into some sort of … of … *God* at *our* expense!"

Sawyer shrugged. "I wouldn't say at your expense. I'd call it more giving your life for the greater good."

"Oh, the greater good? You really want us to believe you're interested in the greater good?" Whitney snapped. "You're insane!"

Sawyer's eyes drifted past Whitney, almost like her words hadn't even reached his ears. "Ah, Dr. Weeks, delighted you could finally join us," he grinned.

Thursday turned around and instantly set her sights on the psychotic doctor who had tortured her in the asylum. Before anyone could stop her, she marched right up to the woman and planted an almighty slap across her face. It gave Thursday a sick satisfaction when it made Weeks yell in pain.

"You cow, why didn't you tell me Sawyer was involved in your evil schemes!" Thursday roared angrily.

Dr. Weeks rubbed her red cheek begrudgingly. "I am not an idiot. I knew if I so much as mentioned Sawyer's name you'd have blown the entire asylum up."

Thursday rolled her eyes. "Do you honestly think I'm that scared of him?" she asked seriously. She looked over her shoulder and scowled at Sawyer. "He's as intimidating as a mouse."

Sawyer barely flinched at Thursday's words. Instead, his grin widened. It was reaching comical levels of width. It was getting extremely off-putting. "Good thing I'm not here to proposition you, Thursday. Not yet anyway. I'm here for number one."

"Over my head body," Matthew shouted, forcing himself to the front of the group to protect Finn. He was back to his ordinary form, no longer looking like some stranger amongst the group.

Sawyer flexed his jaw, lifting his eyes to the ceiling as if conversing with God. "I can arrange that, you know," he said with a bored tone of voice.

"God, you're all so melodramatic." Finn didn't move from where he was standing. Thursday could hear the tremble in the healer's voice from where she stood. She didn't know what he found so terrifying about Sawyer. "Look, Sawyer, I'm not going with you. I didn't want to do this back when you were semi-sane, and I still don't. If you had my ability, you wouldn't be able to heal yourself. We all know that's what you want it for. That's not how it works, and you know it."

Finn's eye was completely drenched in blood now. If it had been anyone else, he could have easily fixed it up. It was Finn's Achilles Heel. It was an odd catch. It made Finn the most open to attack and death, but without Finn himself, the rest of them would be more open to attack and death.

"I want to see if I can get around it. As you know, my luck is stellar." Sawyer's sickly smile exposed all his teeth, giving him an almost shark-like appearance. He always acted so smug, like he had already won. Most of the time it was because he knew that he already had. His ability made luck favour him often.

"Yeah, not through natural odds," Sybil snapped.

"That's like claiming that your telekinesis is an unfair advantage because it's not natural," Sawyer reminded their leader. "I just want to play around a bit and see what I can discover."

"Most likely killing me in the process," Finn added flatly.

Sawyer looked genuinely hurt. "You really believe that I want to hurt you," he said. "Do you think so lowly of me that you believe my loyalty has died?"

"Yes," Thursday deadpanned.

"You would hurt us to achieve your insane endgame," Titus said.

Sawyer rolled his eyes. "I don't want to hurt you; I want to make us better!"

"Make you better, more like."

"I think you'll find that this is more than just Sawyer's endgame," Dr. Weeks spoke up.

Thursday looked at the woman with disdain and lifted her hand to slap her again. Sybil stopped her, freezing her hand in place without even needing to remove her eyes from Sawyer. Thursday hated how Sybil knew her. She'd have to get more spontaneous with her actions if that were possible.

"This is our endgame, too."

"The asylum's?" Thursday had never been more confused in her entire life. "What has Sawyer becoming some sort of overlord got to do with the asylum?"

Dr. Weeks shrugged, her glasses practically falling off the end of her nose. "Sawyer has agreed to further fund us if we help him with his experiments."

"*Further* fund? *Further* fund?" Thursday spun around once more and pushed past Finn and Sybil, her gaze set solely on Sawyer. "*Further* fund?" she roared at the top of her lungs. "You've been funding that hellhole?!"

Sawyer didn't even flinch as Thursday came right up into his personal space. They were so close that their noses were practically touching. "I make logical decisions that aid my intentions. I funded United Arms because I knew that some of you would end up there at one point in your lives." He looked down his nose at Thursday, his lip curling into a small snarl. "I didn't expect for you to break out before I could get there."

"Thank my dear friend Mattie boy here for that," Thursday grinned. She had finally gotten some sort of reaction from Sawyer besides bored indifference or unsettling happiness. "He had the foresight to discover your plan before you could even execute it."

"Matthew and foresight don't belong in the same sentence," Sawyer sighed.

"You just feel bad because I beat you! Ha!" Matthew laughed. "For once it's Mattie who has the insight and power!"

Sawyer rolled his eyes again. He liked to make sure that people knew that he wasn't at all bothered by what was going on around him. It would be a tragedy if people knew that he had actual human emotions. "I should have known that none of you would cooperate. I had held onto the hope that you all would have the same love for me as I have for you and would wish to help me."

"Love," Thursday repeated incredulously. A massive grin broke across her face, and she flicked Sawyer's electronic eyepiece. "I don't know the meaning of the word."

Sawyer caught Thursday's arm before she could retract it. "Then why are you still here?" he asked with a tint of amusement in his tone.

Good lord. What was he trying to insinuate? That she loved these people?

"I'm repaying a debt," Thursday answered. "Matthew and Whitney rescued me from the Asylum. My repayment for that is helping them in the request of reunion."

"Well, you're all reunited." Sawyer cocked his head and frowned, mockingly pursing his lips. "What are you going to do now?"

"I don't know, Sawyer. You know I am not a forward-thinking person!" Thursday exclaimed. "I don't know what I'm doing in five seconds let alone five minutes." Just to prove her point, she slapped Sawyer across the cheek. "See? I didn't know I was going to do that ten seconds ago."

Sawyer rubbed his cheek ruefully, barely any reaction flickering across his face. It frustrated Thursday how she could never invoke so much as surprise from the man. "Wow. You slapped someone. You're so impulsive," he muttered dryly.

"No one said anything about impulse. I just work on instinct."

Thursday's eyes zoned in on Sawyer's eyepiece. There was no pupil or iris, just a red screen that occasionally flashed like there was an LED malfunctioning behind it. Around the eye itself was blue metal, sculpted perfectly to sit on Sawyer's browbone without the need for a string or strap.

Thursday wondered if it had a purpose. Nothing was purely coincidence with Sawyer and, judging by how the eyepiece was flashing like a Christmas tree, it was obvious that there was some sort of reason he was wearing the piece.

Thursday snatched the eyepiece off Sawyer's face and jumped backwards before he could react. He was fast, only a tiny bit slower than her, his arms brushing her own as he yelled angrily and tried to grab it back.

"Funny little trinket," Thursday commented, throwing it behind her and hoping one of the others would catch it. She didn't hear it smacking the floor so that was reassuring.

Sawyer glowered. His real eye was now sealed shut; his skin crinkled as he refused to allow it to open.

"Did I just find your Achilles Heel?" Thursday cackled.

"I have plenty back at my place," Sawyer growled.

"Why do you look so mad then?" It occurred to her as soon as she finished the sentence. Thursday stepped backwards. Not out of fear, but concern. "Have you done something to your mark?"

Sawyer had been born with a birthmark on his right eye. It resembled a Viking rune, except a lot thicker, and it cut diagonally down his eye like someone had slashed at it with a knife. It couldn't have anything to do with his power, or the fact he was one of the Seven, as none of the others had a trait like it. They eventually just assumed it was like any normal birthmark, just on a rather unusual part of the body.

"I experiment on the unusual," Sawyer snarled. "You know this."

"What have you done to your eye, then?" Sybil frowned.

"Sawyer has been using the facilities at The United Arms to discover the purpose and origin of the strange marking on his eye," Dr. Weeks explained plainly. "Things didn't go as smoothly as we would have hop"-

"That's enough," Sawyer interrupted, holding his hand up to silence Weeks.

"Oh no, go on! Continue! I want to know!" Thursday declared. She took the eyepiece out of Titus' hands and waved it a distance away from Sawyer. "I'll give this back if you show us!"

"I don't know if that's a good idea," Sybil started to say.

Sawyer's face twisted into a wretched grin. "You want to know what happened to my eye?"

"Duh!" Thursday said excitedly.

Titus stepped forward. "No, I don't think that's smart"-

"Show us!" Thursday demanded.

"Stop it, Thursday!" Titus snapped.

"You don't know that it's dangerous!" Thursday accused.

"*You* don't know that it's safe!" Titus threw back.

Thursday didn't know why she was so keen to know what had happened to Sawyer's eye but now that the question had been posed, she needed to know. Maybe it was a product of her insanity, or just pure curiosity overweighing everything else, but there was an incessant pulling at the edge of her being that demanded she find out what Sawyer had done to himself.

"Stop it!" Sybil roared, silencing the bickering going on between Titus and Thursday. "No one is doing anything, especially not you, Sawyer!"

Thursday reluctantly decided that Sybil was probably right, and this wasn't the place to determine what had been done to the marked eye, especially since whatever had been done had been done through artificial means. It didn't staunch her curiosity in the slightest, but it was going to have to be something she returned to later.

She pocketed Sawyer's eyepiece. Sawyer noticed this and smirked. "Please, do take it, I have plenty back at home. Let me know if you can figure out what it does," he said.

"Don't you know what it does?" asked Finn.

"Of course, I do. I'm interested to see how you'll react when you find out."

Sybil stuck her hand into Thursday's pocket, clearly not trusting the madwoman to handle the possibly dangerous eyepiece. She focused her eyes on Sawyer. "Let us pass," she said firmly.

"I'll let five of you pass," Sawyer answered. "I need number one for my experiments to succeed."

"Shut up, Sawyer, really. This mad scientist spiel has gotten old," Whitney spoke up. "You honestly think Finn or me or anyone is just going to go *'Oh, well, he says he needs us, well then jeez we better go!'*"

"No. Hence why I've brought Weeks and her goons to help me." Sawyer's grin took a sudden dark, twisted turn. "By force."

Matthew started forward. "To hell you wi"-

Finn grabbed the scruff of Matthew's neck and dragged him backwards before he did something stupid. Sawyer seemed partially relieved by this, his patience never being its usual impeccable self whenever Matthew was running his mouth. "I've already handed in your resignation," the madman pointed out.

"You did what?" Finn released Matthew so suddenly that the shifter almost stumbled into the wall.

Sawyer looked rather insane, standing there with one eye open and one eye tightly shut. Thursday wondered if he truly needed to keep it closed like that or if he was doing it purely to unsettle them. If that was his intent, it wasn't working. For her, anyway.

"I handed in your resignation. Do you think I'm going to leave a trail behind once I take you? I'm not an idiot," Sawyer explained. "Esteemed doctor such as yourself? There would be so many questions if you just vanished."

"So, you quit my job?" Finn's voice was shaking with anger. Thursday didn't know the full story about Finn's history in medicine, but she did know that he had been studying every development since he was old enough to train, which was a very, very long time ago.

"You'll be part of a larger medical cause, now!" Sawyer beamed.

"First my house, now my job?!" Finn shouted. "What else are you going to destroy?!"

"Why just Finn?" Thursday asked with a frown. "Surely if you were trying to ruin our lives, I would have thought you'd have given us all equal treatment."

Sawyer shrugged. "Call this … an incentive. I mean, where else are you going to go without a house or a job? First, I'll take one." His dark eyes moved to Whitney. "Then two." Then Sybil. "Then three."

Thursday started to laugh. She couldn't help it. Did Sawyer honestly think such a thing would affect her? No house? No job? That was basically how she had been living her life ever since they'd all split up. She found jumping from one place to the next much more entertaining than settling down and developing a normal life.

It was no secret that, to most of the Seven, living a normal life was the goal. Thursday had never needed to ask to know. Most of them reeked of domestication. They all blended into human culture so easily, like it was second instinct to them, that it was obvious that they wished their powers weren't in the way of them leading an ordinary life.

Thursday never understood this desire. Maybe it was because she never blended in as easily as they did, or her madness was just impossible to domesticate, or she just flat-out couldn't comprehend it. In her eyes, they had been *blessed*. The others didn't see it like that. They saw their abilities as a curse more than anything else.

"If you think you'll be able to take me that easy, you've got another thing coming," Thursday plainly replied. She glanced over her shoulder and sighed. "If you think you can take *any* of us that easy."

Sawyer shrugged. "I will get what I want."

"You sound pretty sure about that."

"That's because I am."

Sawyer being sure about something could make even the most secure of people squirm. His ability didn't work all the time, if it did then he'd have taken over the world by now. However, it does favour his desires and self-confidence. Sawyer being one hundred per cent positive about capturing them one by one meant that his ability was a lot stronger.

Sybil pushed past Thursday. She simply stood there, staring at Sawyer. He stared back, his eyebrows lifting almost in invitation. The redhead lifted her hand. "Let all of us pass."

Sybil tried not to raise her hand against anyone, especially not against one of her own. So, seeing her hand up, ready to act, sent a chill down Thursday's spine. It made her proud to see their leader standing up for herself with her ability. Sybil usually only used her ability to end violence, rarely to initiate it.

"Or what?" Sawyer asked.

"You know what."

Sawyer sighed. "You won't do it."

"It's been a long ten years, Sawyer, things have changed."

"You know I'll just find you again."

"Then we'll fight you again."

Sawyer's one open eye gleamed maliciously. "Go ahead, then."

Sybil clenched her jaw. Thursday watched the woman endure an internal battle. Not only was it against her morals, but there was a lot of emotion behind Sawyer and Sybil's history. Thursday found emotions rather useless, especially in this type of situation, and she wished Sybil felt the same way.

It was clear Sawyer knew that Sybil would be conflicted. He was smirking again and was about to open his mouth-probably to gloat-when Matthew spoke up. His voice was almost timid, but the corridor was so quiet that it rang out like a siren.

"It's the only way."

Sybil's face scrunched up. She released her fingers. Sawyer barely had a chance to react as his entire body was flung against the nearest wall, but Thursday was fairly sure she saw the smug bastard's face drop like a stone as soon as Sybil acted. The only person to react was Dr. Weeks, who yelped with shock and horror as Sawyer's head cracked off the wall, knocking him unconscious.

Thursday whistled. "You could have done that sooner, you know."

"Shut up, Thursday."

"Come on, we need to go right now!" Whitney shouted, flying past them.

As the others disappeared up the corridor and around the corner, Sybil lingered. Thursday had to give her a hard push to get her going. Emotions got in the way of a lot of things and that was why Thursday had smothered hers to death decades ago. It kept her alert. It most definitely came in handy when idiots like Sybil were distracted by such gooey feelings.

When Sybil shook herself into reality and ran after the others, Dr. Weeks came rushing forward. She had been waiting for Sybil to leave in case she threw her against a wall next.

"You're a pack of animals," the doctor sneered angrily. She threw herself to her knees beside Sawyer and started examining his head.

If Thursday's eyebrows had shot up her forehead any faster, they'd have popped right off her head. "If we're all animals, you're currently conspiring with the snake."

"You would say that, wouldn't you?" Dr. Weeks was cradling Sawyer's head against her chest.

Ah. So, Thursday's torturer *wasn't* involved in this for Asylum funding. Thursday had to admit, it was ingenious of Sawyer to get a woman of Weeks' position attached to him to the point of doing his bidding without question. It was certainly something the madman was good at.

Thursday looked down on Dr. Weeks. "He doesn't love you, you know," she said.

Dr. Weeks glowered. Her hands were practically shaking as she brushed Sawyer's dark hair from his eyes. "You would say that, wouldn't you?" she repeated.

Thursday rolled her eyes. She sighed. "He only loves us."

She hated pointing it out, but it was true. All of this was a product of Sawyer's insane version of love. He believed himself capable of loving every one of the Seven equally and irrevocably. Somewhere in that mess, he believed his experiments were an extension of such love. "No one else."

"You're lying!" Weeks accused, pulling Sawyer closer to her body, if that were possible.

"You're being used, Weeks!" Thursday barked.

"Thursday!" Whitney was back. "Hurry up!"

Thursday spun to Whitney and plastered a smile on her face. "I was just shooting the breeze with my old pal!" She began to back away from the slobbering woman and repeated, "He only loves us. No one else."

Weeks buried her face in Sawyer's hair, as if she was going to wake him up by sheer force of will. Thursday curled her lip. Pathetic. She could already see Sawyer waking up and slapping the doctor silly for not giving chase.

Thursday turned her back on the doctor and ran after Whitney.

CHAPTER SIX

THEY DITCHED THE CAR THEY'D HIJACKED. They didn't know who had seen them leaving the hospital, nor did they know if Sawyer had copied the license plate before ambushing them. It was easier driving in the car, but it was not wise. They needed to hide while they figured out what to do next.

This posed to be a harder quest than any of them had previously expected. Sawyer had said that he knew where each of them lived and even worked, so going back to anyone's house was out of the question.

It made things more difficult, but not impossible. It was simply a challenge, one that Thursday knew the exact solution to.

"Are you sure this place is abandoned?"

"It should be." As Thursday pushed the door open, the entire structure fell off its hinges, hanging off the doorframe with a rusted yelp. "It's been empty for the past twenty years. The only problem I've ever had are squatters and they are usually quite friendly."

"What about unfriendly squatters?" Matthew asked from somewhere behind her.

"Easily dealt with." Thursday didn't elaborate, and no one asked her to.

Thursday entered the empty living room. It was the same as it had been before she had been arrested if a bit unruly. Wallpaper peeling off the walls in long strips; furniture with giant chunks bitten out; and a fireplace filled with trash instead of a fire. It was not a homely home by any means, but it was where she went whenever she was in a jam and if this current predicament didn't count as a jam, then Thursday didn't know what did.

"How did you even find this place?" Titus asked, looking through the next door to make sure there weren't any of the unfriendly squatters lurking around.

"*Find?* Excuse you, I own this place," Thursday said indignantly.

"*You?* A homeowner?" Whitney scoffed in disbelief.

"To be fair, if Thursday were to own a home, I'd say this is exactly how I imagine it would look," said Titus.

Sybil crouched in front of the fire and pulled out an empty chicken box. "Is this Del Monte Forest Manor?" she asked.

Thursday looked down at their leader with a grin. "Bing bing! You get first prize!" she declared.

Finn made a noise at the back of his throat. "*This* is Del Monte? What did you do to it?!"

Thursday gave the healer a withering look. "It's called ageing with grace," she said.

"Aging? I think it has already died," Matthew commented.

"*You* try and upkeep an entire manor while constantly getting arrested then!" Thursday threw back.

"Many would argue that the solution to such an issue would be don't get arrested," Finn pointed out.

"Many would say shut the hell up," Thursday childishly responded.

Thursday would be the first to admit that she was an awful homeowner. The only reason she had bought Del Monte Forest was because there used to be a man across the road who she suspected her girlfriend had been visiting. It had cost her a heavy penny, but she had believed it would all be worth it once she had castrated the man for daring to touch her girl. She thought she'd be able to sell the building once she had finished with it, but her girlfriend ran away with the man and the property market plummeted and …well …she was stuck with Del Monte Forest Manor.

She liked to use it as a shelter for the insane now. She allowed homeless people to stay for as long as they needed, especially if they had been kicked out by their families for whatever reason. It wasn't an act of kindness, they had to provide for themselves in the house, and the shelter was the only help she provided. A lot of them took many liberties in her absence, explaining why the house was in the state it was in. That *also* explained why the entire manor was in complete disarray upon their arrival. Thursday had been gone for a *very* long time.

Thursday sniffed blood in the air and wondered if there was another stabbing victim upstairs bleeding out on her toilet floor. She cast her eyes to the ceiling as if she would be able to see through the yellowing paint to the room above. Rolling her head on her neck, Thursday stared at Finn. "Oh yeah," she said vaguely, "you're hurt."

Finn's hand was still pressed against the wound on his head. "How nice of you to notice," he responded, his tone just as flat as hers had been. To his credit, he hadn't been a baby about the cut, but Thursday supposed they were going to have to do something about it.

"I think I have medical stuff around here somewhere."

As previously mentioned, every so often, Thursday would find a stab or murder or assault victim dying upstairs, and she eventually left a box of supplies in her toilet-they seemed to frequent there-to stop them staining her floor with their blood. It was rather rude to just bleed all over a stranger's floor, but she had yet to find a dying person willing to be lectured about their mannerisms.

Thursday left the room with Sybil in close tow. "I'll help you look," the red-headed woman muttered.

"Oh, goody, because I've got questions for you!" Thursday beamed.

Thursday hopped up the gigantic staircase two at a time, Sybil's heavy sigh following her like a ghost. Once upon a time, these stairs had been coated in thick, scarlet red carpet that felt like clouds between your toes. Now it was flat; dirty; and drained of all colours. Thursday's feet made loud thumping noises against each stair, her bare feet pulling some of the carpet out from the corners as she went.

That reminded her, she'd have to find clothes soon. Walking around with a strait jacket tied around her torso was only going to suffice for so long…

"Questions?" Sybil echoed.

"Who; what; where; when; why; you know, the usual," Thursday responded.

"Of…?"

Thursday spun around at the top of the staircase and raised her eyebrows. "Do you have to ask?" she replied.

Sybil stared back at Thursday from a couple of steps down, brown eyes narrowed irritably. "Is now really the time?" she asked.

"Well, there isn't going to be a *'time'*," Thursday answered, beckoning Sybil to follow her as she headed down the hallway to the toilet. The door to said room gave the impression that it too was going to collapse off its hinges through the loud screech it exuded upon opening. "I mean, look at the situation we're in."

Sybil looked over Thursday's shoulder into the toilet with mild disdain. "Have you ever thought of investing in an oil can?"

"Yeah, when I was chewing the cushioned walls in United Arms, one of the most important things on my agenda was *get an oil can for my decrepit Manor*," Thursday sarcastically responded. She nudged the door open completely and stepped inside.

The floor was stained with a variety of questionable substances. A mixture of blood and dirt and other strains of germs Thursday didn't wish to consider in the presence of Sybil. She turned to the leader and grinned at how the woman's nose was upturned. Thursday threw herself onto the broken toilet and kicked open the cabinet, releasing an army of woodlice and beetles.

"Be free, my minions!" Thursday cackled as the bugs made a break for whatever corner they could find.

"This is disgusting," Sybil sighed.

"Hey, when the world is decimated by whatever the hell is going to end us, these guys will rule all," Thursday pointed out, referencing the horde of bugs. She crouched in front of the cabinet and rummaged around inside for the medical box. Hopefully, her squatters hadn't used all of it, or else Finn's head would have to bleed until it was empty. "So, tell me, who's the lucky guy?"

Sybil propped her hip on the dirty doorframe as the last of the bugs made their escape. "You wouldn't know him," was her pathetic answer.

Thursday rolled her eyes. "That's not what I asked."

"It is, however, what I answered."

Thursday exhaled through her nostrils. "*Fine*. How?"

"How?" Sybil wasn't confused by this question. She was just prolonging the answer.

"Is it possible?"

Sybil made an odd, chuckling noise at the back of her throat. "I'm the immaculate conception."

This made Thursday burst into hysterical laughter. Well, at least Sybil had a sense of humour about the situation. "Did Finn diagnose it that way?" she chuckled.

"Yes, because you know how medical science and religion meld so perfectly," Sybil answered, the humour in her tone fading. "No, Finn hasn't been able to diagnose how it's possible. Not through lack of trying…"

Thursday raised her eyebrows. "But you know how, right?" she asked. She stopped rummaging and looked back over her shoulder at the woman. Sybil didn't need to say anything; the expression on her pale, freckled face was enough. "You just won't tell him."

"It'll make him angry," Sybil sighed.

"Ooooh, will it make him question his reality as a physician?" Thursday grinned. "Will it make him mad because he's been studying lies all his life?"

"No. It will make him mad because he's a decent human being. The same goes for Titus. And Whitney. And Matthew. You? I don't know…" Sybil's voice trailed off.

"You forgot Sawyer," Thursday reminded Sybil, turning back to the cabinet and dragging things out regardless of what they were. "I'm sure he's seething since you two used to be so close and a"-Thursday stopped. She glanced back at Sybil. "It's not his, is it?"

Sybil snorted. "No," she replied.

"You got lucky there."

"I'm aware."

Thursday grabbed the medical box. It had been sitting at the back of the cabinet covered in such a thick layer of grime that it had melted into the black backboard. As she stood up, her knees crackled with age. Despite being immortal, her body sometimes reminded her of how many years she'd lived.

She spun on her heel to face Sybil again. "You still haven't answered me."

Sybil folded her arms. "Thursday, I have been lying through my teeth to Finn-a trained physician-for months now, what makes you think in that insane brain of yours that I'm going to tell *you*?"

Well, the answer to that was easy.

Thursday wasn't the first person anyone would go to spill out their deepest, darkest secrets to. Mainly because she could not take things seriously and would most likely make light of whatever the situation was. Thursday didn't know what to do with severity and she found it suffocating. Her humour was the only weapon she had when she couldn't blast off into the sky with her hands. The answer to Sybil's question, though? It was quite simple.

"No one would believe me."

Sybil glared. She had nothing to say in retaliation. Thursday grinned.

It must have worked, though. Sybil opened her mouth, as if about to respond, but was rudely caught off by a male voice.

"What is taking so long?"

Sybil closed her mouth in the presence of another person.

"Titus, I could kill you!" Thursday shouted, pushing past Sybil and taking a swing at the dancer with the medical box. Titus dodged the blow by weaving beneath it like he'd seen it coming before Thursday had even moved. "Did your mother never teach you not to interrupt conversations?"

"My mother told me not to interrupt *ladies,* Thursday, a group who I question your inclusion in every day," Titus dryly answered. He grabbed her wrist as she tried to take another swing at him, squeezing it tightly to force her to release the box. Titus kicked the box as it hurtled to the floor and caught it in his free hand as it bounced back up.

Thursday sneered at him. "Glad to know I'm in your thoughts every day," she said. She wrenched her wrist out of his hand. "Got impatient, did you? What, is Finn dying on the floor or something?"

"He has concluded that he could be concussed," said Titus, turning his back on her and heading back to the stairs. "He wants to stitch his wound before he can't even see straight."

"Concussed? How did he even…?" Thursday groaned and stomped after Titus. Sybil's footsteps echoed hers, letting her know that she was following. For the healer of the group, Finn was the most prone to goddamn injuries. "Moron. Absolute moron."

Sybil's footsteps stopped. "What does that mean?"

Thursday looked over her shoulder and stopped as well. Sybil was gazing at the wall in front of the stairs. The wallpaper was torn down to the floor and words had been scrawled across the wall itself. Thursday backtracked and stood beside Sybil to take in the message. It wasn't long before Titus' curiosity had gotten the better of him and he was standing with them.

"'You have to die to truly live'," he quoted from the wall.

"Huh. My last visitor must have left it there," said Thursday. She snorted. "How pathetically dramatic."

"I wonder what they meant by it," Sybil muttered.

"I wonder how many people offed themselves thinking it would help them 'live'," Thursday countered.

Sybil gave Thursday a despondent look. What? Surely there had been someone who had read the graffiti and decided that it was telling them that they had to literally die to live. There were plenty of stupid people out there who would take such a statement to the extreme.

"Maybe it means that sometimes you need to abandon your beliefs, thus 'dying', to live the life you truly desire," Titus said thoughtfully.

Thursday and Sybil's heads rotated simultaneously to stare at the dancer. How long had he been mulling over *that one*?

A pause.

Thursday snorted again. "Nah, it's just some weirdo who's taken too many happy pills and is trying to act like they're philosophical and deep," she answered. "Come on, let's go before Finn's brain melts out of his ears."

Back in the living room, Finn had taken up residence on the floor. His hand was above his eyes like he was trying to blot out a light only he could see. Whitney had taken the one couch that was useable and didn't look to be interested in the debilitated man in the slightest. Matthew, on the other hand, was being his usual hover parent self, silently watching from the fireplace. He seemed to be immensely concentrated as if he expected Sawyer to suddenly burst into the house and steal Finn from right beneath his nose.

Thursday clamped her hand down on Matthew's shoulder, causing the shifter to jump out of his skin in shock. "Held down the ranks while I was gone?" she joked.

"Did you get the box?" Matthew asked.

"Yeah." Titus snapped the box open to reveal, thankfully, a bunch of untouched medical supplies.

"Sterilised?" Finn's voice floated from the floor.

"Probably not."

Whitney sighed and snatched the box out of Titus' hands without needing to even get up. She picked the needle out of the box and lit a fire in her free hand. She then held the needle over the flame. "Dry heat is one of the earliest forms of sterilisation," she informed the other four when she noticed them gaping at her. "Right, Finn?"

"Right," the healer muttered. "While she's doing that, was anyone else hurt?"

"I mean, I knocked my elbow but no big deal," Thursday shrugged, examining said elbow for bruises.

"Worry about yourself. I know I'm not having your hands anywhere near me while you're concussed," Titus added as Whitney passed the needle back to him. She also tossed him the thread.

Finn sat up and rubbed his hand over his face. "Pass me it."

Thursday snorted with amusement. He had thrust his arm out towards Sybil instead of Titus. "Dude, you're messed up," she laughed. She took the needle and thread from Titus and fell to her knees in front of Finn. "I'll do it."

Finn's blue eyes were narrowed and unfocused. Thursday was still baffled that he had somehow managed to get concussed in that small kerfuffle in the hospital. One would think someone so vulnerable to injury would have at least trained to fight. Learn karate or Tae Kwan Do or *anything* that could aid him in a fight. He took his damn pacifism too seriously.

"What qualifies you?" asked Finn.

"I'm not concussed," Thursday flatly answered.

—149—

Thursday climbed into Finn's lap and pushed his head back to get a better look at his wound. He must have cleaned it while Thursday and Sybil had been upstairs because she could see it a lot clearer. It looked like a cut now as opposed to a mass of red. It wasn't extremely deep, but it had been over an hour and the bleeding hadn't stopped so the idiot had hurt himself badly. With an irritated sigh, she threaded the needle.

Another product of being on the run from the authorities was learning how to do some basic survival procedures for oneself. Thursday had spent a few weeks a couple of years ago teaching herself how to stitch a wound; avoid hyperthermia; tie a tourniquet; survive for weeks on nothing but a cracker, that kind of thing. Since the Seven parted and she didn't have Finn at the helm for her healing needs, it had been essential and posed to be quite useful over the years.

"If you stick that needle in my eye, I'll be really mad," Finn muttered.

"Yeah, yeah, whatever," Thursday replied.

Finn sat quietly like a trooper while Thursday stitched up his wound. She could feel four sets of eyes burning into the back of her head as she worked. It was almost like they genuinely believed that she was going to stab Finn in the eye with the needle.

Her face had never been as close to Finn's before, and she was enjoying how awkward she knew it was making him feel. For someone who could be so assertive, Finn could be a very sheepish man. It made her wonder, not for the first time, how he had coped with dating Matthew, one of the most extravagant, overly affectionate, and over-the-top people Thursday had ever met.

Thursday finished with an extravagant sigh and leaned back. Her stitching ended up being a tad messy-she never claimed to be an expert at it-but at least the wound was closed.

Finn released a breath and lightly touched the wound with the tips of his fingers. He winced but nodded, approving of Thursday's stitching. "Now don't let me sleep," he murmured. "At least for tonight."

"You mean we have to stay up with you all night?" Whitney laughed. "Screw that."

"I'll do it," said Sybil.

"No, you won't," Finn answered. "You need rest."

Thursday rolled her eyes, chucking the needle into the fireplace. "Who cares who stays up? Even if one of us did volunteer, clinger over there will stay awake anyway. It's a guarantee."

Matthew said nothing, but even his silence spoke volumes. He probably *couldn't* sleep more than he chose not to. Besides, there was no one more equipped to stand guard than the obsessive who would rip a lion's jaws open if his affection's head was being consumed.

When Matthew didn't answer her, the silence stretched on. The six of them sat in the ruined room, silent as the dead. The air was heavy, the weight of the situation settling around them like dust from the furniture. Everything had been so quick paced up until this point. They hadn't stopped, they had been constantly moving for the past day and a half. Now that they had stopped, their current predicament was becoming more…real.

Sawyer was looking for them.

"Titus, I'd recommend closing your studio," Finn said quietly. "It might end up like my house."

Titus lifted his head from between his knees. "Your house? Oh. Right. Yeah. It'll be closed tomorrow. It's always closed on Tuesdays because …well…" Titus gestured to himself and shrugged. "…Soul Day and all. I'll call Cate tomorrow and tell her to take the week off."

Whitney turned onto her side on the sofa to look at Titus. "Why not do it now? Get it over with?"

"The instant we make a call on any of our phones, our location will be tracked, I'm sure," Titus said. "It's not worth the risk. I'll find a payphone tomorrow."

Whitney sighed and rolled onto her back again. "This sucks."

"That's one way of describing it," Matthew muttered.

Another pause. Each one was more awkward than the last.

Thursday sighed and began to pick at her fingernails. "I'm sorry about your job, Finn."

Finn shrugged with one arm. "Nothing can be done." His answer was nonchalant but the expression on his face told a different story. Even Thursday knew when not to push a topic. "He's going to do the same to the rest of you, too."

Thursday chuckled. "Good luck to him, I'm unemployed."

"I've been out of work, too," Whitney muttered.

Thursday frowned. That was new. Last, she heard, Whitney had been working in advertising. She was more out of touch than she realised.

Matthew slid down the wall and sat on the dirty carpet. He folded his arms around his knees, nestling his chin on top. "You're better off, it seems. The more you have going on in your life right now, the more Sawyer has leverage over you. He intends to flush us out by taking away what we have. He's going to keep taking and taking until there's no other choice but to run to him for help."

"I'd rather eat my own intestines than ask that man for help," Thursday muttered.

"I agree. In a more …eloquent …way," Sybil replied.

Thursday chewed vigorously on her thumbnail like she could take out her pent-up rage on her thumb. Sawyer thought so highly of himself that he believed that all he had to do was remove a couple of essential factors from their lives and it would be all they'd need to crawl to him on their hands and knees to beg for help. He believed himself to be so above everything; so superior; so …so …much *better* than the rest of them. It was infuriating. Thursday didn't need him. She barely needed the five people surrounding her. She didn't need anyone but herself.

She'd survived for ten years on her own. She'd survive ten more once this was over.

"So …what now?" asked Matthew.

"Who knows," Thursday murmured. "I'm not going to hide from him. I'm not going to give him the satisfaction of thinking he has me scared."

"Ah, good old pride," Whitney muttered. Her voice dripped in its usual sarcasm.

"We *can't* hide," said Sybil. "Not for the same reasons Thursday has said, but we really can't. We don't know what sort of technology Sawyer has at his beck and call. For all we know, he could know exactly where we are no matter where we go. Hiding isn't an option."

Technology…

"Hey, Sybil, let me see that eyepatch," said Thursday.

Sybil didn't look too eager to do as Thursday asked. She dipped her hand into her pocket, as if just remembering about the eyepatch herself, and clasped her hand around the small device.

"I'm not going to break it, I promise," Thursday insisted. "I just want to look at it."

Sybil surprised Thursday by relinquishing the eyepatch. What did they honestly expect her to do to it, anyway? She had good control over her motor facilities, so she wasn't going to drop it and even she wasn't stupid enough to attempt to break it for no reason.

The blue patch was made of a heavy sort of metal and the red screen was still blinking away despite not being in use. Thursday turned it over in her hands, tracing every dent and edge in the hopes that a clue was going to jump up at her and scream "THIS IS WHAT I DO!"

Whitney reached over and took the eyepatch off Thursday.

Whitney let the patch rest over her eye. It didn't fit right and slid right off her face. "I'd say the only way to know what it does is to wear it," she said.

"Which is impossible," Sybil sighed.

Whitney was probably right, wearing the patch would most likely have shown them what it did. Even if it didn't, it would give them some sort of clue as to why Sawyer didn't want anyone but himself to wear it. They just needed Sawyer to wear it without Sawyer wearing it. If that made sense.

"Not impossible." Finn pointed to Matthew.

Matthew straightened. "I can't just *turn* into Sawyer."

Thursday's eyes bounced between Matthew and the eyepatch. There had to be some way for him to be able to shift into Sawyer. It was too infuriatingly close to having someone who could shift into any possible form and then just have them …not do it because of a minor setback.

"We would need someone who desires Sawyer to look at him," Thursday concluded.

"Yes, because you know how we gained the ability to mind read over the past decade," Whitney dryly answered. "Go ahead, Thursday, find someone who desires Sawyer."

Thursday wasn't listening to Whitney. She was too busy trying to think of a solution to this. Of all the lovers and suitors Sawyer had had over the years, there had to be someone still out there who desired him …

Thursday looked at Sybil. "I guess it's stupid to ask if you"-

"Yes, Thursday," Sybil interrupted. "I'd have volunteered if I thought it would work but, as I've said, ten years is a long time. A lot of things die in ten years, especially in terms of emotion."

"What about that woman who you said worked at the Asylum, Thursday?" asked Titus. "That doctor woman."

"Oh yeah," mused Matthew, "she stared at Sawyer when he was talking like the sun shone from his ass."

Suddenly, the image of Dr. Weeks cradling Sawyer's head in her lap exploded in Thursday's head. She slapped the faded red floor, making the others jump. "That's right!" she exclaimed. "Sawyer is using her! She's rapt with him! I'd say he made her obsessed with him so that she'd do whatever he told her to do. You know how good he is at that."

"She already saw Matthew at the hospital, surely," said Whitney.

"Most of the time I was in the form of someone else," Matthew admitted. He scratched his head. "And when I wasn't I'd say I was blocked from view because I was standing in front of Finn, and she was at the other end of the crowd."

Thursday hit the floor again. "There we go, then! We kidnap Dr. Weeks, force her to look at Matthew and when he shifts into Sawyer he can put on the eyepatch and find out what it does."

"And if Matthew *doesn't* shift into Sawyer and instead turns into someone else?" asked Whitney. "I don't know, instead of desiring Sawyer she desires a six-foot-five beach hunk with an eight-pack who saves puppies from high trees?"

Thursday shrugged. "At least we can say we tried?"

Titus sighed. "Seems a bit farfetched just to find out what that dumb patch does. Especially since we don't know for sure that it will work."

"If you have another plan, I'd gladly hear it."

No one proposed anything. Sure, the plan wasn't bulletproof, and they'd be going around the world for a shortcut, but

Thursday certainly couldn't think of anything else they could do given their current situation. They would have to keep moving anyway since Sawyer was most likely going to be tracking their every movement. They were taking a risk spending the night in Del Monte, but there wasn't anywhere else for them to go, so it was a risk they had to take.

Since they had to be on the move anyway, they might as well spend that time trying to achieve something.

"And how, may I ask, will we figure out where Sawyer has gone to?" Whitney asked. "Since Dr. Weeks will most likely not be far behind him?"

Sybil reached up and snatched the eyepatch off Whitney. She tossed the device into the air and caught it again with an airy grin. "I think I know exactly the guy we can ask."

~T~

"There's a song for this, I know there is," Thursday chimed, jumping up and down at the back of the procession to catch the others' attention. Of course, besides a thoughtful expression from Matthew, her lovely friends ignored her.

It was the next night. It had been an extremely boring day that they had spent running around from A to B tying up loose ends. Titus contacted Sharon at his studio and told her to shut up shop for the week; Matthew contacted some old flames and told them to be careful and maybe try to get out of the city; Finn tried to make some calls to get his job back; and Sybil made a mysterious call that she didn't let anyone listen in on. Thursday would have tried to eavesdrop, but Titus didn't allow her to.

So now they were following Sybil. She hadn't divulged much information on this guy who could help them catch Sawyer yet, but they were heading in his direction now. Thursday wondered if that was what the call had been about or if it had been about something else entirely…

"Right," Sybil said loudly, stopping on a street corner and allowing for the rest of them to catch up.

"We're going to a gay bar!" Thursday burst into song. That was the tune she'd been thinking of!

Sybil's eyelids fluttered, and her nostrils flared, the universal neon warning that she was agitated. "Right," Sybil repeated pointedly, "Sawyer's old flame works at this bar and we're here purely to see if we can wheedle him about Sawyer's possible whereabouts. It's quite a diluted plan but- Thursday, *shut up*!"

Thursday had been humming the tune to the song while Sybil had been talking. She grimaced and pressed her lips together. "Your lack of appreciation of music disturbs me," Thursday stated, folding her arms.

"Your lack of appreciation for my authority disturbs me," Sybil threw back angrily. Her voice sounded like a mother scolding her child.

Thursday opened her mouth, smart-ass response on hand, but she stopped when Sybil raised her hand to silence her.

Thursday wasn't scared of Sybil. She did have a hilarious lack of respect for Sybil's authority, though. The effort that would have to go into struggling in Sybil's invisible grip just wasn't worth it right now.

Holding her hands up in faux surrender, Thursday smirked at Sybil and lifted her eyebrows in a gesture that said, "*Go on.*"

Titus sighed heavily. "You were saying?" he sternly asked.

"It's a pretty diluted plan," Sybil continued, irritation boiling on the edge of her skin like a cheap marinara sauce left in the pot too long, "but after our failure at the hospital, it's all we've got."

Thursday glanced at Matthew. He had this transfixed expression of pure confusion on his face.

"What makes you think this old flame knows what's up?" the shifter asked.

Sybil sighed, almost reluctant to divulge the answer to such a question. "When Sawyer and I were engaged, he constantly blabbed about this bloke and how if there could be an eighth day of the week this guy would be it"-

"Obsessed much?" Thursday frowned.

"It's Sawyer, of course, he was obsessed," Whitney counterpointed.

"You all know what he's like," Sybil continued. "I'd have been surprised if he *hadn't* gotten as attached as he did. He used to insist that we could trust this guy with our plans, but I never trusted it. I always figured that when he left us, he ran straight back to Bas."

Bas? Thursday chuckled. "Sawyer fell for a freak called *Bas*? What a loser!"

"So, you think this Bas guy is still working with Sawyer?" asked Finn.

Any sign of the maybe concussion from the previous night seemed to have disappeared, the only evidence of Finn ever having been thumped on the head being Thursday's untidy stitching job on his forehead.

"Of course not," Thursday surprised them by answering on Sybil's behalf. "If Bas was still working with Sawyer he would have been at Sawyer's side when he cornered us at the hospital. But he wasn't. Besides, at the rate Sawyer eats through humans, gaining interest then getting bored, I'd be shocked if they were still together."

Matthew; Titus; Finn and Whitney stared at Thursday with mild bafflement before slowly turning to look at Sybil for confirmation.

Their leader shrugged. "Pretty much what she said."

"Don't look so shocked!" Thursday snapped. "I have a brain, too!"

"Yeah, a brain that has endured copious amounts of shock therapy," Whitney commented.

Thursday peered across the road, to where their destination sat, flashing bright multi-coloured lights like some sort of city lighthouse. "Well, let's go, then!" the madwoman declared. She took a step forward to cross the road but was stopped by a strong hand dragging her back.

"Male access, only," Sybil said.

Thursday could have sworn she heard the leader mutter, "*Thank God*," beneath her breath but she dismissed the notion.

There was a momentary silence. Sybil turned pleadingly to face Titus, but he was immediately shaking his head. "No. Not even if you paid me," he said.

"Titus"-

"No."

"I'll do it!" Matthew stuck his hand in the air.

Sybil's face was frozen as she continued to stare at Titus. "Please, Titus," she begged.

Titus did not flinch. "I will not. I am of no use in there and you know it."

"I can do it!" Matthew insisted.

Sybil's eyes flickered briefly in the shifter's direction before returning to Titus. "It's your Soul Day," she pressed. "You're the strongest today."

"Yes, and when kicking the crap out of everyone in there without so much as a trip becomes useful for interviewing Bas, Sybil, I will be glad to oblige," Titus answered.

Thursday exhaled, making her irritation well known. For the love of Pete, why must everything be so complicated? She could understand why Sybil was weary. Sending Matthew off on a mission on his own was only a bit saner than sending Thursday herself off on her own. Matthew was a socialite, though, this was right up his street. He could flirt with the Queen if he was given enough time to work on her. Surely, this Bas guy would be no problem.

"Just let Mattie go," Thursday groaned.

Sybil shook her head. "Yes, because millions of fresh, adrenalin-fuelled eyes on the shifter is *exactly* what we want. I don't think you've thought this through."

"I can try to control it." Matthew didn't even believe what he was saying. He was already deflating like a balloon.

"I'll go with him."

Thursday grinned at Finn, despite the reluctant look on the healer's face.

Over the years, the Seven's abilities constantly developed. Thursday started only able to shoot sparks from her fingers, while

Sybil had only been able to move tiny pebbles and inkwells. They worked on their powers and as they grew older, the stronger and more confident they got. Matthew's ability had been the same right from the start. It was rather lucky since only being able to transform one part of the body did sound quite uncomfortable indeed.

A development did come for him, eventually. All those years ago, when Matthew and Finn started dating, whatever emotion or fluffy nonsense passed between them in that time … it changed the dynamic of Matthew's ability. Whenever in Finn's presence, Matthew could hold his real image. Matthew could look like Matthew, no matter who else was looking at him.

"How can you be sure it will still work?" Whitney asked.

"I can't," Finn shrugged. "But someone will need to be with him anyway and if there's a possibility it could work then why not try?"

For once, Matthew was silent.

"Well, then," Thursday grinned. "Sorted!"

CHAPTER SEVEN

MATTHEW HAD BEEN TRANSFORMING INTO DIFFERENT PEOPLE FOR SO LONG THAT HE BARELY NOTICED WHEN THE CHANGE HAPPENED. Due to having had his ability since the day he was born, his appearance had always been constantly in flux. He identified as male, no matter what body he was in, but enjoyed the fluidity that came with his talent for changing bodies.

Environments like the establishment they were about to enter, however, made everything so much more complicated. So many people. So many thoughts ran wild in their heads as they grew intoxicated and danced and desperately sought partnership, even just for the night. Thoughts such as passion and desire and sexuality would be at the forefront of nearly every patron's head, and Matthew had to focus on not turning into the heart's desire of every single sod in that damn club.

Normally, Matthew would have been up for a party. He was always up for trying to fill the hole that Finn left behind with alcohol and sex, but the fact that they were on a mission made it different. The fact that Finn was there, right beside him, made things different.

A part of Matthew had been dying to ditch this entire plan from the moment Thursday flew them to the hospital. He had planned to reunite them, sure, but Matthew wasn't going to pretend he was a hero. A part of him had hoped that the others would take over trying to thwart Sawyer and he could continue his life of greed in peace. It would have preyed on his mind if he hadn't done anything, but in getting Whitney and releasing Thursday he had thought he had done his bit. Then the temptation had kicked in and he continued to the hospital.

As predicted, as soon as Finn came into the picture, Matthew was a goner.

"Do you know what you're supposed to say?"

Matthew regarded Sybil with a cheeky smirk. "Sure."

Sybil, not in a playful mood, didn't respond to his gesture. "Repeat it back to me."

She was always so uptight. Before Sawyer left, the group's leader had been softer, and Matthew would have gotten away with a few mishaps, but after? The stick in Sybil's ass grew so long it would have made Vlad the Impaler wet himself with excitement. "I have to find out what Sawyer's planning, right? I just need to ask questions, try to poke it out of him."

"Repeat what I told you to say!" Sybil insisted.

Matthew sighed and swung himself up off the pavement to stand. He was much taller than Sybil but what she lacked in height, she made up for in anger. "You can't plan out seduction, Sybil. No matter how hard you try to draw up diagrams and plans, it just won't work that way. You need to let me do what I need to do. You can't tell me what to say or do, it won't be natural." Matthew snickered. "Especially since you aren't exactly the master of seduction yourself."

Thursday pouted. "I wanted to write your script, but Sybil said no."

"I wonder why," Titus responded blandly.

Sybil groaned and rubbed her face irritably. "Matthew, please just follow the script. The last thing I need to worry about is having to start aga-"

"You won't have to. Don't you trust me enough to do this one thing on my own? Seduction is the purpose of my gift; it always has been. Whether it be of the mind; the heart or the body no one can deny that Monday's gift is to entice through appearance!"

"The most superficial of all," Whitney said with a tight smile that held no warmth.

Matthew looked at her angrily. "Why do you guys never trust me? Why do you never seem to understand that I know exactly how to work my gift? You never tell Thursday how to fly or Titus how to fight. I don't see you looming over Finn with notes on how to heal!"

Sybil sighed but before she could speak, Finn started talking first. "We do trust you, dummy," the healer snapped. "You just have to understand the importance of this mission. Without this man's help, we don't have anywhere to go. Dead end. Done. Do you think we'd give a job like that to someone we didn't trust?" Finn rolled his eyes. "Fool."

Matthew was so dumbstruck by being addressed directly by Finn that he just stared at him blankly. As stupid as it sounded, Matthew wanted Finn to keep insulting him. If it meant that the younger man continued to address him like he was there, then Finn could be reciting a breakfast menu for all Matthew cared.

"You can remind me, then," Matthew smirked back. "It's why you're coming with me right? I'm sure Sybil is absolutely thrilled that she has someone to babysit me."

"Maybe if you didn't need babysat then things would be easier," Finn threw back.

"Yes, because I know how hard it is for any of you to be in my presence!" Matthew snapped.

Why did everyone have to act like he was such a burden, anyway? Not only was he the reason they had any form of transport but without him, they would have no way of talking to this Bas man nor would they have any means of discovering what the eyepatch did.

Finn rolled his eyes. "Oh, lick your wounds, Mattie."

Matthew lifted his finger to point at the healer and snarl his snippy remark back, but he was interrupted by Whitney. "Will you both quit with the lovers' quarrels? It's sickening."

Matthew rolled his head to stare at Whitney. He threw a queasy grin in her direction. "Oh, sorry, I forgot you hated to witness human emotion, Whitney."

Whitney glowered, not rising to his bait and starting a fight of her own as he had hoped.

Sybil stepped forward. "Look, Matth"-

"No, Sybil. I do this my way or not at all." Matthew didn't allow the glare that Sybil was currently branding into his face to deter him. It solidified his stance more than anything else.

"I'll be there, Sybil. I won't let him do anything stupid," sighed Finn.

Matthew couldn't hate Finn. Not true, deep hatred. There was nothing on this Earth that could make Matthew truly despise Finn, no matter what he said or did. However, that didn't mean that sometimes he didn't want to slap the smug git right in the mouth. The way Finn had been acting since they had reunited had been nothing short of cold and, in a way, Matthew hadn't expected any less. He knew he deserved this treatment because of what he did, but that didn't exactly make it any easier to cope with. Especially since it was coming from someone, he used to be so close to.

Sybil glanced at Finn and the two exchanged a look. Matthew wished he knew what sort of understanding was passing between them. It was probably something along the lines of, *'What an idiot, right? Make sure he stays on his leash.'*

Finn exhaled and turned on the edge of the pavement. "Come on then," he said to the oncoming traffic. "Let's get this over with."

"We're going to go find some clothes for Thursday while you're doing this. We'll be back as soon as we can," said Sybil.

"What? I must change?" Thursday looked mildly hurt as she clutched the dirty sleeves of her destroyed strait jacket. "But I love this jacket!" Her momentary pain quickly evaporated as an insane grin grew on her face. "Fine, but no skirts!"

Matthew huffed but didn't comment. He quickened his pace to stay in step with the healer, who almost looked like he couldn't wait to get into the gay bar. They were pursued by Thursday's voice, which echoed through the half-empty streets as she yelled after them.

"Try not to pull anyone, okay?"

"If I can shake this one off, I can't promise anything!" Matthew called back, winking over his shoulder at his friend.

When Matthew turned back to fact front, he felt all energy drain from him. If the circumstances were different, this would have been fun. Back in the day, the two of them had gone to plenty of clubs like this one. This time was different. Not only because they weren't partners anymore, but because they were on a mission.

"You didn't have to volunteer like that," Matthew muttered under his breath petulantly.

Finn sighed heavily. "Yes, I did. It's the only feasible solution to the problem."

Matthew pulled to a stop. Finn stopped, too, giving the shifter a puzzled look in response. The streetlamps cast a shadow across the healer's face, highlighting not only the exasperation in his eyes but also a great deal of exhaustion.

"Do you think it will still work?" Matthew asked. "I mean, the only reason it worked before was because"-

"I know why it worked," Finn interrupted briskly.

Matthew waited for Finn to continue, almost scared that the healer could hear how loud his heart was beating in his chest. Finn didn't finish his sentence; his blue eyes burning into Matthew like rods of sapphire flame.

Matthew raised his eyebrows. "I mean … if this works … does that mean …"

Finn looked away. "We've got a mission to be"-

"*Finn,*" Matthew pressed.

The healer looked back to Matthew; the blue had darkened to a glistening cobalt. Matthew held his breath. This was the kind of thing he had daydreamed about so often when he allowed his mind to wander. That moment where not repressing his feelings would be worth it. A scenario that was almost too good to imagine it didn't even dare to enter his dreams.

"You need to get over it, Matthew."

Matthew had been punched in the gut many times in his long, tired existence. He'd even been hit with large, hard objects once or twice, too. That pain had nothing on those words. He didn't understand how Finn could ditch everything they used to have … He almost wished he could do it as easily as the healer had done as well. At least then they would both be on the same boat. That way Matthew wouldn't be carrying around this ball and chain of yearning and regret.

What hurt the most was that Matthew knew it was all his fault.

Finn had turned and was walking away again.

"I didn't leave you because I wanted to!" Matthew blurted out., giving chase. "I left because I couldn't ...I didn't ...I didn't know how to ..."

Finn spun around again. "I'm not having this conversation with you in the middle of the street!"

"Then have it with me later," said Matthew. "Tonight. When we're resting for the night." He narrowed his eyes at Finn. "You can't keep running from this."

The healer clenched his jaw. "I'm not the one who ran."

With that, Finn spun around for the final time and walked to the bar.

Matthew didn't know how to answer that. He honestly didn't know what he had expected. Those words were like a blow to his chest. He'd *rather* it be a blow to his chest. Matthew would prefer it if Finn would just come out with it and be angry with him. Matthew wanted to be yelled at; screamed at; even hit once or twice. Something, *anything* at all. At least then Matthew would be comforted in the fact that he got what he deserved.

Feeling a lot more miserable than he had done five minutes prior, Matthew followed Finn to the bar.

Finn stopped at the back of the line outside of the bar and folded his arms. He looked completely out of his element. Everyone else in the line was dressed ready to party: crop tops; shorts; glow-in-the-dark paint; the works. Then low and behold,

Finn was standing at the back of the line, dressed in a white dress shirt and dark jeans. The only informal element of his attire was his red sneakers which, in comparison to the people surrounding them, still made him the most formal person there.

"What if they don't let you in?" Matthew smirked, stopping at the back as well. "You look like you're about to attend a board meeting." He flicked Finn's bloodied blue tie over his shoulder and raised his eyebrows.

"Then I guess we'll have to break in through the back entrance," Finn answered.

"That's what she said."

Finn stared at Matthew blankly. "Your ability to joke in this situation does astound me."

"What situation? We're in line to enter a gay bar where an ex of Sawyer's works who may or may not know where Sawyer is while you're dressed like a substitute teacher, and I may end up shifting into God knows what. As far as situations go, this one is pretty humorous to me."

Finn took off his tie, deciding that it wasn't appropriate to be worn in its bloodied state. "I don't look like a substitute teacher," he muttered.

"Yeah, you do. Not one of those old musty ones who smell of B.O. and fall asleep in class, though. The young, smart, sexy ones who have all the girls under their thumb as soon as they enter the classroom," Matthew insisted. "It's the shoes that do it."

The healer looked down at his sneakers as if they were going to confirm or deny Matthew's statement for him. "Your ability to flirt in this situation really astounds me," he repeated, looking as if he was speaking to the ground.

Matthew grinned. "You underestimate me."

Matthew didn't care about Finn's standoffish attitude. As much as the healer could try to deny it, the way his cheeks had flushed slightly pink at the compliment had been unmistakable.

"Clearly." Finn narrowed his eyes. "What about you, anyway? You aren't exactly dressed to impress, either."

"At least I look casual and not like I'm about to conduct a slideshow about appropriate behaviour in the workplace."

If Matthew knew he had been going to a bar he would have dressed a lot differently. He was comfortable enough in his jeans, though, and they would let him into the bar wearing them without a problem. Especially since he hadn't coupled it with a white button-up like Finn had done.

"Maybe they'll think the stitches are some sort of outrageous fashion statement," he suggested.

"Yeah, because I'm going for the 'concussed moron' look," Finn answered.

"You're not a moron," said Matthew. "More of an idiot. I mean, Thursday has been offering to teach you Karate for years now, so you can defend yourself…"

"Because we all know how reliable Thursday is when it comes to violence…"

Matthew knew that Finn was a pacifist because of what happened to his mother, but the lengths that he took it to were going to lead to his destruction. The fact that he couldn't heal himself meant that he *had* to find some means of defence even if it was just acquiring a big stick and waving it around to keep potential threats out of the way. It was either that or healing at a normal pace which, considering their current predicament, wasn't an option.

"I mean, Thursday is insane, but she does know how to fight," Matthew insisted. "Or even Titus! The man can't even trip, he'd be the perfect tutor! Titus doesn't hate you, too, so he'd probably be happy to do it."

Finn eyed Matthew wearily, moving forward as the line edged up. "Titus doesn't hate you either, you know," he said.

Matthew snorted. "Of course, he does. I don't blame him. We just don't mesh well. It's the same reason Sawyer doesn't like me. They just can't …swallow me."

Titus and Sawyer had similar personalities in the sense that they were both very…*proper*. They had a way of doing things and anyone who didn't fit the certain conditions they had in mind was wrong. In all fairness, Titus didn't just hate Matthew, he had an extreme distaste for Thursday as well, which was reassuring. At least Matthew could take comfort in the fact that it wasn't just him who got on the dancer's nerves.

Sawyer, on the other hand, did like Thursday because they were both insane. Matthew didn't care about that as much. He hated Sawyer right back. Even when he was in a relationship with Finn, it was no secret that Sawyer had been working behind the scenes to try to separate them. Matthew knew that Sawyer didn't think that someone of Finn's stature should be with someone as filthy as him.

You see, Matthew was *dirty*. Matthew had slept with humans. He'd had relationships with people outside of the Seven. So that, in Sawyer's eyes, made him the filth of the group.

Matthew didn't care. He didn't regret his past relationships just because some crazy pounce thought he was dirtying his deluded idea of what should be the Seven's morale. Matthew enjoyed the company of humans; they were just the same as him just without an ability. He hated even calling them 'humans.' It sounded wrong. Matthew was just as human as those outside the Seven. He just had a powerful add-on.

"Titus is hard to please," said Finn.

"That's a way of putting it, for sure," Matthew muttered. "But my point still stands, you know."

Finn shrugged, a petulant look on his face. "I know basic self-defence."

"Yeah, and look at your head." Matthew poked Finn's arm. "You trusted Thursday to stitch your head, you should at least consider letting her teach you how to fight."

Matthew could tell from Finn's expression that he still wasn't keen on the idea. Harming another human being was against everything Finn believed in as a healer. This made sense in principle but in the ever-evolving world, it grew more and more difficult to enforce. With every passing year, the world grew more hell-bent on self-destruction.

Matthew had lived for so long, but he had never seen the world so keen to destroy itself as it had been in the past decade.

"At least consider it?"

"Okay, will that stop you harping on about it?"

Matthew grinned. "I'll be checking in on it."

"I don't expect any less from you."

Matthew glanced up at the line of colourful characters waiting to enter the club. He was intrigued by every one of them. Was that man with the blue feather boa here looking for a rebound or was he meeting a partner inside? Were the two men with the blue and green hair a couple or two friends going out for a guys' night out? Why was that man on the phone alone, had he been stood up? They were surrounded by so many different lives, so many different stories. Matthew sometimes wished he had been born a psychic instead of a shifter.

What would this line of people do if they knew that there were two members of the Seven with them? Would they scream? Run away? Would anyone dare to remain and speak to them? Matthew and Finn couldn't do any harm when they weren't with the rest of the group, so no one had anything to fear.

Explaining your innocence to a person is one of the hardest things to do, especially since all the humans have ever seen of them in their lives were *"THE UBER DANGEROUS SEVEN! DON'T APPROACH THEM, STAY AWAY AT ALL COSTS IF YOU VALUE YOUR LIVES!"*

These people didn't even know what they *looked* like, but they still felt they knew enough to claim that they were the most dangerous souls to ever wander the streets of Castlebrooke. Sure, they had never been the safest in their endeavours, but they never went out intending to harm innocents. They tried to help as many people as they possibly could. They had an honest-to-God *pacifist* in their group! But, sure, don't approach them. Extremely deadly and all that.

When did lack of understanding equate to fear, anyway?

What did all these lives and stories think of them? When they glanced at the two men standing at the back of the line, could they see through them? Matthew hoped not. He had enough skeletons in his closet, and he didn't need anyone snooping around trying to find them. Not to mention he couldn't cope with a mob at the moment. *Oh no! It's the shifter and the healer! So dangerous!*

Matthew did a double take as realisation dawned on him. He fought off a smile as he turned to Finn and dutifully pointed out, "They're looking at us."

"So?"

"Well, I don't know, maybe hazard a guess?"

Finn brushed his hair back from his eyes. "You haven't changed," he sighed. "It still works…"

Matthew didn't know what to decipher from Finn's tone. There wasn't any relief there. Why wouldn't Finn be relieved, though? It meant that they could go forward with their plan and there was no risk of being exposed. The only reason Matthew could think of for Finn's lack of relief was that he almost didn't want it to work. Why would that be, though? Would it …expose something? It made Matthew wonder if Finn had been lying when he said that it didn't mean anything…The implications of such a thing made Matthew's heart skip a beat with excitement.

No. He couldn't read into this too much. Getting too hyped up would only lead to devastation if it truly did mean nothing. Besides, if it did mean that Finn's true feelings had not died either, then this was probably making him extremely uncomfortable. Matthew wasn't going to be the one to force Finn into admitting something that might not be true nor was he going to force Finn to admit anything that could be true, but he wasn't ready to reveal yet.

A decade had been a long time, for sure, but Matthew had too much respect for Finn to do such a thing to him. He could wait.

"Thank you for lending me your protective bubble." Matthew flashed Finn his best gooey grin, prompting the healer to roll his eyes.

"Yeah, yeah, whatever," Finn muttered.

They were met at the door by a bouncer. He was your classic burly bloke: no hair; muscles that filled the doorway; and a constant scowl on his face. Immediately, he was taken aback by Finn's formal attire. "I didn't know we were due for an inspection," he said.

Matthew snickered. "You're not don't worry. My friend here is just out of a tense day at work, and he needs a drink."

It was like the bouncer's entire demeanour changed. He grinned at them and said, "I know what that's like," he commented, opening the door for them. "Go on in."

As they were entering, the bouncer suddenly grabbed Matthew's arm. What? Was he going to let them in and then chuck them out?

Matthew sighed and turned to the man, ready to start talking his way out …or more so talk his way *in* …like he had done on so many occasions before now.

"I just need to say, by the way, your eyes are stunning," said the bouncer.

Matthew stared, completely blinkered for a moment. His first reaction was to panic. Had he shifted in front of this man and that was why he was flirting? He looked to Finn for help, but the shifter didn't look at all freaked out or distressed. He was quite the opposite. More …irritated at the distraction.

Matthew turned back to the bouncer and flashed a winning smile. His eyes did garner a great deal of attention from other people and, as his most defining feature, Matthew couldn't help being proud of them.

"Why, thank you," he purred.

The bouncer smiled. He leaned closer as if checking the authenticity of both eyes. He was so close; Matthew could smell the strong mint scent coming from the gum he was chewing. "I've never seen it so pronounced before. Like they're distinctly green and blue. It's amazing."

"Yeah, well, that pretty much sums me up," Matthew replied with an easy shrug.

"If you stick around, my shift ends in an hour. I'd love to talk with you more…."

Matthew laughed. "Uh"-

A hand grabbed the scruff of his jacket and dragged him backwards. Matthew yelped as he was roughly thrown in through the entrance to the bar.

"We're on a mission," Finn hissed as he let the door clang shut behind them. "It's not a time to be collecting numbers."

"Who says it meant anything? Maybe he just wanted to talk. I have friends, you know," Matthew glowered, shrugging Finn's hand off his jacket.

"Do it in your own time." Finn walked past Matthew and went straight to the bar without saying anything else.

Matthew glared at the back of the healer's head. Finn could be so obnoxious, it boiled Matthew's blood. He wouldn't have sought anything out with that man right now. If they weren't on a mission …maybe. Matthew did have a shred of professionalism, but no one seemed to believe it. First Sybil, now Finn. Titus did too for sure. The only person who would probably vouch for him would be Thursday and they trusted her word as much as they trusted Sawyer.

The bar consisted of a dimly lit room dotted with coffee tables and lounge chairs. A pristine jukebox was droning Elvis Presley's music at low volume, adding a sort of chilled vibe to the entire setting. It seemed to have a sort of retro theme, as there were old records and their cases taped to the walls, with the occasional dog-eared concert poster. Pink Floyd; Meatloaf; Queen; David Bowie …Whoever owned this joint certainly had wicked taste in music.

Finn stood at the bar and, from his stance and expression, seemed to be struggling to get information from the bartender. Matthew rolled his eyes and strolled up to them, jumping into the barstool closest to his companion.

The tender that Finn was talking to was a short girl with fiery red hair. The closed-off expression on her pale face reminded Matthew of Whitney. "Hey," Matthew grinned, "is my friend here annoying you?"

Finn gave Matthew a look that could crack concrete. He chose not to meet the angry gaze.

"No. He's just asking for Bas but, as I keep saying, he is on his break," the girl answered.

Matthew raised his eyebrows. "And?"

"I don't know when he'll be back."

Matthew snorted. "You don't know how long the place you work for allows its employees out for breaks?"

The girl was annoyed by Matthew's sniggering at her. "I do," she stubbornly answered.

"So, you *do* know when Bas will be back?"

"I didn't say that."

"I hate to say it, but you have no logic, lady. What's a girl doing in an all-male establishment anyway?" Matthew tipped his head curiously.

The girl looked uncomfortable. "My dad owns this place."

"Oh, I see." Matthew nudged Finn. "Privilege gets you far in life, doesn't it?"

Finn didn't answer him.

"Look, we're going to sit over there," Matthew gestured to one of the leather couches at the back of the bar, "and when Bas shows up, you tell him that we're here by Sawyer's order. That's *Sawyer*. Understand?"

The redhead scowled. "I'm not some message dog. Especially not for that arrogant idiot Bas!"

"What about me?"

Matthew looked over his shoulder. A man stood behind them, eyebrows raised to his hairline with interest. Turning in his seat, Matthew asked, "Are you Bas?"

"Who's asking?" the man asked back.

He was a tall man, towering over both Matthew and Finn. He made the redhead behind the bar look like a dormouse.

"We're here to talk business. It's very important and we don't have a lot of time, so"-

"Business?" Bas flicked his golden hair out of his eyes, which were narrowed with suspicion. "What sort of business?"

"Sawyer," Finn said shortly.

The man's expression changed from intrigued to sombre. "You better come with me," he said.

Matthew flashed the redhead a victorious grin as he hopped off his stool. She rewarded such a gesture with a sour scowl. She must have been nearing the end of her shift or something and didn't want to have to deal with such irritating customers. Either that or she was just sour like that on a day-to-day basis. Matthew would bet his eyes that it was the latter.

Bas led them through a set of red double doors that brought them out into a garden. Fairy lights twinkled in every corner; the cables wrapped around white gazebos like vines. There wasn't anyone outside due to the chilly weather. This would work in their favour since they couldn't afford anyone listening in to what they were going to be talking about. There was a 'click' as Bas locked the door behind them to keep it that way.

The grass bristled in the breeze as Bas jumped behind the bar that ran along the far wall. "Do you want anything to drink?" he asked, pulling a glass out for himself and making a vodka and coke.

Matthew opened his mouth but the voice that came out was not his, it was Finn's. "No, we're fine, thanks."

Bas propped both elbows up on the bar and rested his chin on his threaded fingers. "So," he said, his voice slightly reserved, "what about Sawyer?"

"We want to know if he's been in contact with you lately," asked Finn.

Bas' eyes lowered to the bar top. "Are you the authorities?" he asked back.

Matthew snorted. "Do I look like an official to you?"

Bas wasn't convinced. He began drawing patterns on the top of the bar like he was trying to occupy his hands while his mind worked. "Why do you want to know, if you're not law enforcers?" was his next question.

Matthew watched Finn struggle to come up with an answer that didn't expose who they truly were and what they wanted with Sawyer. There was no way around it, even Finn knew that, but it was worth trying, at the very least. "We're looking for him," Matthew eventually answered. "He has something we need."

Bas raised an eyebrow. "Oh? What's that?"

"That's classified," Finn intercepted.

"I don't know if I can help you if I don't know the context."

Bas took a sip of his drink and there was a glint in his eye that Matthew recognised all too well. A sparkle of mischief, the sort he used to see in Sawyer's dark eyes regularly back in the old days. Bas knew something. He was simply entertaining himself by pretending that he didn't. No wonder Sawyer liked this guy so much. Bas was like the human version of Sawyer himself. Who better to love than oneself?

"Who are you, anyway?" Bas enquired.

Matthew sighed. "I'm Matthew, that's Finn, we just want to know"-

"You're the Seven."

Matthew momentarily forgot to breathe. It took Finn asking, "What?" to remind him that breathing was necessary for life. The chill in the air suddenly intensified and Matthew shivered. How did Bas know simply from their names that they were members of the Seven?

Bas pointed at Matthew, "Monday's child," he stated, before dragging his finger lazily over to Finn, "Friday's child."

"Why on earth would you think that?" Finn quickly deflected.

"Because it's true," Bas shrugged.

"Monday's child shifts, everyone knows that," Matthew insisted. "Do I look like I'm shifting anywhere to you?"

Bas laughed. "Stop lying. Do you honestly think Sawyer didn't tell me everything there was to know about the Seven of you when we spent time together? Of course, he did. I know that Monday and Friday are called Matthew and Finn."

"Purely coincidence," Finn insisted, an edge to his voice.

Matthew looked around. Thankfully, there still weren't any humans around or else they'd have more issues than just Bas. The last thing they needed was for the entire bar to go on a rampage. Then they'd never get their information, and they might even end up arrested and thrown into a padded cell just like Thursday's previous homestead.

"Coincidence, huh?" Bas asked. He pushed back from the bar with a tired sigh. "Well, I guess if you aren't Monday and Friday…"

Quick as lightning, Bas snatched a knife from beneath the bar and dragged it across his neck. It all happened extremely fast. Matthew was horrified and couldn't contain his exclamation of shock as an explosion of red spurted free from the human man. No wonder this man got along with Sawyer! They were both insane!

Finn cursed and lurched across the bar almost faster than Bas had grabbed the knife. He grabbed the front of the bartender's shirt in his hand and held his free hand over the gushing wound. Gold sparks exploded from his hand like fire from a blowtorch, the healing glow consuming the fatal wound with urgency and closing it up.

It had all happened so quickly, in a whirlwind of red and gold, that Matthew barely had time to process what had happened. The only remaining evidence of the near-enough attempted suicide was the frantic beating of Matthew's heart. It almost felt like the organ was trying to force its way up his throat it was so desperate to escape his body out of panic.

Finn didn't release Bas once the wound was healed. As the golden sparks faded from his fingers, Bas' head rolled forward on his shoulders, and he grinned dopily at the healer. "What was that all about?!" Finn nearly growled.

"Proved my point, didn't it?" Bas answered.

"And if you had been wrong?" Matthew exclaimed.

"Well, no point considering that since I wasn't, right?"

Finn released Bas with a push and looked at his hand. As the glow faded from his fingers, tiny sparks shot out of his skin like damaged wires. "Don't you value your own life?" he asked.

Bas shrugged, casually dragging a stool over and sitting himself down. "What's life without risk?"

"That was just flat-out stupidity," Finn corrected. He shook his hand off as the last few sparks faded into the night air. "Are you going to co-operate or are you just going to keep behaving like a madman?"

"Where's the rest of your gang?" asked Bas. "I highly doubt it's just the two of you looking for Sawyer."

"They're attending other business," Matthew answered. "We were sent to talk to you."

Bas shook his head, the grin never once leaving his face. "Sawyer would rip his skin off if he knew that you were leading a mission," he commented.

Matthew's eyes rolled in his sockets like marbles. "Yeah, well, tell me something I don't know." He eyed Bas wearily before asking, "Are you still obsessed with Sawyer? I mean, is your loyalty still to him?"

For all they knew Bas could sit here and listen to all they had to say then find the closest phone as soon as their backs were turned to report back to Sawyer. If Bas was still loyal to the lunatic, there was no point pursuing this lead. It would just get them into more trouble than they were already in.

Bas laughed. "No way," he said, snatching his glass off the bar top. "We ended it years ago; I have no reason to remain loyal to him."

"Why did you break up?" Matthew curiously asked.

"I said the wrong thing about Saturday's Child. You know, your girl Sybil? I should have known better. Sawyer made sure I was aware of how beneath him I was. Not just beneath him, beneath all of you ...*superhumans*," Bas bitterly explained.

It seemed that if Sawyer constantly reminded the humans he was dating that they were a sub-species it was an entirely different scenario from when Matthew dated humans as equals. So much hypocrisy. So many lies. Matthew couldn't wait to see Sawyer again, so he could punch him in the mouth for every time he treated him like dirt for dating humans.

"And you stayed with him despite that?" Finn frowned.

Bas shrugged. "What can I say? I'm an idiot," he said.

Matthew and Finn didn't dispute this claim. The man did just cut his own throat on the off chance that they were the children of Monday and Friday, after all.

"What did you say about Sybil?"

"I asked Sawyer to break up with her, so we could become exclusive." Bas pulled a face. "I mean, how dare I ask such a thing? I'm a heartless bastard."

The pieces slid together in Matthew's brain like parts of a puzzle. "Sawyer was dating you and Sybil at the same time?"

"He was with me first," Bas petulantly responded.

Matthew highly doubted that. Sybil and Sawyer had been dating on and off since the group first came together in the mid-nineteenth century. He decided against pointing this out to Bas.

Bas took another drink, raising his eyes from the lip of the glass to keep staring at the two men in front of him. "Be honest with me," he eventually said, "how many of you had he slept with when he was with me?"

Finn shrugged uncomfortably. "Depends on when you were with him," he said.

"We were together for the majority of the 90's."

Matthew cringed. Such an awkward question ...Bas surely knew that Sawyer was ...well ...he got around. He got around but didn't believe in equal relations with the 'human filth', so he spent most of his time with ...well ...*them.*

"Surely you knew he was polyamorous?" Finn awkwardly asked.

"I know about Sybil," Bas pressed, "but I'm no fool. I know she wasn't the only one."

"Sybil is the only one he had a relationship with," Finn corrected.

It was odd to think about Sawyer and Sybil being a thing, after everything that had happened. Matthew remembered a time when the two of them would hold hands; share a kiss; go out on dates ...But it was so long ago. So much had happened since those days. The entire group dynamic had gone through radical changes. They were only echoes of what they used to be now. Sybil couldn't stand the sight of Sawyer anymore, and nobody could blame her.

Finn didn't say anything else. He looked quite uncomfortable as he dithered at the end of his sentence. Bas patiently waited, knowing that Finn was trying to find a polite way to word his next statement.

Matthew sighed. "Sawyer slept with Thursday regularly right up until the group broke apart," he stoically explained. "There was nothing romantic between them, they only did it for fun. Titus had no interest in Sawyer whatsoever however it wasn't for lack of trying on Sawyer's part. It never worked out. Whitney did it once after a bad breakup but never again. Happy?"

Bas stared at his reflection in his drink for a long moment. Matthew and Finn stood by patiently, allowing him time to absorb the information. Matthew had purposely left out the time when Sawyer suggested the Seven of them get married at the turn of the Millennium. Finding out that your ex slept around when in a relationship with you was one thing, finding out there was an actual emotional connection there was another.

Besides, Sybil forbade the marriage and Matthew had never seen Thursday laugh as hard in his entire life.

"But not you two?" Bas asked. He was still staring at his drink, giving the impression that he was talking to his vodka coke.

"I think you know what his feelings for me are," Matthew answered. He liked to think he was the one special exception for Sawyer's claim of irrevocable love for the Seven.

"I was in a relationship," Finn explained. "I don't believe in polyamory."

There was something oddly comforting about knowing that Finn hadn't fallen under Sawyer's spell when they had been dating. Matthew wouldn't have blamed Finn if he had. Despite not believing in using his power against his own, Sawyer was still an incredibly manipulative man on his own. He knew exactly the right buzzwords to make someone gush and smile and fall under his spell. Matthew had always feared that Sawyer would someday succeed in driving that wedge between them and, even though there was most definitely a wedge now, it was not of Sawyer's making, as much as he had tried.

"Why didn't you expose him?" Matthew asked. "If your relationship ended so suddenly ..., Weren't you angry?"

"I was beyond angry," Bas answered. "However, look at the status Sawyer has in this city. Nobody would believe me if I said he was Sunday's Child. I only knew the names of the rest of you, I didn't know where you lived or what you looked like. I was snookered."

On some level, Matthew felt bad for Bas. He'd gotten wrapped up in Sawyer's insanity and power. He didn't know that Sawyer didn't see their relationship as anything more than a project, most likely. Sawyer didn't feel emotions for human beings. They were all ants under his feet. Sybil said that Sawyer always claimed that if there was an eighth day of the week, it would be Bas. Maybe then their relationship would have stood a chance. Bas was still as human as they came, and nothing was changing that. So, Sawyer treated him like a rag doll; playing with him lovingly until the day he grew bored and chucked him away.

"Has he been in contact with you recently?" Finn tentatively asked.

Bas downed the rest of his drink, strands of blond hair falling into his eyes. He didn't brush them back again, he let them hang over his face. "Should he have?" he asked.

"I'm taking that as a no, then?" said Matthew.

"If Sawyer is up to something sinister, I'd be the last person he would contact," Bas sighed.

"Why is that?"

Bas rolled the glass around in his hand, peering at the remaining droplets of drink as they slid against each other along the bottom. "Could be because I told him if he ever set foot in my bar again, I'd kill him," he said. Bas lifted his dark eyes to the black sky above their heads. "When I heard the news that the Seven were rumoured to have broken apart, I was tempted to go to Sawyer's building and shoot him in the face. No healer by his side to protect him … The world is better off without a lunatic like him."

If there were to ever be an example of the damage Sawyer left in his wake, Matthew was staring at him. Were there any more rag dolls they didn't know about? Humans that Sawyer had toyed with and then thrown away like they were nothing?

"What happens when one of you dies? When the Seven is no longer the Seven?" Bas asked.

Neither Matthew nor Finn knew how to answer. It hadn't happened yet, so they weren't sure what the answer was.

There was a knock on the door. Bas rolled his eyes. "Garden's closed!"

There had been a moment when they had gotten close. Whitney had never been able to swim. No matter how much they tried to teach her, she just couldn't get the hang of it. One day they went to the seaside on the edge of Opara City and Whitney was knocked off the pier into the ocean. Sawyer had gone right in after her without hesitance and as soon as he dragged her out onto the sand, Finn had been there to heal her. It took so long, though, that they almost believed it was hopeless.

It felt…wrong. As Matthew had stood in the sand watching Finn desperately try to heal Whitney, suddenly his skin felt like it didn't fit right. It was like he was standing at the edge of the world and all it would take was a tiny push and he'd fall into nothingness. He wouldn't die just because Whitney did, but a piece of him was getting tugged at. Almost as if a dog had latched to his leg and was desperately tugging at him trying to rip a piece of him off.

Even Thursday had been silent. Matthew knew she felt it too.

Then, as Whitney's eyes had shot open and she started coughing, that feeling left. All at once. The tugging stopped, and his skin returned to normal. He no longer stood on the edge of the universe waiting for that push. It was all gone. Just like that.

"We don't know. It hasn't happened yet," Finn answered.

"Let's hope for your sake then that Sawyer doesn't contact me," Bas said darkly. "If it meant ridding the world of his existence, I'd go through you all."

"Has he hurt you that much?" Matthew frowned.

There was that knocking again. "I said the garden's closed!" Bas yelled. He looked at Matthew and narrowed his eyes. "This isn't just about emotional trauma. That man is the reason I am the way I am now."

"What do you mean 'the way I am now'? What way are you now?" Matthew demanded.

"You're talking about your prosthetic arm, aren't you?" said Finn.

"I should have known the doctor would notice," Bas said, smiling at Finn with no warmth.

"Prosthetic … What prosthetic?" Matthew exclaimed. He had suddenly gotten very lost in this conversation.

Bas slammed his glass down onto the bar and pulled his sleeve up. Matthew's eyes widened at what he saw. Bas' arm …It was fake. His real arm ended at his bicep and the rest was fake. How had he not noticed that?

"What's that got to do with Sawyer?"

"Sawyer's experiments," Bas sourly explained. "Don't you know? He's trying to merge all your abilities into his own body."

"Of course, we know that," Matthew answered. He didn't like the direction this conversation was going in. "But why experiment on you?"

"He said he was trying to make me like you guys. He was trying to make me the eighth day. When I asked him to break up with Sybil, he laughed in my face and told me that there was never going to be an eighth day. He was using me to find a way to merge your abilities." Bas stared at his fake hand. "At least he had the decency to let me keep the prosthetic he invented for me when he chopped off my arm."

Matthew had no words. He looked at Finn with shock and found him in a similar situation. However, Finn looked more angry than shocked. It was no secret Finn despised Sawyer's experiments. He'd always viewed it as an insult to medical science. The only time a body should be touched in such a way was if it was necessary for life.

"Did he …succeed?" Matthew carefully asked, turning back to Bas.

"Hell, if I know."

The knocking returned. Bas scowled and stood up. He leapt over the bar again and stormed over to the doors, sticking the key in and throwing them open. "I said that the garden is clo"-

Bas was on the ground before the gunshot reached Matthew's ears. A bullet was fired straight to the head. The sound was like a car backfired in the middle of the garden, exploding right in Matthew's ears like a firework in the night. There was no arguing that the man was dead. No human could survive such a wound.

In an instant, United Arms goons were pouring in like a tidal wave. "On the floor, now!" the leader roared the two of them.

Finn grabbed Matthew and dragged him to the ground. Matthew slapped his hands onto his head in surrender.

"Are there any more of you here?" the leader demanded.

They shook their heads.

Matthew licked his lips and breathed out shakily. His heart was in his throat again. He was sure if he opened his mouth to speak it was going to fall out onto the ground. How had they found them so quickly? Had Sawyer figured out that they might contact Bas? Had they been spotted outside the bar? Were they working on a hunch?

Not believing them, the goons started scoping the garden. What were they expecting? To find the rest hiding up a tree or something?

The goons had been informed by Sawyer that Matthew and Finn were two of the most harmless members of the group. Why else would they be searching the garden without bothering to keep a watch on them? They must have known that their powers weren't violent or dangerous and if they tried to get up and run, they wouldn't get far before they were caught.

"Finn," Matthew whispered as the garden was ripped apart, "close your eyes."

"What?" Finn's voice shook like a leaf, his fear practically radiating off him.

Matthew knew how scared Finn was of being taken first. The first time Sawyer had spoken of this mad plan of experimentation, Finn had been so disturbed that he didn't sleep for weeks. Matthew remembered sitting up on some nights, talking it out with him, assuring him that Sawyer was just being insane, and Sybil would never allow it to happen and if the group remained together, they would never act out against each other.

Sawyer would have to step over Matthew's own dead body before he got Finn or Whitney or Sybil or any of them near an experimentation table.

Matthew had promised.

"Trust me," Matthew insisted. "Just close your eyes."

"You can't beat them, Matthew," Finn replied. "There's too many of them."

"You underestimate me, darling," Matthew grinned. "Just do it."

Finn looked unsure but without any other choice, he obeyed.

Matthew stood up.

CHAPTER EIGHT

A FEATHER SLID DOWN THE LINE OF MATTHEW'S SPINE AS THE FIRST SET OF EYES FOUND HIM, HIS SKIN FOLLOWING THAT PATH AS IT RIPPLED INTO A NEW BODY. To an outsider, the change was instantaneous, barely noticeable, but for Matthew, there was always a moment in between when he was neither here nor there. Not Matthew or the next shape he was about to take. Simply nothing.

Matthew took to his new form instantly, at once latching eyes with the goon who'd incited the change. He couldn't see through their helmet but, judging from how they were staring at him with their hands still in a bush, they were rapt. Desire was so easy to control, especially when lust was one of the most domineering emotions in the human mind.

Matthew didn't need to assess what he'd turned into but as he passed the bar, he caught a flash of long silver hair in his reflection in Bas' glass. He dragged his hand along the bar top and slid the knife Bas had cut himself with into his hand. The goon continued to watch him, completely hypnotised and said nothing as Matthew crouched beside him by the bush.

"Would you mind taking your helmet off for me?" Matthew sweetly asked, batting his eyelashes.

The goon didn't think twice before ripping off their helmet. It was a pasty-skinned male with ginger hair. His eyes were so wide they looked like they were going to pop out of his sockets.

Matthew sighed and leaned into the man's ear. He whispered, "Would you mind if I killed you?"

The ginger did one better. He snatched the knife from Matthew's grip and slashed his own throat. Matthew jumped back as the goon fell forward into the bush, blood seeping from his skin to the floor in a puddle of scarlet.

Sometimes Matthew wondered if he wasn't a shifter at all. Maybe he was a hypnotist who knew how to change shape. There was no other logical explanation for how he could manipulate actions simply based on appearance.

"Hey, lady, what do you think you're"-

As soon as Matthew turned to face the next United Arms Lackey, the feather returned, and he was something new. This guy surprised Matthew, as he ripped his helmet off and dragged him against him for a kiss. It was amusing how some people couldn't control themselves even in the direst of situations.

Then again, Matthew only spoke from the perspective of someone who had trained himself in the art of self-control. He was lucky enough to have dated his idea of perfection for most of his life and the first time he'd laid eyes on him again ...yeah, Matthew couldn't say he wouldn't react similarly.

When he went to the hospital with Thursday and Whitney came to mind and Matthew realised that he pretty much *had* reacted similarly.

Matthew slid his hands up the arms of his eager victim and wrapped his hands around their throat. He squeezed his fingers tight, and he felt them dig their own fingers into his face as they realised what was happening. They grabbed the back of his neck, trying to get him to release them. They weren't strong enough.

Taking human life was a necessity Matthew had grown used to long ago. The Seven were not angels. They did not *intentionally* harm innocents. What they *did* do was harm those who tried to harm them first. Matthew had no qualms with getting rid of people who tried to hurt him or the people he cared about.

Even Finn did not protest as Matthew pushed the guard who'd kissed him on top of the bar top and held tight as he struggled for air. Maybe it was because of his fear of being taken for experimentation. Maybe it was because he knew it was necessary. Maybe it was because he couldn't see. Whatever the explanation, Matthew was glad for it. Even if Finn hadn't wanted it this way, Matthew still would have done it, and the last thing they needed right now was an argument over differences in belief.

As the final etch of life drained from the body on the bar, Matthew gave one final squeeze. Once dead, he pushed the body behind the bar and looked in Finn's direction. The healer was in the same position he'd left him in. Hands-on head; breathing unevenly; eyes shut. Confident that Finn was safe, Matthew returned to the bush and retrieved the knife from the first goon.

Matthew worked as fast as he could. Every time someone new faced him, there was a pause of disbelief, which Matthew used to jump in and stab them. It became methodical. Over and over again. Stab. Stab. Stab. Blood everywhere. It coated the blade of the knife; his clothes; his hands; his face. Matthew didn't feel guilt or remorse for this loss of life. These people took pleasure in the torture of the mentally unwell every day. Now they were working for Sawyer at the command of that woman with the big nose. The world would not grieve the loss of this scum.

Once the front of the garden was clear and the rest of the goons were down at the bottom, still searching for hiding members of the Seven, Matthew ran back to Finn.

"We need to move, now!" he said.

Finn's eyes shot open as Matthew grabbed his hand and dragged him to his feet. Immediately, the feather changed Matthew back to his normal form. They crossed the short distance to the double doors and burst back into the interior of the bar.

The smell of blood was thick inside. Matthew covered his nose with his free hand, only to remember that it too was coated in blood and would do nothing to prevent the metallic stench. Finn made a disgusted noise at the back of his throat and covered his own nose with his tie.

Everyone inside the bar was dead. Not a single person had gotten out alive. Every patron lay sprawled across the tables and sofas, a gunshot wound somewhere on their bodies. People who'd stood in front of them in the line to get in. People who must have entered after them. Even the red-headed bartender lay across the bar, her bright orange hair hanging over the edge like a curtain of fire, her eyes wide open but unseeing.

Something sparked in the corner of his eye. Matthew looked at Finn's hands, which were twitching with a small bright glow. "There's no point," Matthew said quietly, "they're already gone."

Finn pulled a face and shouted angrily, kicking over a table and ripping down a nearby curtain. "This is our fault!"

Matthew couldn't disagree. It was true. If they hadn't set foot in this bar, these people would still be alive. "We need to leave, now," he said, grabbing Finn's hand again and tugging so he would follow him.

As if to answer that statement, the front doors opened and the bald bouncer from earlier entered.

"You're not dead!" Matthew exclaimed. He released Finn's hand and crossed the room. "We need help, there are people out in the garden who killed all these p"-

As soon as he was within reaching distance of the bouncer, the burly man grabbed Matthew by the front of his shirt and threw him across the room. His body hit the bar full force, the impact stealing all air from Matthew's lungs. He heard a crack, and a splitting pain instantly consumed his entire torso as he smacked the floor beneath.

"Matthew!" He heard Finn shout.

Matthew lifted his head and saw Finn quickly approaching him, hands warming into gold in preparation to heal whatever damage had been done.

"Not so fast," the bouncer said.

Finn stopped moving. Matthew inclined his head in the bald man's direction, despite the agony it caused him. The bouncer was pointing a gun at Finn, preventing him from getting any closer to Matthew.

"You're coming with me, right now," he said carefully.

"Who are you?" Finn demanded to know.

"My name is Bram. I work for Mr. Bateman," the bouncer answered.

"You mean Sawyer?" Matthew yelled back. Every breath was currently a marathon, each one causing his chest to rattle and his ribs to scream.

"If you like," Bram replied. "I'm under orders to make sure that Friday's Child does not leave this building free. I was also ordered to obtain Wednesday's Child and Saturday's Child, but they don't seem to be here." He glanced down at Matthew. "Monday's Child could be terminated, if necessary, but it isn't desired."

Finn looked desperately at Matthew. Matthew could be going insane from the agony, but he was quite sure he saw tears in Finn's eyes. Did he look that bad? Was the damage that severe? Even if it was, Matthew couldn't take exterior damage, it was part of his ability. His entire system could be shutting down and he'd still look at the peak of health on the outside

"You spoke to Matthew, you even flirted with him!" Finn accused.

"My job was to separate you both before United Arms reached the establishment. However, Bas came back from his break early and locked the doors to the garden and I couldn't do so," Bram explained. He shrugged casually and looked at Matthew. "Your eyes are incredibly striking; I will say that."

"Oh, well, *thanks*," Matthew sarcastically replied. Bram's compliments were about as welcome as a priest at a gay wedding. "I'll be sure to remember that as my spine crumbles!"

Matthew was unable to contain a scream as a fresh wave of pain electrified his nerves. Bram must have thrown him with the strength of ten men because surely hitting your back against a bar didn't cause this much damage.

Unless …possibly …Bram was one of Sawyer's experiments…

Finn took one last look at Bram and his gun. He pulled a face before lunging across the room towards Matthew's broken body.

Matthew predicted Bram's next move before it happened. If Finn got shot in the wrong place, that was it. Game over. No healing. No second chance. Matthew knew that Sawyer had most likely told Bram that Finn couldn't heal himself. That didn't make the man any more accurate a shot. It was too great a risk. A risk Matthew couldn't allow the lackey to take. Losing Finn over a stupid gunshot wound was not an option.

Another car backfired. The shifter threw himself up off the ground despite the protest of every cell in his body. Shootings don't happen in slow motion like described in books or depicted on television. It's all very fast. Almost faster than humanly possible. Like God or the higher power overlooking them all suddenly pressed their thumb against the fast-forward button.

Matthew jumped in front of Finn as the bullet hurtled towards him, just in time for it to embed itself into his abdomen instead.

Matthew's ears rang as the pain in his back became secondary to the fire in his stomach. Arms wrapped around him so that he didn't slam against the floor again and the descent to the ground was softer than expected. All he could see was the ceiling, the edges of his sight blotted with black, like ink had been spilt in his vision. Matthew couldn't breathe, the agony was so intense it stole every possible breath he could take.

Then Finn's face came into view, scrunched up in a mixture of anger and frustration. Matthew reached out for something, anything, to grab hold of, and Finn immediately grabbed his hand. He was saying something, but Matthew couldn't hear him. With every beat of his heart, there was a fresh wave of searing pain through his entire system, and it was hard to focus on much else.

Matthew squeezed his eyes shut as if it would ward away the pain as well. He knew Finn was going to heal him, but every second dragged on for a century as he waited for that moment to come. He squeezed Finn's hand as hard as he could, and he was sure that Finn was squeezing back. That was all he needed. The anchor to keep him buoyed to reality.

If he still had this hand, and the person connected to it, he would be okay.

Then the bliss arrived.

Being healed by Finn was difficult to explain. Everyone had a unique way of describing it. Some would say that it was a calming sensation. Others claimed it filled them with energy. Each one of the Seven had different experiences with it. Thursday believed it was like a knife, cutting out the poison before it killed her. It usually lulled Whitney to sleep. Titus said it felt like cool water washed over his wound, clearing it completely. Sybil had explained that she felt like she had been injected with caffeine afterwards. Sawyer simply said it was 'inhumanly pleasant'.

Matthew had more experience with the healing ability than anyone else. He had been on the receiving end of it more than anyone else on the planet. Thursday had been right. When they were together, Finn did everything he could to remove any type of pain from Matthew's system whether it be a stubbed toe or a papercut. It didn't matter how small it was.

There had been days when Matthew had laid in bed with his head in Finn's lap, the healer's hands pressed against his forehead to fix an intense headache.

Or other times when he'd banged his hip against the corner of a table and Finn would have stood with his arm around his waist so that his hand would have rested against the assaulted hip to soothe the pain.

Then the moments when Matthew felt down because all he ever did was change and change and change, with no form of stability to his own self. The times when he didn't know what to do with himself and thus stayed up in his room all day just so that he didn't have to face the fresh eyes that would change him. Finn stayed with him; held him beneath a cocoon of blankets and stroked his forehead with his healing hands. The ability did not reach the ailment of the mind but that didn't matter. It was to comfort him, not to remove his depression. Even miracle powers had their limits.

It was euphoric. That was the word to describe it. Completely euphoric. It put a person into an almost docile state and removed whatever ailed them while their conscious brain remained in limbo. It was a painless and almost ecstatic process. Matthew had missed this feeling. These hands that had fixed his broken self so often he had lost count. They had been absent for a decade. The most miserable and lonely decade of Matthew's long existence.

Something cold slid along Matthew's insides and he vaguely heard a soft 'chink' as the bullet was dragged from his body by Finn. The ringing in his ears was fading and new voices were coming through. Familiar voices. Friendly voices.

His vision slid into focus once more, the golden hue that had replaced the ink black receding to reveal Finn's face hovering over his own once more. The younger man was drenched in sweat, the stitched scar on his forehead practically bulging out of his head because he was concentrating so intensely. There was someone else standing over them. Someone with bright orange hair. Hadn't the orange-haired bartender been killed?

Matthew focused harder and realised it was Sybil. Her mouth was moving but his hearing hadn't completely returned yet, so he couldn't discern what she was saying. He rolled his head forward so that he could assess his current situation.

Finn was still healing him, it seemed. That explained why Matthew had not returned to a complete plain of normalcy yet. He felt too relaxed for the situation, a side effect usually brought on by the healing process. Despite knowing that he had just been shot by Bram the psycho bouncer, all Matthew could think about was how chill he felt as he watched the halcyon glow caress the bullet wound in his stomach. It was slowly shrinking, the edges of the wound pushing towards each other bit by bit.

Matthew let his head fall back. He noticed that he wasn't lying on the ground anymore, he was propped up in Finn's lap on the floor. Probably made the wound easier to access. The ringing was nearly completely gone now, and he could hear

Sybil's voice more distinctly. She was giving orders of some sort, probably to the other three.

Matthew smiled stupidly, still under the sedative of Finn's ability, and brushed his bloody fingers through the healer's hair.

"Thank you," he slurred.

Despite his immense concentration, Finn let a smile break through his tough exterior. "It's my job to save your life, not the other way around, you silly man," Finn replied.

Matthew let his hand sit in Finn's hair for a moment, flakes of blood staining the bronze strands like paint. "Most would say thank you back," he said.

Finn shook his head, the smile still not leaving his face. This was the longest Matthew had seen the man smile since they'd first retrieved him from the hospital. "Thank you," he said.

Matthew closed his eyes and brushed his cheek against the healer's arm. "It was my pleasure."

"I will kill you, you bald freak!"

Matthew opened his eyes again, rolling his head in the direction of the yelling. Bram was on the floor, hogtied like a pig about to be spit-roasted. Thursday stood over the bouncer, decked out in brand new clothes, kicking the living shit out of him. There was a maniac grin on her face. Her ebony hair was wild and untamed, flicking around her face as she moved.

"A gun is a coward's weapon, don't you know?" Thursday raged as she continuously booted Bram in the stomach. "You're about as manly as a day-old cheese sandwich! You're lucky that you're needed, or I'd have cut each of your fingers off and fed them to you by now!"

"Thursday!" Sybil barked. "Stop it!"

"You shot my best friend, you freak!" Thursday continued, ignoring Sybil completely. "Your lord and saviour Sawyer would have your eyeballs in his soup if he knew you tried to shoot one of us! I'll have your head when we're done with you! It'll look lovely on my mantelpiece with a golden plaque saying, 'Here lies a Cheese Sandwich'!"

"Thursday!"

Thursday lifted her foot, ready to stamp down on Bram's head as if to prove her point, when Whitney suddenly swooped in and pulled Thursday away.

"We need him sentient," said Whitney, pushing Thursday back. The madwoman was pushing back against Whitney's grasp, but she had gotten her fill. If Thursday genuinely wanted past Whitney, she would never have let herself get pulled away in the first place.

"What about the rest of the guards?" Matthew frowned.

"Taken care of." Matthew hadn't noticed Titus sitting at the bar until he had spoken up. He was seated on the very bar stool Matthew himself had knelt on not even an hour ago. Judging by the beads of sweat glistening on his chocolate skin and the quickened rise of his chest, 'taken care of' was code for 'I-Just-Kicked-The-Ever-Living-Mercy-Out-Of-Them'.

"We're sorry we took so long." Sybil looked disturbed as she gazed around at all the bodies in the room. "I should have known that Sawyer would be able to predict our next move. It was our last option. We should never have left you both here."

Matthew shuddered as a flush of relief slithered through his body. Finn had finished healing the bullet wound and the damage to his back. Both agonies were now non-existent like they had never been there at all. Matthew struggled to sit up and, despite feeling brand new and energised, he felt Finn's hands on his back helping him do so.

"Was I out long?" Matthew asked.

"No," Finn answered. "Bram shot you and had the gun pointed at my head when Sybil and the others arrived. Thursday and Titus took care of the guards and Whitney took care of Bram. It was all very …quick. Almost too quick."

"I wanted to take care of Bram," Thursday pointed out. She had found her way behind the bar and was mixing a drink for herself now. "But *nooooo*."

"You would have killed him, Thursday," said Titus. "You killed the guards when we told you to *apprehend* them."

"Which you say as if it's a bad thing."

"It is when we need information," Sybil reminded her.

Thursday perked up. "Can I kill him once we've gotten the information?"

"No, you know that's not how we do things."

Thursday slumped again. She downed the drink she made and purposely broke the glass against the floor. It reminded Matthew of a child throwing their toys out of their pram. Most petulant children were commonly upset because they weren't allowed a lollipop, not because they weren't allowed to brutally murder a man and have his head on their mantle.

Matthew hauled himself to his feet. Sybil stepped forward to help him, but he waved her off as he slid into the closest chair. He honestly felt fine now. Once the healing process was over, usually the victim couldn't even remember what the pain had felt like. It was almost like a distant dream. If they weren't still surrounded by dead bodies with Bram hogtied on the floor, Matthew probably would have believed that it had been a surreal nightmare of some sort.

Finn rose to his feet as well. "Are you hurt at all?" Sybil asked him as he slid into the seat next to Matthew's.

"Me? No," Finn replied. "Just some bumps and bruises. Nothing to complain about."

Sybil joined them at the table. "Did you get any information from Bas? We found him on the ground outside. I assume they killed him."

"It certainly wasn't me that did it, that's for sure," Matthew responded dryly.

"Why would Sawyer kill him? I would have thought that he'd want a loyal human like Bas at his beck and call," Sybil frowned.

"Bas wasn't loyal, Sybil," Finn told her.

Their leader looked perplexed by this. "Sawyer always spoke so highly of him, though. I would have thought that Bas had done the same. I know Sawyer doesn't like humans all that much, but I had thought Bas was the rare exception. Why, I could never understand, but…"

"Sawyer experimented on him, Sybil," Matthew sighed. "Bas lost an arm because of him."

Whitney, who had been standing by Bram in case he somehow broke his bounds and tried to make a run for it, grimaced. "What?" she asked, gripping her arm as if it was going to suddenly fall off.

"I noticed he had a fake arm as soon as he started making his drink, but I had figured he had been in some sort of accident or maybe fought in the war or something," Finn explained. He massaged his forehead, careful not to disturb his stitches. "I never considered that it had been Sawyer's doing."

Sybil was staring intensely at the table. She looked extremely uncomfortable. Matthew couldn't blame her. Sawyer's experiments had always been a taboo topic between the six of them. They had never been forced to acknowledge any of it up until now. Sure, Sawyer used to talk about it a lot, but they had never actually seen evidence of him having tried any of it. Up until now, they had been able to deny the possibility that Sawyer had gone through with the mad schemes he used to talk about. Now they had no choice.

"Why would Sawyer experiment on a human?" asked Titus.

"Bas knew all about Sawyer's plan to take all our abilities for himself," Matthew explained. "I can only imagine that that had been what he had been working towards."

"That makes absolutely no sense," Whitney said.

"I don't know about you but I'm no scientist so who knows if it actually makes sense or not," Matthew replied.

Another glass smashed against the ground and suddenly Thursday spoke up. "Maybe human DNA is the key. It's no secret that we aren't fully human, as much as you all like to pretend to be, so maybe a human can have all our abilities in the one body. Maybe that's what Sawyer had done to Bas. All it would take would be to inject some of Whitney's DNA into Bas' body and bam as soon as he gets angry, he sets his entire arm on fire, and it has to get amputated."

"Bas would have mentioned if he had our abilities."

"Unless Sawyer flushed it out as soon as he realised it worked."

For someone who was clinically insane, it scared Matthew how much Thursday could sometimes make sense. Matthew hoped she was wrong this time. Such a suggestion would imply that Sawyer already had the means of combining their abilities, all he needed was his subjects…

A cold, harsh laugh filled the room. Whitney looked down at the man lying at her feet as the other five turned to look at him also.

Bram was *laughing*. His body shook against the ground as he chuckled away to himself, a beaming grin on his bloodied face. Matthew was deeply perturbed by the bouncer's amusement. What was there about his situation to be happy about?

"I think someone needs a fresh kicking," said Thursday. She was already climbing over the bar to conduct said kicking, but Titus pushed her back. She stuck her bottom lip out petulantly and crossed her arms over her chest in a clear huff.

Sybil stood up, her chair scraping against the wooden floor behind her. Matthew watched her cross the short distance to where Bram lay, almost holding his breath with anticipation.

Sybil was fair. Sybil was wise. Sybil was collected. Sybil had always been the best person to oversee the Seven. Without her, they wouldn't have even found each other. Whitney would still be on the streets. Titus wouldn't have escaped slavery. Finn would still be doing tricks at that circus and Thursday would have still been in the asylum under the authority of her parents. Matthew couldn't see himself even being alive right now if Sybil hadn't given him sanctuary after Thursday found him at that hovel of an orphanage.

Despite being fair; wise; collected; and the founder of the Seven, Sybil was in charge for a reason. She could get angry just as much as the rest of them, she was only better at hiding it. Matthew knew how to recognise her rage. After spending so long in the company of another person it grew easier to recognise their mask. When angry, Sybil would go deadly quiet, and her eyes would turn the colour of mud after a storm. There was nothing more terrifying to Matthew than a decent person getting angry. That was why, despite his jibes and jeers, he didn't dare push Sybil to her limit.

Sybil planted her foot onto Bram's shoulder and kicked him over onto his back. "What's so funny?" she demanded to know.

"You lot," Bram chuckled. Thursday had certainly done a number on him. His nose was practically non-existent in a mass of thick, scarlet blood and his eye had swollen completely shut. "You're so pathetic. The mighty, terrifying Seven are nothing but a bunch of scared children."

"Children?" Sybil laughed, except hers was empty of humour. "To me, you're nothing but a kid who never learned how to walk."

"I'm old enough to be your great-great-great grandmother," Thursday added.

Bram wriggled against his bounds. He looked like a sad, fat worm writhing on the end of a fishing hook. "You're all so afraid of Mr. Bateman."

"Bateman. Is that Sawyer?" asked Whitney.

"Bateman is his current alias," Titus confirmed. "I've seen his name floating around the newspapers recently. '*Mr. Sawyer Bateman...*'"

Sybil looked down her nose at Bram, clearly unamused by his answer. "I'm not afraid of Sawyer. None of us are," she said.

"Well, that's a lie. The healer looked ready to spontaneously combust when I confronted him," Bram answered. "You shouldn't fear Mr. Bateman. He told me that if I ever found you, I was to tell you all that he loves you. Every one of you." Bram caught Matthew's eyes. "Even that one. Just not as much."

Matthew knew that that was a lie. Sawyer didn't love him. He never had. They had clashed since day one and never found common ground in the centuries the group were together. It was just the way it had gone. This was a tactic of some sort, it had to be. If Matthew had to guess, he'd say that Sawyer was trying to make it look like he loved him like everyone else on the off chance that it would butter Matthew up and make him softer to the idea of taking his family away from him to kill them.

"Sawyer loves me like a bullet to the head," said Matthew.

"That's where you're wrong," Bram answered. "Sawyer does not like you but as a member of the Seven you are still loved."

"God, this lovey-dovey rubbish is making me break out in hives," Thursday complained, scratching her arms as if to emphasize her point. "Since when did this turn into the plot of *The Notebook* anyway?"

Sybil didn't look too pleased with the topic, either. "Sawyer is not capable of love, you silly cretin," she said. "Whatever he has brainwashed you with to convince you otherwise is a lie. Nobody as insane as that man could ever understand the concept of caring for another. Nobody in their right mind would look a person in the eye and say, *'I love you with all of my heart, now let me cut you open so I can steal your organs'.*"

Bram's small blue eye focused on Sybil as if she were the only person in the room. "You would know, wouldn't you?"

What did Bram mean by that? Matthew looked desperately at their leader, but her expression was unreadable.

"I don't know what you're talking about," Sybil stiffly responded.

"Mr. Bateman must be overjoyed that it worked," Bram continued. "Not so much that it is not his but that can be easily remed"-

Sybil flew down and punched Bram across the jaw, cutting off his sentence before he could finish it. "Shut up!" she barked. "You're in no position to be making demands! You will be silent and answer our questions as they're asked if you want to return to the light of day. Don't make me let Thursday have at you again!"

Whitney grabbed Sybil by the elbow. "Careful, Sybil," she warned. "Don't get yourself too worked up."

Bram was no longer laughing but the grin seemed to be irremovable from his face. His teeth were coated in blood, adding a much more sinister look to the expression on his face. "Ask away," was all he said.

Matthew stood up and grabbed his chair, bringing it over to Sybil and making her sit down on it. All this stress couldn't be good for her baby. She tried to stay standing, but it didn't take much for her to concede and sit. Matthew could only gauge how exhausted he was after all of this and he wasn't the pregnant one, so who knew how drained Sybil was?

"How long has Sawyer been experimenting on humans?" was Sybil's first question.

"Ever since the rumours began about the separation of the Seven," Bram shrugged. "Phase One was figuring out how to merge your abilities into his body, which took a decade in the making. Phase Two had originally been to kidnap each of you one by one in order of your ability's value. Somehow you figured him out before he could initiate this and joined forces against him."

"He experimented on Bas before we even thought about leaving each other," Finn said.

"Bas was a special case. Mr. Bateman had a human at his disposal, did you honestly think he wasn't going to take advantage of that?"

"How can you speak of humans as if you aren't one yourself?" Whitney asked. "Have you no humanity?"

"I am not human. Not anymore. Mr. Bateman …he improved me."

"You mean he cut you up," Titus clarified.

Bram didn't seem to mind this description. "I was fixed by Mr. Bateman."

Thursday made an ugly noise at the back of her throat. "Another sod obsessed with Sawyer. Just what the world needed. How many of you does he have enslaved, anyway? First Dr. Weeks, now you? How many humans exactly has he hypnotised to do his bidding?"

"I am not hypnotised; I came of my own free will."

"How long did it take for him to convince you of that, then? A week? A month?" Thursday walked around the bar and approached their bound prisoner, an entertained gleam in her eyes. "How long did you have to spend in his basement until the Stockholm Syndrome kicked in, huh?"

Bram regarded Thursday with a disinterested sneer. "He said you would not understand."

"How can you follow Sawyer even though you know what happened to Bas?" Matthew frowned. "He threw him away as soon as he wasn't of use anymore. What would stop him from doing the same to you, too?"

"I know I am disposable. I am not foolish enough to view myself as a higher being to Mr. Bateman and the six he loves so dearly. That was Bas' problem. He wanted to be a higher being. We are not higher. We are scum; dirt; filth. You are the true Gods of this pathetic city. This immoral world will bow to the feet of Mr. Bateman once he has your faith and your abilities at his disposal."

There were religions out there based around the stories of the Seven, entire faiths born of the stories of the Seven metahumans who wandered the streets of Castlebrooke, hidden in plain sight. It made Matthew rather uncomfortable to think about people worshipping him or revering him as some sort of God. What did they pray for the Seven to do for them? Bless them? Forgive their wrongdoings? Save them from death? They weren't capable of any of that. They were just Seven unlucky sods who got cursed with powers for a reason out of their control.

Thursday flipped her hair over her shoulder with a knowing smirk. "I always fancied myself a God," she said. "Imagine how screwed the world would be if it was based on *my* judgement. Oh, the fun it would be!" She looked down at Bram with a bored expression. "Sawyer will become a God the same day I am given a clean bill of health. Scenarios are fun in 'never going to happen' land, aren't they?"

"Where is Sawyer currently hiding?" Sybil asked. "There's no way he's in his building, that would be too obvious."

Bram coughed and spat blood out onto the floor. "He works from his second home in Opara City."

Whitney didn't look too convinced. "That was way too easy," she stated.

She was right. Matthew had expected Bram to struggle, to refuse to answer. Maybe they'd have to get Thursday to kick him some more, beat him to the point where they'd have to get Finn to resuscitate him before he even considered talking. Bram had just answered them without hesitance. Why was he so quick to sell out the man he worked for?

"You better not be lying to us," Sybil warned.

Bram shrugged. "I have no reason to lie. Mr. Bateman welcomes your arrival with open arms. He wants you to come to him. He hopes for it every day. If I can help hasten his happiness, I will gladly do so."

How were they ever going to get Dr Weeks on her own if she spent most of her time with Sawyer or at the Asylum, two establishments from which once they entered, they would most likely never return? It almost seemed like a trap. Maybe that was Sawyer's plan all along. Give them the eyepatch so that they'd wonder what it did; make the connection between Matthew's ability and Dr. Weeks' obsession with Sawyer; and walk straight into Sawyer's lair to kidnap Weeks.

"Do you know what this does?" Sybil produced Sawyer's eyepiece from the pocket of her jumper. The LED was still flickering away, almost like the eye was active and watching them right that second.

Bram examined the device through his one functioning eye. Blood seeped from his mouth in long, thin strips, joining the cocktail of several types already staining the floor. "No," he eventually answered. "I am not highly ranked enough to be given such information."

"How do we know you're not lying?" Matthew challenged.

"I did just tell you where Mr. Bateman is currently residing, didn't I?"

"Okay, change of tactics, then." Titus still hadn't moved from his position at the bar. Besides Finn, he was the only one not standing around Bram. It was obvious that Finn wasn't standing around Bram because he didn't agree with the inevitable violence.

Too soft for his own good. "Do you know what Sawyer is doing to his eye that makes him need the patch?"

Bram rolled his tongue around his bloodied lips as if trying to pick his answer carefully. "No."

Bram had suddenly closed the book on his helpful answers. He was opting instead to be cryptic. It had to be because Sawyer or 'Mr. Bateman', as Bram knew him, did not wish for them to know what his eyepatch did or what he had done to his eye. What Sawyer did want, however, was for them to find where he was currently working so that they'd walk into his trap like animals in the slaughterhouse, and that was why Bram had shared that information with them. Now they were asking questions that Bram wasn't allowed to answer, it seemed he wasn't willing to play the game anymore.

"Aw, Bram, have you lost your voice already?" Thursday teased. "And here I thought you were going to reveal all of Sawyer's plans to us just like the villains in the movies."

"It is not in Mr. Bateman's interest for you to know such information," Bram simply replied.

Thursday folded her arms. "Can I kick him again now?"

Bram looked past Thursday, and Whitney, and even Matthew. He focused his undamaged eye on Sybil. "Mr. Bateman requires me to return to him with some information," he told her.

"Oh?" Sybil raised her eyebrows with interest. "And what information is that?"

There was a glint in Bram's eye that made Matthew uncomfortable, and he wasn't even the person on the receiving end of it. Sybil shifted in her chair, holding the disconcerting gaze with a firm stare of her own. Matthew didn't know how people could stare at each other like that for so long without speaking. What was it for? Suspense? Were they speaking telepathically? Speaking with their eyes only?

"He wants to know whose it is," said Bram.

The mortified look on Sybil's face was drowned out by Thursday's maniacal laughter. "What makes you think you'll even escape us to return such information to Sawyer?" she cackled.

Bram ignored her, his eye still set firmly on their leader. "Your baby. It's not Mr. Bateman's. That deeply disturbs him. He must know who it belongs to."

The baby wasn't Sawyer's. None of them had interacted with Sawyer in years until the hospital. What was this? Was Sawyer baffled by the fact that Sybil wasn't barren like the rest of them had been and needed to know how it had happened? Or was it an act of bitter jealousy because his ex-fiancée was pregnant, meaning that she had gotten over him?

Sybil stood up, drawing herself up to her full height so she loomed over Bram's broken form like the reaper about to steal a soul. Matthew stepped backwards and even Whitney had retracted the hand she had been about to put onto their leader's arm for aid. The venomous expression on Sybil's face made their blood turn cold.

"Thursday," Sybil said, not breaking her gaze with Bram.

"Yes?" Thursday asked, perking up like a dog.

"You can continue kicking him."

Thursday didn't need to be told twice. She lifted her brand-new boot and kicked the bouncer in the back, slamming him back onto the ground with relish. Sybil turned away, her face emotionless, and returned to the table she had been sitting at before Bram had started laughing at them. She seated herself beside Finn and laid a protective hand on top of her stomach.

Without being told, without even looking at her, Finn reached out and placed his hand on top of hers, that familiar golden glow momentarily appearing before fading as fast as it had arrived. As soon as it disappeared again, Finn removed his hand, covering his eyes with it as the sound of Thursday's boot connecting with Bram's body grew louder and louder.

Matthew couldn't look for too long. He wasn't squeamish, but Thursday had a way of doing things where it was all or nothing. She also didn't know when to stop. Bram wasn't making any noise, but the state of his face was growing too gruesome to continue watching. All Matthew could see was red and, honestly, he couldn't wait for it to be over. He had seen enough red tonight.

Whitney seemed to have the same thought process as she quickly rounded the body being beaten on the floor and joined the three of them at the table. Titus crossed the short distance from the bar to the table to join them also.

Matthew suddenly noticed that Whitney was dressed differently from before. She'd changed from her skirt and jacket into black shorts and a matching sports jersey.

She must have noticed him staring at her because she said, "We were raiding the store anyway, I figured I had time to change my clothes as well." She gestured to Matthew's blood-drenched clothes. "You'll probably need to do the same, to be honest."

Changing his clothes was the last thing on his mind right now. "When do we stop her?" Matthew asked Sybil.

"When I call it," was all Sybil said.

"And that would be...?"

"When I call it."

Titus leaned over the table, so he was closer to Sybil. "I get that it's upsetting that Sawyer is trying to gain information about your baby, but I don't think letting Thursday beat Bram into a bloody mess of flesh is going to achieve much. Sorry to be harsh here but we could decapitate Bram right here right now but that wouldn't change the fact that Sawyer would still be trying to find out who the father is. Nothing we do here will change that."

"He's right, you know," said Finn.

"No offence, Finn, but you'd say that anyway," Whitney answered.

"Do you agree with letting Thursday go buck daft on him?" Finn threw back acidly. His fingers were picking anxiously at something on his chest, beneath his shirt. Matthew wasn't sure but from where he stood, he could see a small lump, like a charm or locket, beneath his shirt.

Whitney shrugged. Her eyes had always reminded Matthew of a snake. Dark; green; and venomous. "He has it coming. He shot Matthew. He shot Matthew intending to shoot *you*, Finn. You can't heal, I feel we constantly must remind you of this. That man could have killed you right there on the spot and there would have been nothing any of us could have done to stop it."

"But he didn't," Finn stubbornly answered.

"No, he just shot Matthew instead." Whitney rolled her eyes and walked away, muttering something unintelligent under her breath.

Matthew felt eyes on him. He met Finn's entrancing blue gaze with a shrug. "I don't agree with it, either," he conceded. "But it's Sybil's call."

Sybil's hand tightened on her stomach and her head dipped to stare at the bump she was hiding beneath her black sweater. "What did he mean when he said that Bas wanted to be a higher being?" she asked.

It was a random question considering their background soundtrack was currently the happy grunts of Thursday as she continued to beat Bas.

Matthew and Finn exchanged a look. "He kind of spoke out of turn," was all Finn said.

"In what way?"

"He, ah, asked Sawyer to dump you," Matthew explained, awkwardly scratching his head. "He believed Sawyer was experimenting on him to make him become like us ...I suppose it made him think he could start making demands."

Sybil nodded. "I see," she mused.

The information that Sawyer and Bas had had their fling during the same time Sawyer was dating her didn't seem to come as a shock to Sybil at all. Matthew didn't find this too hard to believe. Sybil was not an idiot. She had probably known about Bas and Sawyer before Bas and Sawyer knew about Bas and Sawyer. Besides, Sawyer made his interest in polyamory abundantly clear through his belief that the Seven should have been some sort of relationship unit.

"Oh, shit."

Matthew spun around in the direction of Thursday's voice. The madwoman had stopped kicking Bram. She was no longer looking down on him, either.

The bouncer must have finally had enough, for he had ripped clean through his bonds and was now getting to his feet. The grin still hadn't left Thursday's face as she watched the human rise from the ground, dripping blood from nearly every visible orifice. She reversed, more out of self-preservation than fear, Matthew assumed, and banged into the front doors of the bar.

When Bram turned towards Thursday, Matthew and Titus both took a step forward, but stopped. Bram didn't make a move to hit her or lash out. He simply stared at her for a long moment. Thursday gawked back, the grin fading into a confused grimace when Bram ignored her completely and turned back in the direction of Matthew and the others.

"Why didn't you do that before now?!" Matthew exclaimed. Not that he had wanted Bram to escape earlier than now but the question was still extremely valid.

"I can't return until you tell me who it belongs to," Bram said.

Sybil watched the bleeding man from her seat. "That won't happen," she informed him. "You won't be returning to Sawyer."

Bram scowled. "You cannot keep me from my leader. I will leave by force if I must."

As if to prove his point, Bram turned and raised his hand to hit Thursday. Matthew did not doubt in his mind that Bram had been enhanced through Sawyer's experiments. The fact that he had been able to practically break Matthew's back with one throw and breakthrough tightly bound ropes like they were nothing but liquorice confirmed this. Who knew what would happen to Thursday if Bram so much as got one hit in on her? Thursday was an adept fighter but all it could take would be one hit.

Titus suddenly flew past him, whipping up an artificial breeze that ruffled Matthew's hair. He leapt onto the closest table and jumped to the next, then the next, and the next. Matthew gaped as Titus then kicked off the edge of the table closest to Bram and spun, using the momentum to kick the artificial metahuman across the face. Bram was floored again, with Titus landing neatly on their prisoner's back.

"Please stay down this time," Titus sniffed. "It's getting late and kicking your arse is truly getting exhausting."

Watching Titus fight was almost the same as watching him dance. He did it so easily, without a single falter, it would lead one to believe that it had all been rehearsed. Titus didn't need to think what his next move would be, it was almost like his body decided for him. Honestly, Matthew was kind of jealous of it. As someone who constantly tripped and stumbled daily, he could kind of use the grace that came with being Tuesday's child.

Thursday crouched in front of Bram and cocked her head. "You know what they say," she sweetly said, lifting a finger and twirling it in front of his face. "An eye for an eye."

And in her finger went, squishing Bram's only functioning eye into nonexistence. Matthew's stomach flipped, and he turned away, having to go as far as to cover his ears so he didn't have to hear the squelch of the eye-popping in the socket. He could see Thursday's insane grin even with his back turned, her expression not even flinching as she blinded Bram for good.

Thursday was Matthew's best friend, but sometimes her ability to conduct such brutality without remorse terrified even him.

"So!" Thursday cheered once she'd finished, jumping to her feet and finally joining Finn and Sybil at the table. She slammed her hands onto the table, her finger still dripping in blood and eye goo. "What's for dinner?"

~M~

Matthew sat nestled on a couch in the corner of the bar. The only seat untouched by human blood from the massacre. They'd collected the bodies hours ago and left them in the garden. They had no choice for now. This bar had to be their refuge for the night, and it was unanimous that they weren't going to sleep with a bunch of dead bodies watching them. They didn't just dump them; they lined them all up in a respectful procession on the grass. Once they were leaving the next morning, they'd call the authorities. There was no doubt that they'd get the blame for it anyway. Unsolved massacre? Must be the Seven!

Bram was bound up again and locked in the broom closet. The man seemed to have gained some sense and realised that he couldn't escape. It didn't matter how much brawn Sawyer's experiments had given him, there was no escaping a skilled fighter, a mental patient and a telekinetic. Besides, until his bruised and swollen eye healed, he was blind thanks to Thursday. He wouldn't get far even if he tried.

Whitney had ventured into the kitchen and was currently cooking up whatever was in the back cupboards. Thursday had offered to help but it was, again, unanimous that Thursday had to stay away from potentially dangerous appliances of any kind.

Matthew didn't know if he was all that hungry. After everything that had happened, food was the last thing on his mind. When was the last time he'd eaten, anyway? He had raided Finn's fridge when Thursday had disappeared off to bed a couple of days ago. Everything since then had been so mad, for once in his life Matthew hadn't thought to eat, nor did he feel hungry.

While scoping out the rest of the bar, they found a flat upstairs. It was empty. They could only assume the occupants had been somewhere amongst the fray when United Arms broke in since it was now midnight, and no one had returned home. Sybil had been wrangled into the bedroom by Whitney and Titus and made to rest for a while. She had insisted that she wasn't tired, but it hadn't been hard to see that she was lying. Especially since once they'd finished lining the bodies up outside, they'd come back in to find her snoozing into her folded arms by the bar.

"What's up, mopey?"

Matthew looked up at Thursday, forcing a smile to match her own. "Nothing," he said. "What about yourself? I see you've got new clothes."

"Yup," Thursday replied, dramatically popping the 'p'. She threw herself into the armchair opposite Matthew and slung her leg over the arm. She picked at the black and red plaid button-up she had on. "Plaid is the universal sign that a woman is a lesbian."

Matthew chuckled. "Well, you aren't proving that theory wrong, as such."

Thursday rubbed the fabric between her thumb and forefinger thoughtfully. "If plaid is a sign that a woman is gay, what's the sign that a man is gay, do you think?"

"I'd say skinny jeans."

"You think so?"

"Well look at me," Matthew said, gesturing to his black jeans.

Thursday snorted. "Not to mention Finn is rarely seen without a pair on," she added.

"And consider Titus," Matthew insisted.

"Never wears 'em." Thursday nodded with finality. "Well, that's it then! Plaid means that you're a lesbian, skinny jeans mean you're gay."

Matthew picked at a loose thread in his discarded jacket. For a moment, everything felt normal again. Like he had somehow travelled back in time to before the Seven had separated before Sawyer even lost his mind. The times when he and Thursday used to be able to sit and talk about nonsensical rubbish for days on end.

"You okay, big bro?"

Matthew shrugged. "I don't know. It's all rather crazy. One day I'm living my life; dating random people; having fun; and the next I'm responsible for the massacre of a room full of humans. I don't know how to process it."

"You weren't responsible for the massacre, Sawyer was," Thursday reminded him.

"If we hadn't entered this bar, everyone would still be alive. Sybil wouldn't be sleeping in the bed of a dead couple. Titus wouldn't be scrubbing blood off the floor. Whitney wouldn't be cooking in a kitchen that we had to drag the dead chef out of." Matthew shrugged helplessly. "It's like every step we take leaves a bomb behind."

"If you want to get technical, Sawyer was looking for Finn. So, if you're going to blame someone who's not Sawyer himself…" Thursday stopped talking at the look that Matthew was giving her. "What?"

"It's not Finn's fault," Matthew snapped.

"Sybil also should have known that Sawyer had figured us out before sending anyone in here…"

"You can't blame Sybil, either!"

Thursday leaned back in her chair and folded her arms. "I don't think you're looking for who's truly responsible for this. I think you're just looking for a reason to blame yourself."

Matthew looked away. "So, what if I am?"

"Don't be pathetic, Mattie, it doesn't suit you," Thursday responded. "It wasn't your fault, nor was it Finn's or Sybil's. Sawyer sent those men with the orders to do what was necessary to obtain the target. The blood of the people who died tonight is on Sawyer's hands, no one else's. Now please stop making me play counsellor, I can't stand it."

Matthew didn't know what to think. He knew that Thursday was right. There was no way he could have known about or prevented the deaths. If they had known that Sawyer had predicted their next move, they would never have entered a bar full of innocent people.

Matthew still couldn't shake the feeling that they could have done something differently …Anything that would have prevented all those people from dying.

"I'm sick of all of this," Matthew muttered.

Thursday cocked her head. "Sick of what?"

"I'm tired of people dying because of us, because of him." Matthew rubbed an exhausted hand over his face. "When is this disaster going to end?"

"Don't start wishing for things like that," Thursday warned. "Your prayers will be answered but you know what happens when someone makes a wish without properly thinking it through. They end up turning to ash when they wish to live forever."

Matthew shuddered. Thursday's words put him in mind of all his years suddenly catching up with him. He had lived so long that if he suddenly lost his immortality …he dreaded to think what he would end up like. All the Seven stopped aging when they had turned twenty-one years old but for Matthew, it was one step more. It was a natural part of his ability to constantly look good. It was why he couldn't take exterior damage, his ability made sure that he constantly looked …appealing. Monday's child is fair of face, after all.

When he turned twenty-one, Matthew stopped gaining and losing weight; his hair stopped growing; his nails stopped elongating; someone could waltz right up to him and smack him with a metal pole and his face would remain unblemished. He still couldn't exactly wrap his head around how he felt about it. In a way, it made his life easier, but in another, it made him feel …less human.

Matthew would never tell Thursday such a thing. He knew that she had never been able to understand his desire to be like everyone else. Thursday was insane. Like, proper, off the wall, lost her meds in a dumpster fire, insane. Matthew didn't expect her to understand. When you spend a good deal of your life being constantly altered to fit the desire of another person, Matthew liked to think it was natural to yearn to be normal. He would have given anything to be ordinary.

"Come on, buck up." Thursday nudged Matthew's knee with the toe of her boot. "It could be worse."

"How could it be worse?" Matthew bitterly asked.

"We could be dead."

Matthew snickered, despite himself. He could always rely on Thursday to be the realist. He had missed her company over the past decade. He had considered finding out where she was, in the same way he discovered Finn's work schedule and often passed Sawyer's building on the way to his usual date spot, but Thursday never stayed put long enough for him to find her. Usually, she was getting herself into trouble and, despite having missed her dearly, Matthew couldn't let himself get arrested.

With an ability like his, being thrown into prison would be a death sentence.

"I plan to die grandly, too," Thursday explained. "Hopefully in a nice Villa in Spain somewhere holding a cool bottle of cider in my hand. Finn will have died the previous day and I'll have finally overstepped my mark and gotten stabbed or shot or something. It's inevitable."

Matthew didn't want to think about anyone dying anytime soon.

Finn was immortal like the rest of them when it came to age but since he was so much more susceptible to damage, it was a no-brainer that he would most likely be the first to go. Without their healer, the Seven would have to then be a lot more careful with themselves. Matthew could see Sybil and Titus living on for decades after Finn goes, but Thursday was too reckless, and Whitney was too careless.

"That's centuries from now," Matthew replied.

Thursday raised her eyebrows. "*Centuries*? Doubt it. I say we have one or two centuries left in us but that's about it."

Matthew shuddered. "I can only hope you're wrong."

"Oh, don't worry, I'm sure you and Finn will have reunited long before then and will have banged plenty of times," Thursday waved off.

"Surprisingly, that wasn't really what I was concerned with…"

"Oh, good! At least if we ever return to living together as a group, I might finally get a decent night's sleep!" Thursday beamed.

Matthew remembered having the room beside Thursdays back in the day. They'd decided it to be that way since they had been such good friends and thought it would be fun. What they hadn't predicted was that Matthew would start dating Finn and Finn would then become a resident in Matthew's room. Thursday used to purposely barge into their bedroom wielding a baseball bat at the most awkward of moments, declaring that she heard them in pain and had come to help.

The funny thing was, that they never actually did anything in Matthew's bedroom. They saved that for when they were in Finn's room, as it was the attic room far removed from everyone else on the floor, so it wouldn't disturb anyone. Thursday never believed them when they said this, though, and believed to this very day that they had no regard for her sleeping patterns and prioritised their, in her words, 'hormones.'

"Do you think we'd ever live together again?" Matthew asked.

Thursday shrugged. "Probably not," she admitted. "I mean, I suppose it all depends on how this mess turns out."

"I guess. I don't know if I'd want to or not. As Sybil has said before, ten years is a long time. I feel like everyone has changed, in a way." Matthew grinned when Thursday exaggerated looking offended. "Except you, of course, my dear."

Thursday winked at him. "Too right. I just keep getting better."

"Oh, aye, completely," Matthew sarcastically replied.

If the near-enough impossible occurred and the six of them somehow managed to outsmart Sawyer, Matthew didn't know if he could see them living together like they used to. For one thing, their house had long since been sold so they'd have to find fresh accommodation. Not only that, but everyone seemed to have built lives of their own away from each other in the decade they'd been apart. They couldn't just drop the homes they'd bought or the jobs they'd accepted just to return to the life they used to live.

That was the thing about the past. It was history. No going back.

Thursday flipped a pocketknife out of her trousers and carved a grid into the wooden arm of the chair she was sitting in. Then, without asking Matthew if he was willing to play, tossed him the knife. "Noughts and crosses, you go first."

So, they sat and played noughts and crosses. Matthew absorbed himself in the simplicity of the game and nothing else, not even registering how long they were doing it for. It was nice to almost have himself convinced that the only problems he had in life were that Thursday could claim she was crosses before he got a chance to. Maybe it was foolish to take part in such childish games when there were bigger problems at hand, but it honestly did make him feel better.

When there was barely any space left on Thursday's armchair, and the two of them were crouched behind the seat like children hiding from their parents just to carve a tiny grid into the small space that remained, Finn appeared.

"Hey, Thursday, Whitney's soup is ready if you want to grab some," he said.

"Right," Thursday jumped to her feet. "Don't cheat!" she told Matthew as she weaved around Finn and headed to the kitchen.

Matthew straightened up and dropped Thursday's knife onto a nearby coffee table. Why would he cheat at noughts and crosses? Especially when he was winning.

As he threw himself back onto the sofa, Matthew noticed that Finn was holding two bowls of soup.

Immediately noticing that Matthew saw the second bowl of soup in his hands, Finn thrust it out towards him. "I didn't know if you were hungry, but I brought you some anyway," he said.

"Thanks," Matthew accepted the bowl from Finn. The soup was red, so he could only assume-more like *hope*-that Whitney had found some tomatoes in the kitchen and hadn't just thrown tomato sauce in for colouring.

Finn eased himself into the chair Thursday had previously sat on, now covered in copious games of noughts and crosses. The two of them sat in silence for a while, eating their soup without words. Whitney was a good cook. Even if it had been tomato sauce in a bowl, it was hard to tell. Matthew missed Whitney's cooking. The things she used to be able to make from the most basic ingredients ... Even a vegetarian would have to concede that her burgers were amazing.

"So," Finn eventually said, "do you want to have that talk?"

Matthew frowned over his spoon. "Talk?" he repeated dubiously.

Finn put his bowl down on the floor and shook his hair from his eyes. "Uh, yeah," he nervously replied. "Y'know, the conversation that doesn't take place in the middle of the street?"

Matthew eyed Finn wearily, slowly pushing his spoon between his lips and taking the final mouthful. After swallowing, he asked, "You're not going to get mad, are you? I'm not emotionally prepared for yelling right now."

Finn shook his head. "I won't yell. We're going to do this like adults."

"Adults, right," Matthew agreed. He put his bowl down beside Finn's. His stomach had started churning with nerves and he could already feel his heart speeding up with anticipation. "Ah, where do you want to start, then?"

Finn sighed and pulled his tie out of his back pocket to occupy his hands with. "I want to know why, Matthew. It's been ten years, and I still can't figure out why."

Matthew chewed his lips anxiously. He had had this conversation in his head so many times. There were so many things he wanted to say to explain his behaviour. He had imagined falling to his knees at Finn's feet, pleading with him to understand that he had never meant to hurt him like that; that he had meant to come back but because he was a piece of chicken shit he didn't; and insist that he didn't deserve Finn's forgiveness at all. Matthew had been so ready to explain himself to Finn but now that he was here, sitting in front of Finn and being watched by those annoyingly captivating blue eyes, he couldn't get half the words straight in his mind.

"Did I do something to you?"

"No," Matthew quickly said, "you didn't do anything to me."

"Was it your awkward way of breaking up with me?" Finn enquired.

Matthew shook his head. "No, no. I wanted to stay with you, I did. I even told you I'd come back. Which, in hindsight, was wrong of me … It's just … I was terrified of the commitment settling down would have needed."

Finn was confused by this. "Matthew, you had been my partner for over a century. I don't understand how that is any different from asking you to live with me and settle down without the surroundings of the Seven."

Matthew directed his eyes to the floor. He couldn't hold Finn's gaze, he felt too ashamed to do so. "I was scared," he shrugged. "The Seven were my first proper family. I felt like we were safe. But then Sawyer left, and then Thursday decided to go too, and Sybil asked if we thought there was a point in us still being together ... The Seven were my rock, the only people who truly felt like family and suddenly we were all falling apart. Then you asked me to settle down with you and I just sort of ... flipped. I don't know why, because I *wanted* to stay with you, I *did*. I was miserable because I'd lost my family and, I don't know, I just kind of just freaked out and I ran."

"Why didn't you come back then? Once you weren't miserable anymore?" asked Finn.

Matthew shuddered. "I thought you would have moved on. If I returned to you and discovered that you had found a life where I didn't fit anymore ...I couldn't handle it." He looked up through the strands of hair in his eyes to stare at Finn. "Has there been anyone...?"

Finn shrugged; his eyes focused on the fabric in his hands. "A couple of men," he admitted. "It's not easy to date someone for over a century and then simply move on like it was nothing but a fling."

The thought alone made envy swell up inside Matthew like a disease. He coughed, directing his face downwards so Finn didn't see the sour expression on his face. "What went wrong?" he curiously asked.

"They told me I didn't spend enough time with them," Finn shrugged. "I wasn't avoiding them, per se, but every time I was in a relationship I found myself taking extra shifts at the hospital. I just didn't have the energy to deal with romance. Most of the time they dumped me because I was too focused on my job or whatever."

Matthew frowned in confusion. How could someone view a person being dedicated to saving lives as a burden? Although Finn normally took extra shifts at the hospital anyway so that meant that when he was dating, he took *extra* extra shifts which was, admittedly, a lot of shifts.

"Besides," Finn slouched in the armchair, tracing one of the grids that Thursday had carved into the wood with his fingers, "their eyes were boring."

Matthew fought back a smile. His eyes, he knew, had been the first thing that Finn had noticed about him all those years ago. "I'm sorry," he said. "I should have known the effect it would have had on you."

"I just wish you would have talked to me instead of running," Finn sighed. "Who knows where we would be now if you had."

"Thursday seems to think we'll be banging in the room next to her again in no time," Matthew said, gesturing to said madwoman. She was currently at the bar trying to eat her soup upside down.

Finn pulled a face. "She still believes we did that?"

"Do you expect anything less from her?"

Finn unbuttoned his collar and rubbed his neck. It had only been a couple of days since he lost his house, but he already seemed to be growing stubble. This was a feat Matthew himself had never been able to achieve due to his ability.

Matthew watched Finn carefully for a few minutes, wondering what was going on inside his head. Had he accepted Matthew's explanation? He hoped not. Matthew didn't believe he deserved Finn's forgiveness for what he had done to him. Receiving it would almost feel …wrong.

"Where do you think we'd be now if I hadn't run away?" Matthew curiously asked.

"Probably exactly where we are now, I'd say," Finn said, making Matthew's heart sink a little. "Except I'd probably be sitting there beside you on the sofa."

Matthew couldn't hold back the smile this time, especially since Finn was embarrassed by his own words if his pink face was anything to go by. "Can I ask you something? It's kind of personal so you don't have to answer if you don't want to."

Finn looked weary but nodded, nonetheless. "Okay. Ask me," he said.

"My ability … I could control myself when you were with me. I didn't change shape despite the many eyes that were on me," Matthew explained. "I asked if that meant anything, but you told me to get over it. I was just wondering … am I still … your …"

"Idea of beauty?" The words rushed out of Finn's mouth like an avalanche. "Yes."

Matthew honestly didn't know what to do with this information. He hadn't expected a straightforward answer. He had expected Finn to get angry and tell him to stop asking such personal questions when they were trying to sort out their tangled history. So now he was stuck with an answer he had not expected to get. An answer he hadn't thought he would get in a million years.

"But why?" the shifter eventually asked.

"It doesn't just change, Matthew," Finn answered flatly. "I'm not like Thursday, I don't have a new idea of physical perfection every week. I'm pretty sure emotional composition plays a large role in the fact that you still are, even in the eyes of your ability. It's why you can control yourself in my presence and it's why you turned back to normal when I looked at you after you stole the car."

"Does that mean that we …?" Matthew dared not let himself say it. There was still room in this conversation for a 'but' or 'however.'

"I don't know, Matthew," Finn answered, knowing what the shifter had been about to say without needing him to have said it. "Certainly not right now while all this Sawyer ridiculousness is going on. Who knows where we're going to be by the end of it."

Matthew conceded that Finn was probably right. They didn't know where this Sawyer malarkey was going to lead them. They could only hope that they were able to get out on the other side in one piece. Emotions were the last thing that should be on their agenda but now that Matthew knew the possibility was there, he couldn't stop thinking about it. It almost felt too good to be true. It could be snatched away from him so easily that it almost made him feel sick.

"Hello, boys." Thursday threw herself into Finn's lap and slung her arms around his neck. "Did you miss me? Of course, you did. Who wouldn't?"

"I lament every minute you're not in my life, dear Thursday," Matthew grinned.

"As expected." Thursday tugged Finn's tie out of his hands and began trying it around her head. "What did I miss? You didn't play the final grid without me, did you?"

"Don't worry, it's still empty," Matthew chuckled.

"Good. I'd have cut your hands off if you'd cheated," said Thursday, a serious glint in her eyes. "It's the only way cheaters learn." She cocked her head. "You seem happier. What changed?"

Matthew shrugged, knowing that the smile on his face was probably unmissable. "Nothing."

"Has Finn promised you a strip tease since you saved his life or something?" Thursday pressed.

"I would have offered but I left my music in my office," Finn sarcastically answered.

"I could sing it if you want," Thursday insisted, nudging the healer with a playful grin. The madwoman opened her mouth as if to begin but was promptly silenced by Finn's hand engulfing her mouth.

"Yeah, no thanks," Finn chuckled.

Matthew felt a lot better. The conversation with Finn had lifted his spirits expeditiously, even if it was still, in a way, left open-ended. He was comforted by the knowledge that Finn didn't hate his guts for what he did and while Matthew would never accept his ex-lover's forgiveness, he would most definitely accept being on decent terms with one another again. There was a chance those decent terms could flourish if they all got out of this mess alive.

Titus approached them. The knees of his trousers were stained with blood from the ground. They'd be raiding stores for him next. "Whitney has informed me that since she cooked, she's not doing the dishes and I'm certainly not doing it since I just spent an hour and a half scrubbing the floor. So, who's doing it?"

"*Dishes?*" Thursday looked horrified. "A bunch of dead bodies in the garden and you're worried about *dishes?*"

"We need to make it look like we were never here," Titus told her. "We can't leave a trace of ourselves behind."

"They're going to blame it on us anyway," Thursday complained. "Who cares about a couple of dirty bowls?"

"Can someone just do them, please?" Titus asked pointedly, ignoring Thursday's complaints.

"I'll take care of it," Finn volunteered.

Thursday beamed. "There. Sorted." She leaned forward and planted an exaggerated kiss on Finn's cheek in thanks.

Finn cringed away from her. "Never do that again," he told her.

"Charming. Absolutely charming," Thursday huffed, the grin that hadn't left her face exposing that she wasn't truly annoyed. "Whatever did you see in this man?" she asked Matthew.

Matthew shrugged. "Free health care."

"You're hilarious," Finn sarcastically replied. He grabbed Thursday and deposited her in the armchair as he stood up. "I'd recommend going to sleep soon. Who knows when we'll have to leave tomorrow? My guess is when Sybil wakes up. Best get some rest in now before she does."

Matthew didn't feel all that tired, but Finn had a point. He wasn't an early riser on a normal day, never mind a day where they'd have to get up at who knows what time and immediately be on the move.

"Aye, aye, Captain." Thursday saluted Finn and, without saying another word, smacked her forehead. The madwoman threw herself backwards as if the force behind the slap had been too powerful and as soon as her back hit the backrest of the chair, she was asleep, snoring away like she had never been awake.

"Did she just knock herself out?" Titus asked mildly. There was no concern in his voice.

"I guess we'll see in the morning," Matthew frowned.

Titus shook his head and walked away, muttering under his breath about crazy women. Matthew rolled his eyes and kicked his legs up onto the sofa, ready to settle in for the night. He glanced at Finn, who was turning to walk away from them.

"Goodnight," the shifter said.

Finn looked over his shoulder, blue eyes seeming to have brightened into an electric azure as opposed to their usual sapphire glow. He smiled, and Matthew's stomach flipped like a pancake in a pan, his heart bursting into a race like the Starter just blew their pistol. It was a sin that Finn didn't smile a lot because, even though the effect it had on Matthew was ridiculous, it lifted his entire face.

Finn looked a lot younger when he smiled.

"Goodnight," the healer answered.

Matthew watched the back of Finn's head as he retreated to the kitchen, his heart still running the race long after he'd disappeared. The shifter slouched down onto the couch and buried his face into a silk pillow, hiding the smile that he couldn't remove from his face.

Long after he'd closed his eyes, he could still see Finn's smile.

CHAPTER NINE

THE CAR RIDE WAS LONG.

The rumble of their newest stolen vehicle as it tumbled along the open roads of the Meadows caused the window Matthew had his head resting against to vibrate. Finn had been right about the early start. Sybil had gotten everyone up at the crack of dawn, telling them to prepare to leave. Once the call to the police had been made, the six of them had piled into the new car and taken off.

In what direction?

Well ...they didn't quite know yet.

They had left Castlebrooke behind and were currently driving through the Meadows that separated Castlebrooke from Opara City. The Meadows were endless and easy to get lost in if not travelling in a vehicle of some sort. The children at the Orphanage used to tell horror stories about people disappearing amongst the tall green grass of the Meadows, never to be seen again. Matthew never paid attention to such silly tales, especially when the kids used to turn it on him and claim it was probably the shifter sent by Satan who made the people vanish.

"What are we doing, anyway?" asked Whitney. "Are we going to Sawyer's base in Opara?"

"We can't just waltz on up, that's what he wants," Titus muttered.

"We can't exactly drive around the Meadows for the remainder of our days, either. We need a plan," Whitney argued.

"The plan is to obtain Dr. Weeks, but Dr. Weeks is most likely with Sawyer and Sawyer wants us to find him because it aids his mission so really, we're kind of stuck," Thursday rambled. She had been forced to take a backseat so that Sybil could sit in the passenger side of the car. Now wedged between Titus and Whitney in the second row of seats in the vehicle, the madwoman had been constantly squirming for the past few hours now, unable to stay still. Like she had a persistent itch that she couldn't reach.

"You don't think this was part of his plan?" Titus suddenly asked.

Matthew lifted his head from the window and frowned at the back of Titus' head. "What do you mean?" he asked back.

"Well ... Sawyer wanted us to take his eyepatch because he 'wanted us to figure out what it did.' He made a big fuss out of being ambiguous about its purpose like it's some big, massive deal. Almost like he was purposefully trying to get our interest in the device piqued. What if that was intentional? What if he figured out that we would realise that we needed Dr. Weeks to find out what it did, leading us right into his hands through Bram's revelation of his location?" Titus explained.

Sawyer couldn't possibly have thought that far ahead, right? Matthew felt uneasy, his palms beginning to sweat as Titus' scenario became more real in his head. It made perfect sense, even if it relied a lot on their actions and had surely been based on a lot of guesswork. That was exactly it, though. Sawyer's guesswork wasn't really guesswork at all. His ability gave him such insight if he so desired it.

"There would be only one way of debunking that," said Sybil, "and that would be through getting Matthew to wear the eyepatch anyway. We have nothing else to go on. Even if this is an elaborate trap, it only means we will need to be on higher alert. We can't hide from Sawyer forever, as easy as that option is. We must devise a plan to get into his second house in Opara that won't get us caught."

Matthew let his head rest against the window again. "Why don't we go to United Arms, first?" he asked.

"What?" asked Titus.

"There's only two possible places Dr. Weeks could be. With Sawyer in Opara City or working from United Arms Asylum. As dangerous as United Arms would be since we're harbouring a fugitive that escaped from there, at least we wouldn't be at risk of being kidnapped by Sawyer just yet," Matthew explained. "It's the lesser of two evils and hopefully Sawyer won't have expected it. He's good at guessing but he's not a psychic."

"Whoa, I never thought I'd ever hear Matthew make sense," Whitney muttered.

"Do you think she'll be there?" Sybil asked.

Finn, who had been focusing on driving more than talking, spoke up. "It makes sense for her to be there. Despite being enamoured with Sawyer; she still has a job to do. She must keep up appearances, after all. I'm sure there are plenty of people at United Arms who don't go on the Sawyer missions conducted by Weeks. They have to be convinced that nothing weird is going on."

Matthew glanced up at the rear-view mirror. He caught Finn's eyes in his reflection in the glass. The healer smiled, and Matthew automatically smiled back.

"Oh goody, I get to go home!" Thursday cooed, clasping her hands together. "I wonder if they've rented my room out already."

"Something tells me that they have it specially reserved for you," Titus flatly answered. "Greatly awaiting your return, I'm sure."

Thursday punched Titus' arm playfully. "You think so? Maybe they'll finally give me a full cell block to myself!"

Sybil leaned forward in her seat and rubbed the nape of her neck. "I guess we're going to United Arms, then. We better turn around now before we get too far away, and we can devise a plan on the way there."

"There's a turning up here," Finn said. "I'll just"-

The earth shattered.

Glass exploded everywhere as something rammed into the back of their car. The force of the impact sent Matthew flying straight into the window he had only seconds ago been leaning his head against. A white light slashed across his eyes as his head cracked, and the world started spinning around him. Except this wasn't because of his head injury, the car was literally spinning.

The car rolled out of control, crashing into the tall grasses of the Meadows, and flipping onto the roof. Matthew, never having been one to wear his seatbelt, was thrown around the vehicle like a bouncy ball, until finally falling up onto the upended roof.

Matthew lay on his back with his eyes sealed shut, chest heaving as he forced himself to calm down. What had just happened? Had some moron veered off the road and crashed into them? His skull felt like it was splitting open and every one of his limbs were roaring in pain. Finn had always told him to wear his seatbelt, why had he never listened to him?

It was hard to determine how long Matthew lay there, cowering in the darkness behind his closed lids. All he could register was agony and with every passing second, he grew worried as to why Finn hadn't reached him yet. He didn't expect the healer to come to him every time he was hurt like he was some sort of dog at his beck and call whenever he needed him, but it was still very odd that he hadn't been at the very least pulled out of the wreckage yet.

Matthew forced his eyes open and looked around. Everyone was stuck in their seats, belted into place by their seat belts. Slowly, his hearing returned, Thursday's shouts and cruses fading into his ears like someone was slowly turning the volume back up.

"Matthew! Are you okay?" Sybil shouted.

Matthew groaned in response. He didn't feel up to speaking just yet.

"Unbuckle you stupid thing!" Thursday roared at her belt.

Thursday's belt released and she, too, fell upwards onto the roof. Her body thumped against Matthew's and even though he shouted in pain, she didn't seem to care. She was crawling to the window that had been shattered by Mathew's head.

Chest still heaving with panic, Matthew saw Whitney struggling with her own belt while Titus sat unconscious in his chair. Sybil was clinging to her belt, not trying to unbuckle herself at all. The warm purple of Thursday's Glow began to seep through the metal by Sybil's window. Thursday must have been trying to remove a portion of the window so there was more room for Sybil to get out.

That was when Matthew noticed.

The seat beside Sybil was ...empty. The belt for the driver's seat was disconnected, the buckle sitting on the ceiling above Sybil's head.

Matthew was filled with dread. His stomach churned. His heart began to pound. "Where's Finn?" he cried.

"His belt was tampered with," Sybil answered. She was trying to remain calm but the rapid rise and fall of her chest was unmissable. "It completely broke free and..."

As she spoke, Matthew noticed the massive hole in the window right in front of the steering wheel. Big enough for a body to fit through.

Nausea swept through Matthew like a virus. Despite the blinding agony that coursed through his veins with every breath he took, the shifter reached out and grabbed the edge of the broken window, dragging himself over to it. Broken shards of glass bit into his skin like hundreds of bugs. He did not bleed. He hauled his heavy body out of the car and onto the dented grass of the Meadows.

Slinging himself to his feet, Matthew desperately looked around. He could hear every beat of his heart pumping in his ears as he dragged himself around the car and back onto the road.

There he was.

Finn was on the road a couple of metres ahead of the wreckage.

"Finn!" Matthew roared. "Finn, are you alright?"

Matthew tried to run to the healer, but his ankle screamed at him, and he collapsed onto the ground. He must have sprained it! Screaming in frustration, Matthew clawed his way up the road, desperately trying to reach Finn to make sure he was okay.

Finn wasn't dead. Matthew would know if Finn had died. Never mind the tugging he felt when Whitney almost left them, if Finn was gone, Matthew would have lost an entire half of himself. Finn's death wouldn't just happen without Matthew's notice.

Despite that reassurance, Matthew was extremely worried about how Finn wasn't moving. Was he unconscious? Was he getting his bearings? What if he was in a coma and was never going to wake up? Was he paralysed?

Matthew's fingers scraped the rough tarmac of the road, the skin of his fingertips complaining as he dug his hands into the ground to drag himself along. His hands were covered in blood anyway, which wasn't a good sign, but he wasn't concerned about himself now. The love of his life had just been thrown from their car and now lay lifeless on the ground. The universe could drop dead for all Matthew cared if it meant that Finn could wake up unharmed.

As if answering his prayers, Finn's head suddenly lifted from the ground. Matthew froze, his pounding heart lurching into his throat as it tried to escape his body. The entire right side of Finn's face was scraped, probably from where his body had slid across the unforgiving ground. His stitches had also ripped free, and his cut was bleeding relentlessly once again.

The healer's tired blue eyes met Matthew's blue and green ones. They both stared at each other, their bodies about a metre apart in the middle of the road in a random part of the Meadows. Finn weakly smiled, clearly disorientated, and let his head thump onto the road again.

A shadow suddenly appeared, a silhouette against the blinding morning sun. It loomed over them like a grim reaper. Matthew momentarily wondered if he had died and was about to be taken to wherever the metahumans went. The shadow then stepped out of the way of the sun, and horror filled Matthew like a disease infecting an infant.

The red LED in Sawyer's new eyepatch blinked, almost as if he were winking at Matthew. The dark-haired man looked down on Matthew with a sly smile, clearly enjoying towering over the shifter like a giant.

"You …You could have …killed … us," Matthew stammered.

"You know that's not true. My plans usually work in my favour," Sawyer smirked back, his voice sickly sweet. He glanced up, beyond Matthew to the car wreckage he had caused. "I see you all survived. Good. Just as planned."

Without another word, Sawyer bent down.

Matthew recognised what the madman was doing, and he hysterically shouted, "Don't touch him! I'll kill you if you dare touch a hair on his head, Sawyer!"

Sawyer chuckled, the sound dark and menacing. He ignored Matthew and scooped Finn up into his arms like he weighed nothing. It was such a surreal image. Sawyer towering above Matthew, carrying Finn in his arms like how a groom carries his bride over the threshold of their first house. Finn had gone unconscious. His head hung limp over Sawyer's elbow and there was no struggle.

"I was hoping to also obtain Whitney and Sybil, but Sybil is too close to Thursday, and I doubt approaching Whitney on her Soul Day is very clever." Sawyer tsked, clearly bothered by this unpredicted flaw. "No matter. Finn will make me invincible and then I'll come back for you all."

Sawyer turned, set on walking away.

"Don't take him, please!" Matthew shouted. "Please, you can't do this!

Sawyer looked over his shoulder, dark eyes focusing on Matthew as if only truly realising he was there. "The last thing I wish to do is cause harm to any of you. I will take care of him. I won't hurt him," he said.

"Yes, you will, you'll hurt him, I know you will! This is all part of your demented, sick plan! You're going to hurt him to get his ability, so you won't ever die!" Matthew was so overwhelmed; tears were streaming freely down his face as he pleaded. "It won't work, it doesn't work like that, he can't heal himself, so you won't be able to either please don't take him, it's not worth it!"

Sawyer was smiling down at Matthew. "It amuses me how deluded you are. I have my ways and means. Yes, I want Finn's ability, as I want Sybil's and Whitney's and Thursday's. However, do you think I don't have a plan for altering the flaws to fix them? Of course, I do. They will be sacrificing their lives for a higher cause and that makes my love for them grow even more."

Matthew didn't know what to do. His entire body had gone numb, and he couldn't move. Had he gone into shock? He stared at Sawyer with wide eyes, tears soaking his face and dripping onto the road beneath him. "Please," he croaked, his voice nothing but a tiny whisper.

There was a cruel sparkle in Sawyer's eye. He didn't say another word to Matthew, he just continued his way with Finn in his arms. There was a car a few yards away from where Finn had fallen, a chauffeur holding the door open for Sawyer to climb in. They couldn't be any old chauffeur that you can book out of the Yellow Pages, as she did not even blink as Sawyer slung Finn's unconscious body into the backseat. That, and she had driven her car straight into the back of theirs without question if the emotionless expression on her face was anything to go by.

"Sawyer!" Matthew screamed at the top of his lungs as if somehow the volume of his scream would bring the psychopath back to him. He tried to pull himself to his feet, but his body would not respond. The shock of the crash was beginning to have an impact on him.

Someone flew past him in a blur. Whitney was hurtling after Sawyer, her hands boiling with hosts of fire. On her Soul Day, her powers grew a lot more unstable. Usually, she could keep it in check, despite each of her elemental talents being controlled by her emotions. On her Soul Day, it was a lot more difficult.

Matthew's heart lifted, daring to hope that maybe she'd get to Finn on time. There was a reason Sawyer hadn't wished to confront Whitney on her Soul Day. He knew if he got her angry enough, she would be capable of blowing them all up on the spot without even really meaning to. Sawyer was desperate to start his experiments, but he wasn't stupid. He wouldn't fight her today.

It was a vain hope.

Sawyer's car was already driving away by the time Whitney reached the place where it had been parked. She screamed with frustration and slammed her hands together, sending a rocket of flame after the vehicle. The car swerved out of the way of the fireball with a deafening screech of tyres against the tarmac. Matthew choked as he watched it disappear into the distance.

Whitney's hands were still boiling as she turned and despondently walked back. With each step she took, the flames slowly turned clear and within seconds her hands were dripping with water. She crouched in front of Matthew, emerald eyes shining with sympathy.

"I am so sorry," she said quietly.

Matthew simply stared at her. He didn't have words. Everything had fallen apart so quickly. He didn't know how to process it. He wanted to start over. Rewind time. Get in the car and put his belt on so he could reach Finn before Sawyer did. No, even better, go out to the car the previous night and fix the seatbelt on the driver's side of the car.

It had to be some sort of horrible nightmare. He was going to wake up on the sofa in the bar and see Finn standing at the entrance, holding the door open with that same celestial smile on his face. Safe. Unharmed. Out of Sawyer's grasp. There was no way Finn had just been kidnapped. After all those nights promising that he would never allow the psychopath to touch him ...for nothing. Matthew had failed.

Whitney grabbed Matthew's arm and threw it over her shoulders, helping him to his feet and walking him back to the car wreckage. As Matthew stared at the car lying on its roof; at Thursday dragging an unconscious Titus out; at Sybil sitting on the flattened grass with a pained expression on her face; he slowly filled with rage.

When Whitney let go of him, he supported himself by leaning against the front of the car. By the time Thursday had finally rescued Titus, he was practically shaking with anger. Why hadn't they gone to help Finn when he was lying on the road? Why had it taken Whitney so long to chase after Sawyer? What took them so long to get out of the damn car?

Thursday laid Titus on the grass and immediately turned to Matthew. She must have felt her ears burning simply from his thoughts alone. Her brown eyes bore into him. "There's nothing we could have done," she told him.

Matthew glared at her. "Lies. You could have helped him when you got out of the car."

"Stop being irrational, Matthew. Sybil was the priority, and you know it," Thursday replied.

"You should have done it faster, then!" Matthew threw back.

Anger was like poison. It could fill you very quickly or slowly affect you in trickles. Matthew felt sick with rage, the word 'irrational' rattling around in his brain and making him even more resentful. Mainly because he knew Thursday was right. Anger made him irrational. He couldn't help it. He just needed someone to shout at.

"Matthew," Sybil said firmly, "we'll get him back."

"When? Once we've found out what the eyepatch does? How long will that take, do you think? A day? Two? Three? All while Finn is stuck with Sawyer!" Matthew yelled back. "Whatever Sawyer has created to give him our abilities could only take an hour to enforce! For all we know as soon as Finn was in the backseat of that car, he was a goner!"

Sybil was annoyingly calm. Matthew wanted her to yell back at him, so at least his own shouting would seem justified. "You know that's not true, Matthew. We would have felt such a thing. Finn is strong, he is more than capable of enduring Sawyer and his nonsense until we can reach him."

"You don't get it!" Matthew's voice shook with fury. His emotions were a jumble. He didn't know whether to laugh or cry or scream. "I said that I wouldn't let Sawyer touch him! I told Finn I would die first before I let that happen! I promised! Don't you understand that?"

Sybil looked away from Matthew like she suddenly felt ashamed of herself. "I know you probably did," she answered, sympathy in her voice. "But getting upset and yelling at us isn't going to solve anything. We need to work together now, more than ever. We'll get nowhere if we're constantly tearing lumps out of each other."

Matthew knew she was right. He looked from her to Thursday, and to Whitney desperately, as if trying to search for some sort of answer that he knew he wasn't going to find. He sank to the ground and covered his head. He wanted to blot out all of this with the barrier of his hands.

Someone sat down beside him and wrapped an arm around him. "We'll get him back," Thursday said, a determination in her voice that Matthew had never heard before. He could only wish that he was that confident. "We just need to find Dr. Weeks first."

He had never felt so helpless before in his whole life.

CHAPTER TEN

FINN HAD GROWN USED TO THE HARSH NATURE OF WHITE WALLS. He had worked in hospitals for most of his life, buildings completely made up of white walls, green oil cloth floors and pale blue doors. Every colour in a hospital always felt like it had been dulled, drained of all its life as if every time someone died; or was given a Cancer diagnosis; or were told they couldn't have children or needed a limb amputated, the misery and fear of the patients took a piece of the colour with it.

Even though he had only regained consciousness half an hour ago, Finn knew what was going on. Someone had crashed into the car and suddenly he was in an unfamiliar room tethered to a bed. This was Sawyer's doing. The walls of this room reminded him too much of the hospital he loved working in. It made him feel almost comfortable, which a part of him knew was probably the point. Sawyer was trying to make him feel safe.

Finn was surprised that he wasn't dead. He had been thrown from the front window of a moving vehicle because his belt malfunctioned. He should have been dead or severely injured at the very least. Every limb was still working, though, and he didn't appear to have broken anything, despite how his body felt like it had gone through a woodchipper. A human would probably say his Guardian Angel had been looking over him, or that Lady Luck had favoured him today. It wasn't either of those things.

Finn wasn't dead because Sawyer needed him alive.

Sawyer's ability was very tricky. He had copious amounts of good luck and if he wanted something, fate usually gave it to him. It wasn't that Sawyer physically changed anything himself, it was almost like fate moulded things around him to fit his desires. Sometimes it worked, sometimes it didn't. It was a slippery ability that even Sawyer sometimes couldn't control, and sometimes he had to take risks and hope for the best.

Finn wasn't dead because Sawyer didn't want him dead. He would be no use to him dead.

Finn touched his forehead and winced. His head was stitched up again, much more neatly than when Thursday had done it. He wished for a mirror, so he could analyse the depth of the damage to his face, but the room was completely bare apart from the bed he was tethered to and a sink and toilet in the corner of the room. The last thing he could remember was his face tearing open before everything went dark. He could also vaguely recall something to do with Matthew, but he wasn't completely sure about it.

It would be a lie to say that he wasn't afraid. Finn knew it was no secret to anyone that Sawyer's unstable plans had always sat with him the wrong way. He couldn't help it. Despite everyone's constant insistence that there was no way Sawyer would physically go through with half the schemes he claimed he would, Finn had always had a niggle at the back of his brain, a constant worry that it could happen. 'What ifs' were dangerous to a person's sense of security, Finn knew this from when he studied cognitive behaviour therapy but watching Sawyer experiment on bugs and spiders didn't exactly lessen Finn's concern over the years that the group was whole. It had always been present in his mind that Sawyer had an intention to combine their abilities, which would result in every one of them dying. Apart from Sawyer himself, of course.

Finn looked at his wrists, which were bound to the steel bedposts with a dark purple ribbon. It wasn't tied tight enough to dig into his skin but tight enough so that he couldn't free himself. He'd tried ripping it; biting it; and he even attempted to unthread the knot with his teeth, but it just wouldn't give. He suspected it was some sort of special ribbon Sawyer developed. If the man could make artificial metahumans, then a piece of indestructible ribbon was probably nothing.

The only reason Finn wasn't completely tied down was because Sawyer knew that he wasn't violent. Finn was almost thankful for this as he knew if, say, Thursday had been kidnapped first, she would probably have been forced into another strait jacket with every limb shackled down and a muzzle over her mouth. Finn had a bit more leeway which ...didn't do much. Sure, he could kick Sawyer in the head as soon as he entered the room, but it wouldn't make him any less trapped. He would just have to sit and wait for the man to regain consciousness again. Finn couldn't guarantee how far the loyalty of Sawyer's human lackeys stretched, either. In injuring Sawyer, he could put himself at risk of having to endure the rage of the poor sods Sawyer had hypnotised.

Above everything else, Finn was worried about the others. They had been in a car accident, and he hadn't gotten the opportunity to heal any injuries they may have had. Nobody was dead, he knew that. He would have felt it if someone had died. They would have to heal like mortals which, sure, they had been doing for the past decade, but the past decade hadn't involved severe car accidents where the car was upended and left smoking in the grass.

Finn tried to stop thinking about it. Sawyer needed all of them alive, not just him, so nobody would be in a severe condition after the accident, surely. Except Matthew hadn't been wearing a seat belt at the time and Sawyer didn't need Matthew. Sure, if he had him, he would use him, but it wasn't a necessity. No one was dead yet but that didn't mean that one of them wasn't dying and if most of them were protected by Sawyer's desire for them to survive, then for all Finn knew Matthew could be in trouble. And what of Sybil's baby? Sawyer needed her alive, not her child.

A door appeared on the white wall in front of the bed. It was like a panel being slid open. Finn subconsciously pulled against the ribbon around his wrists, as if he could suddenly rip free like they were nothing but noodles tying him down. His body complained, still in extreme agony from being thrown from the stolen car.

On the other side was Sawyer, looking far too upbeat for the situation. The psychopath entered the room, tossing a bottle of water up into the air and catching it again repeatedly. It was maddening how happy Sawyer looked. A brand-new eyepatch covered his marked eye, that annoying LED blinkering away like a broken light bulb.

Finn opened his mouth, ready to unleash all hell on his captor, but was silenced by the madman's lips landing on top of his own.

Finn was stunned into silence, his eyes bolt wide with shock as Sawyer gently pulled away from the kiss, his one uncovered eye fluttering open and a lazy smile drifting onto his face. "I've missed you," the madman murmured. "I've missed all of you."

Words wouldn't come just yet. Finn didn't know how to respond. Of all the years he'd known that Sawyer had wished to have intimate relations with all of the Seven, he had never anticipated such an action. Maybe the point had been to shock him into silence. If that was the case, it worked.

"I can't wait for us all to be reunited," Sawyer continued. "I will bring us together." He leaned forward and stole one last kiss from the healer before pulling away. Finn had the sudden urge to scrub his mouth until it bled if only his hands were free.

Stepping back, Sawyer gestured around the room. "I trust the room is to your liking."

Finn simply stared. Words still failed him.

The bottomless pits that Sawyer called eyes (or, well, more so *eye*) twinkled with what Finn could only discern as excitement. "It's kind of bland, I know, but since you're my first resident I gave you the best room. You should see Thursday's cell. It isn't pretty."

Slowly, his voice returned. "So, you admit that you're imprisoning us," Finn said slowly.

Sawyer shrugged. "Well, yeah."

Finn pulled a face. "Yet you still claim to love us?"

"My love is exactly why I'm doing all this." Sawyer frowned, looking genuinely confused by what Finn was trying to say. "I *do* love you all."

Maybe imprisonment and love were synonymous with one another in Sawyer's warped mind. Finn shook his head. "Are the others okay? Do you know? Was anyone severely hurt?"

Sawyer sat down on the edge of Finn's bed, flicking his long strands of black hair out of his face. "Thursday and Whitney are fine. Sybil seemed okay, too. I didn't get to see Titus and your boyfriend was putting on a ridiculous amateur dramatics performance when I took you."

The disgust in Sawyer's voice when he referenced Matthew was almost palpable. The temptation to kick Sawyer off the bed grew strong. Finn managed to restrain himself, only because he was more distracted by what Sawyer had said.

"Amateur dramatics?"

"It was really sad," Sawyer answered, turning his nose up at the thought. "Dragging himself across the road like some sort of urchin and bellowing at the top of his lungs at me. Such a rude man."

Conversations with Sawyer usually went this way. He spoke of being rude yet was trying to converse with someone he had kidnapped and strapped to a bed in the hopes of later experimenting on them like it was a completely normal thing to do. He was a raging hypocrite. Finn had tried to decipher what went on in Sawyer's mind decades ago through therapy but not even he could diagnose what made Sawyer so ...unhinged.

"Is he dying?" Finn asked quietly.

For a moment, he could feel Sawyer's eyes on him. Simply watching. Finn didn't know what the madman was looking for but didn't allow it to deter him. He needed an answer.

"No, he is not," Sawyer eventually answered. He didn't even try to hide the disappointment in his tone.

"You would have preferred it otherwise," Finn stated.

"Not necessarily," Sawyer answered. "It wouldn't have affected my plan, but it would have been of great aid to me if the shifter had died."

Finn's teeth scraped against one another as he forced himself to keep his cool. "Am I dying?" he decided to also ask.

Sawyer's black eye shone with concern. "I hope not," he replied. "No, no, dear, I need you alive. Just some bumps and bruises. I have top surgeons at my beck and call who dealt with anything that could have been considered serious or life-threatening."

"You need me alive ...yet you decided that the best course of action was to fling me from the front window of a car?" Finn asked with disbelief. He didn't like the condescending way that Sawyer was speaking to him. He didn't go through decades of medical school to be talked down to by a psychotic who was hoping to kill him and steal his very essence.

"Sometimes we need to take some risks..."

"You didn't intend to kill us with that crash," Finn said. "What was your true intent?"

Sawyer pushed himself up and over Finn's legs on the bed so that he could rest his back against the wall. His casual attitude was what made his company so disconcerting. The world could be crumbling beneath Sawyer's feet, and he would hold a conversation like he was sitting at home having a cup of tea.

"I wished to obtain you," Sawyer explained. "Sybil and Whitney also."

Finn couldn't help feeling amused. "So, you failed?"

"I don't fail," Sawyer replied, "you know that. It's a setback."

"What stopped you from getting the girls?" asked Finn. "Not that I'm not glad you didn't get your hands on them."

"It's Whitney's Soul Day," Sawyer answered. "I'm determined but I'm not an idiot. As for Sybil ... She was too close to Thursday."

Finn rolled his eyes. "You still fear Thursday?"

"I don't fear Thursday." Sawyer plucked his eyepatch off his eye and rubbed it against his trouser leg. He kept his marked eye sealed shut, just like he did in the hospital until the patch was back in place. "I told you, I'm not an idiot. Thursday would have blasted anyone who got too close. You were alone on the road, apart from the shifter, so I made a strategic decision and only took you."

Finn sighed. "I'm assuming you tampered with my belt?"

"Not me," said Sawyer. "My slave Bram did so, under my order. It was obvious that you would steal the closest vehicle you could find but, just to be safe, I had him disconnect all the belts of all the cars in the nearby carpark."

Dread filled Finn as he realised that at least a hundred humans were now travelling in cars with damaged seatbelts. How many of them were going to die or be severely injured because of Sawyer's safety measures?

"You do realise that you have endangered so many lives with your stupid quest?" Finn snarled.

Sawyer shrugged. "C'est la vie. I will hardly mourn the loss of filth."

"Humans aren't filth, Sawyer! Without humans for you to experiment on, you wouldn't have gotten to where you are now! You wouldn't have been able to disconnect my seat belt in the first place!" Finn exclaimed.

"I said they were filth; I didn't say they were useless."

Trying to convince Sawyer of the value of human life was like trying to convince him that an apple was orange or that the grass was pink. Finn would never know what had bred such hatred in the man's heart for humans, but the loathing was extrapolated by Sawyer's insanity, for sure. It was one of the many reasons that Finn had always felt uncomfortable in Sawyer's presence.

When Sybil and Whitney rescued him from the disgusting hovel that had been the travelling circus where he had been forced to work, Finn used the opportunity of new life to save lives. He had seen too much life being stolen in the circus for no good reason. Times when the ringmaster had gone too far and hurt beyond even Finn's ability. He had known since his rescue that he had to prevent as much death as he possibly could, even if it meant he had to study it so that no one knew he was one of the Seven.

Sawyer seemed to have the opposite philosophy. To him, humans were useful but disposable. They were more like toys than beings of actual sentience. Finn wished that Sawyer had been the one forced to see people tortured for the sake of a show, then maybe he would understand exactly why every life was important. Then again, maybe it wouldn't. Maybe someone as sadistic as Sawyer would enjoy such a performance.

Finn thumped his head back against the wall. A jolt of hot pain slashed across the back of his skull and his brain felt like it had been rattled. He didn't dare try to think what sort of damage was causing such soreness.

"How did you know I would be driving?"

"There's no way you could have allowed Thursday or Matthew to drive, that would be too dangerous. As for Whitney and Titus, they have lived in the heart of Castlebrooke for most of their lives, they've never needed to get a licence." Sawyer smirked darkly. "And I knew you would never have allowed Sybil to drive in her condition."

As Sawyer explained himself, his uncovered eye moved from side to side, almost like he was reading his words from a book only he could see. A book of the future that his ability allowed snippets of intel from. What else could Sawyer see? What probabilities was he aware of? What next move was his ability going to bless him with?

Finn looked away. Seeing Sawyer's ability at work made him uneasy. "Good guess."

"Thank you," Sawyer practically purred.

Sawyer lay down on the bed, wedging himself between the wall and Finn's body. Finn winced, his aching body complaining about the slight shift that Sawyer caused. If the situation were different, it would look rather comical as since Sawyer's head was at Finn's hip, his legs dangled over the end of the bed. Finn tried tugging the ribbons again as if the more time that passed, the looser they'd get. They still held firm.

"I know you don't understand right now," Sawyer began, staring at the ceiling like the lines between the tiles were stars to gaze at, "but I have confidence when you all become a part of me you will begin to do so."

Finn peered at the man lying by his hip. "Become a part of you?" he repeated.

Sawyer nodded, still gazing at the ceiling. "I will combine you all into myself. We'll be together forever, and we will be unstoppable."

"You'll be killing us, Sawyer. We won't be a part of you," Finn replied measuredly.

Sawyer didn't respond. He barely moved. Finn watched him carefully, half expecting him to explode into a manic episode like he used to do when faced with facts he couldn't dispute. This didn't happen. Sawyer simply stared at the ceiling as if the meaning of life was somehow engraved somewhere in the tiles.

"You're frightened of me."

Finn felt sick. He had been trying to hide his fear. Sawyer enjoyed people fearing him. Finn focused on controlling his breathing and keeping his heartbeat regular, despite how difficult such a thing was to control.

He won't hurt you. Not yet, at any rate.

"Am I really that scary?" An amused smirk cracked across Sawyer's face. Sawyer turned onto his stomach on the bed so that he could see Finn properly. "What do you fear, Finn? Is it me? Or the solidity of your future with us?"

"There is no future and stop saying 'us' as if you already have us all trapped!" Finn snapped.

Sawyer let his head roll to the side, supporting it on the wall to his left. "Who says I haven't?" he drawled.

"I know you haven't."

"What makes you say so?"

"You wouldn't be wasting time here with me if you had! You'd be with Sybil!" Finn clenched his fists as anger overwhelmed him. "We know that you're annoyed about her being pregnant, you'd be pestering her to know who the father is. Not to mention you must still be hung up on her if you're worried about such a thing!"

Sawyer gazed at Finn coolly. "Good guess, my dear healer. Maybe you have a touch of Sunday in you."

"Gods, I hope not."

"However, that is only the half of it."

Finn eyed Sawyer dejectedly. "How so?"

"You all act like I love only Sybil. Like I have some sort of favouritism towards her because we had a relationship. This is not true, and I know you know it's not true. I love every one of you, not just her. You must believe that."

The passion in which Sawyer spoke, the desperation in his tone of voice, tempted Finn to believe him. He had always known that Sawyer had been obsessed with the idea of them all being together, but he still believed that Sybil was a special exception. That Sawyer couldn't help loving her more. Finn knew he wasn't the only one who thought this. They all did, even Sybil herself at one point.

But Finn had never heard Sawyer speak of his love with such pure adoration before. Like he was prepared to jump off the very bed they sat on and kneel before him and the rest of the Seven like they were Gods. Sawyer believed they were more than Gods. He believed that their abilities were a blessing that made them so much higher than anything else on the planet. In his own warped way, Sawyer probably did love them all, which just made his plans even more twisted.

Besides, there was one flaw in his claim.

"You don't love Matthew."

Sawyer's lip curled. "I do," he contradicted. "I just simply do not like him."

"You wanted him to die."

"For his own good."

"How can that be for his own good?" Finn barked, losing his temper. "You claim to love us, yet you wish to kill us. You claim to love Matthew, but you want him to die. You don't make any sense, Sawyer, you never have! You're insane!"

"I have no need for Matthew's ability! It's more of a burden than an asset. So, when your souls are taken from the fleshy prisons you call bodies and brought home to my own, Matthew shall remain! He is the one with no purpose, he always has been," Sawyer snarled, his voice having taken a sinister tone. "I will have no choice but to leave him behind. He'd be better off dead."

Matthew … left alone? Sawyer was just going to ditch him simply because his ability wasn't of any worth to him. The idea of Matthew being alone, having to carry the knowledge that the rest of the Seven had been killed by Sawyer's hand … such a hardship would kill him. Finn's heart clenched at the very thought of it.

Finn raised his eyes to meet Sawyer's. "I'll die before I allow that to happen."

Sawyer didn't look too amused by this. "Why do you care? He left you. He threw you away like rubbish on the street and spent the following decade running around with the human filth."

"You know nothing of our relationship so don't even try," Finn glowered.

He wasn't an overly sensitive man, but the topic of his relationship with Matthew had always been touchy. A decade-old open wound that, if poked too hard, stung so badly it almost crippled him. It used to hit in waves like somehow the ghost of his ex-lover would pass over him at the most spontaneous of times and touch the wound, reminding him that he had been abandoned and left alone by the only person he had dared to let in.

Sawyer surely knew this and that was why he was saying what he was saying. Finn forced himself to remain calm, as remaining calm was the only front he had left. Not giving Sawyer a rise was the only way he would be able to fight back, even if it meant swallowing the agony as the wound was reopened and taunted.

"Don't tell me you're taking him back…" Sawyer rolled his eyes. "Such a waste."

"Of what, exactly?" Finn demanded. "You don't stand a chance. Not with me, not with any of us! We've all moved on, Sawyer! Even Sybil has gotten over you! She's having a baby that's not yours! The only person wasting anything here is you!"

An explosion of pain right across his face. Finn almost smiled, even though his skin was on fire. He had finally gotten Sawyer to crack. This wasn't exactly a good thing, for who knew what the madman would do to him because of this, but for one moment, he was victorious, and that was what mattered.

"You are lying!" Sawyer yelled. He lunged forward and grabbed Finn by the throat, slamming him back against the wall behind them. Finn tensed up, his beaten body screaming in protest, and shut his eyes as if it would lessen the brunt of Sawyer's rage. "You all love me just as much as I love you, you just don't know it yet! You'll understand the importance of my cause even if I have to make you understand by force!"

Sawyer's fingers dug into the skin of Finn's neck, almost drawing blood by how hard he gripped him. Finn was nearly trembling with the effect of keeping himself calm, his voice shaking as he breathed out, "I'll never love you."

"Oh yeah?" Sawyer growled.

There was a snip and suddenly Finn's left arm was free. Before he could even contemplate taking a swing at Sawyer, the madman had already grabbed his wrist and forced it between them.

Agony exploded across his hand. Finn screamed, his eyes flying open to see what Sawyer had done.

There, on the fourth finger of his left hand was a ring. This was no ordinary ring, though. Attached to the inner circle of the band were tiny metal rods which had embedded themselves into the flesh of Finn's finger, sealing the piece of jewellery into place. Blood and pus seeped out from where the rods had broken his skin, the rods driving in deep and attaching themselves to the bone.

This ring was not going to come off.

Finn couldn't breathe, the pain was so bad. He was going to throw up and, as if expecting this, Sawyer grabbed a bin from beneath the bed and shoved it under his captive's chin.

It felt like his finger had been amputated. Finn vomited into the bin, the acidic burn of his vomit searing his throat and corroding his nostrils. His body violently shook despite already being exhausted and in pain, his system trying to cope with the intrusion of the ring.

"I invented it myself," Sawyer soothed, stroking the healer's trembling hand in his own. He lifted his free hand, so the band on his finger caught the light. "I have five more. Each individually designed for the wearer."

"Why..." Finn was too wrung out to speak, his voice echoing tiredly into the bin. The attack on his finger-despite small in comparison to the beating his body had endured from the crash-was the final straw his system could take.

"Well, you can't have a marriage without an engagement period, right?" Sawyer beamed. "I can't wait for the others to see their rings!"

Finn's head was heavy as he lifted it out of the bin. He was sweating from shock and his eyelids drooped as he glared at Sawyer. "I'm not ...engaged ...to you ..."

"Yes, you are, silly," Sawyer laughed. The madman leaned forward and kissed the healer's bleeding appendage, licking up the blood that came off Finn's skin. "Why else are you wearing your ring?"

Finn tried to swat Sawyer away, but his vision was sliding out of focus and too much sudden movement made it blacken around the edges. The ring forced into his skin-the harsh cold of the metal surging through his seeping flesh and digging into his bone-was completely unwelcome but not in any position to move.

"I'll let you get some rest," Sawyer decided. "If you behave, I'll bring you some healing solution later."

Finn wanted to argue but the black edges of his vision were getting larger, like a piece of parchment being burned away. He knew he was going to pass out from the pain.

A different ring, one that he had worn around his neck every day for ten years, burned against his chest like fire. This ring used to sit proudly on his finger, the finger that had now been violated and ripped apart by Sawyer's contraption, happy for anyone to see it. It held so much meaning to him but for the past decade, it had been hidden away. Never taken off, no, of course not, but hidden, nonetheless. Finn could never have brought himself to take it off, but he hadn't been able to display it either. So instead he wore it around his neck, where only he would know it was there.

Sawyer cupped both sides of the healer's sweaty, shaking face and pressed their foreheads together. "I can't wait for us all to be whole."

Matthew took Finn's hand and slid the ring onto his finger, threading their hands together as he did so. "Hopefully you won't take it off," he joked.

Finn's eyes crossed as his head hollowed out. They rolled up behind his lids and he succumbed to the dark of unconsciousness again.

Finn laughed as his lover drew him over for a kiss. "Don't worry, no ring will ever replace yours, I promise."

CHAPTER ELEVEN

THEY HAD GOTTEN LUCKY.

Thursday stood by the campfire, cracking her sprained wrist back and forth to keep herself focused. The burn of the injured muscles helped her brain concentrate as she surveyed the shoulder-length grass for possible threats. She didn't expect anything to come lunging out of the field in the middle of the night, however, the rumours of disappearances hadn't fallen on deaf ears. There was no harm in being safe rather than sorry, especially now that they were down one man.

Humans would claim that they had gotten extremely lucky, considering the severity of the crash and the fact that none of them had died, not even the man who had been flung from the front window. Not one of them was critically injured, either. A sprain here, a concussion there, but nothing major. This was why humans were naïve. Nothing happened purely out of chance. There was no such thing as luck. It was all Sawyer.

"We shouldn't be resting."

Thursday looked down at Matthew, who was sitting the closest to the campfire. The glow of the flames bounced off his blond hair, making him look more celestial than normal. He wouldn't remove his eyes from the flickering tongues of fire, each one reflected in the unique iris'.

"Yes, we should be," she flatly responded.

"How long is it going to take us to walk to the asylum?" Matthew asked.

"Most likely days." Thursday didn't see a point in lying. It just put off the inevitable.

"Days in which Sawyer will do what he needs to do to Finn." Matthew inhaled, his chest inflating as he held a breath there for a long minute. As he finally released it again, he said, "We need to leave now."

Thursday shook her head. "Titus has a concussion. We need to stay put until at least the morning."

"It could be too late by then."

"It could be too late right now!" Thursday snapped back. "We don't know anything, Mattie! Quit your gurning."

Thursday's patience had been running thin ever since they had decided to stay put in the Meadows until morning. Matthew had blown his top, kicking out and threatening to go to United Arms on his own if they didn't immediately set off. Of course, when Sybil called his bluff, he didn't go anywhere, mainly because he didn't know how to get to United Arms from their current location. That hadn't stopped him from griping and complaining at every possible interval from that point onwards.

Matthew suddenly jumped to his feet, so fast that even Thursday hadn't anticipated it. He grabbed her by her plaid jacket and shook her. "Why aren't you doing anything to help him? Why are we sitting here like ducks when for all we know Finn could be dead! How can we sit by a campfire and sleep when one of our own could be in danger!"

Thursday clenched her fists, resisting the urge to smack Matthew across the face. She knew that he was emotionally charged after what had happened today, after having witnessed Sawyer carrying Finn away while the rest of them had been trapped by the car. Thursday didn't regret her decision to help Sybil out of the car instead of going to Finn. Thursday was no doctor but hanging upside down with a seatbelt digging into your baby bump was surely not good for the foetus inside.

"You're not thinking logically, you're letting emotions cloud your judgment!" Thursday snapped.

"Maybe I want emotions to cloud my judgment since the rest of you seem to be acting like emotionless robots!" Matthew roared. His voice echoed into the night, like a ghost screaming for help. There was a pain in his heterochromatic eyes that ate through Thursday's skin like acid. She couldn't stand being pinned down by it.

"Titus is concussed," Thursday repeated, lowering her voice, and trying to regain her calm, "unless you suggest doing deeper damage to him, I'd plant your whinging butt back down onto the ground."

Matthew's chest rose and fell rapidly as he glowered at Thursday. The pain melted into desperation, and he asked, his voice barely above a whisper, "Don't you care?"

Thursday glared at him. Of course, she damn well cared. Due to the accident, Sawyer had the tools he needed to become invincible. If he succeeded, he would be able to heal any wound he received from them or anyone else. They'd have no means of fighting him unless they got close enough to fire a bullet into his thick skull. That is, of course, hinging on the belief that he had the means of fixing the flaw in Finn's ability.

It was always difficult to know when a madman was lying. The only piece of evidence that Thursday had to go on was that

Finn was not yet dead, meaning that Sawyer had not yet touched him. This was out of character for a man who claimed to know how to fix the only flaw holding him back. Wouldn't Sawyer want to obtain Finn's healing at once? It would certainly make the rest of his plan a lot easier. This surely meant that Sawyer didn't entirely know what he was doing yet, right?

Finn was alive. That was the only evidence they had.

Thursday knew that this was not what Matthew meant. He meant did she not care about Finn, or his wellbeing, or his life? Again, of course, she cared. The only true personal connections Thursday had ever allowed herself to have been the Seven. They were practically her siblings. Finn had always been like a brother to her, even if his prudish ways never gelled well with her recklessness, and he'd certainly healed her out of many near-death experiences.

Thursday liked to pretend that she didn't care about the Seven and that a disconnected life was the sort she'd rather choose. It was moments like these, though, that reminded her that there was a time when these people were all she had. Beneath the crazy, laughing mask that acted like it didn't give a crap about anything or anyone, Thursday would die for her family.

Emotions like that, however, were a weakness. Times like this did not need weakness. It was why Thursday had a mask in the first place. Besides, Matthew had more of a right to allow his emotions to control him right now. If it had been anyone else, Thursday probably would have punched them long ago and told them to grow the hell up.

So, Thursday sucked up her anguish like a big girl and allowed herself to think logically, as opposed to emotionally.

Matthew's fingers tightened desperately around the fabric of Thursday's jacket as if he could forcibly drag an answer out of her. Thursday simply stared back at him, refusing to answer his question, as neither response she could give would do him any good.

A hand suddenly clamped onto Matthew's shoulder, and he jumped, releasing Thursday in the process. She stepped back angrily, straightening her jacket as the shifter turned around.

Whitney's fingers dug into Matthew's shoulder, the skin of her hand-tinged white from the ice that poisoned her being. "Of course, we care," she said in a measured voice, "but we need everyone if we have any hope of rescuing Finn. The only hope we have right now is that he is not dead yet."

"What if we don't get there in time?" Matthew demanded to know.

The hand on his shoulder grew paler and Matthew took a sharp intake of breath. Whitney recognised his discomfort and removed her hand, her fingers rigid from the cold. "Then we don't get there in time," she laid out simply.

Matthew didn't take this well. He sank to the ground again and pushed his fingers into his hair, lifting his eyes to stare at the fire once more. Thursday knew that Matthew was aware that this was the truth. No matter how long it took them, if they didn't get there on time then they didn't get there. That was it. All they had right now was that they had not felt Finn's death. For all they knew, though, it could only be a matter of time.

Thursday gestured to Whitney's frozen hand. "Your ability playing up?"

Whitney shrugged and looked at her hand like it was nothing but an inconvenience. "It happens from time to time," she answered. "Never on this severe a level before, mind you…"

"Ice is … misery?" asked Thursday. "I thought water was misery?"

Whitney nodded. "Ice is misery. Sadness is water. Anger is fire and neutral is earth."

Thursday would kill to have an ability like Whitney's. Control over the elements would be wicked cool. Only if she could choose which she wanted to use. Cut out the whole emotions bull and Whitney could have been untouchable. Every ability came with its hamartia.

"So, your hand has never frozen over before?" Thursday enquired.

Whitney walked around the fire and held her hand over it as if the flames would somehow defeat her ability and free her stuck fingers. She walked with a slight limp, the souvenir she had taken from the car crash. "It's my Soul Day and we just lost Finn to Sawyer. I've never been this miserable in my entire life," she muttered.

"I didn't think you cared about Finn that much," said Thursday. "About any of us."

"Of course, I care," Whitney answered sharply. Thursday was surprised that she sounded offended by her assumption. "We're family." As if unable to allow such a sappy response to pass, she also added, "Besides, I could have used Finn to heal this damn leg of mine."

"I second that," Titus said. He currently lay across from Matthew on the other side of the fire, using the scorch of the flames to stop himself from falling asleep.

Thursday continued to rock her wrist back and forward. The only one of them that wasn't awake was Sybil. They had been keeping a close eye on her since the crash just in case her baby had experienced some trauma. So far there was no sign of any issues, but that didn't mean anything. Another reason they needed to rest: they couldn't move until they were sure Sybil was unharmed. Thursday didn't tell Matthew this during their argument because vocalising the possibility of miscarriage made the idea a lot more …real. Thursday wasn't ready to deal with such a thing.

"What do you think Sawyer is doing?" Matthew asked. He had gone completely monotone, almost not even blinking as he stared into the fire.

"Don't be sadistic, Matthew," Titus groaned. "Let's talk about something else."

"Like what?" Matthew challenged.

An idea popped into Thursday's head. Something she had been meaning to ask since it had been mentioned back at Del Monte Forest Manor. Thursday looked up at Whitney through her hair. "You said you were unemployed," she said. "I thought you worked in advertising?"

Whitney looked uncomfortable with this question. She removed her hand from the fire as her misery ebbed a bit. Quickly busying herself by pinning her hair up in a messy bun, she said, "I did. I don't anymore. I was fired."

Thursday grinned. "What did you do? Talk back? I could easily see you getting fired for answering back."

Whitney looked across the fire at Thursday, a bored expression on her face. "If you must know, I was sacked because I did not wish to be promoted."

Titus lifted his head off the ground. "What?"

Whitney ignored Titus like he hadn't asked her anything at all. Instead, she crouched in front of the fire and warmed her hands against it. She didn't elaborate on her answer and

Thursday didn't push the subject. Whitney had gotten fired, fine. That answered what she wanted to know perfectly fine. Even if the reasoning as to why brought up more questions than it answered...

Thursday didn't expect any less from Whitney. She was an extremely private person. Whitney had never been one to overshare or share at all. The Seven didn't even know where Sybil found Whitney, or what she had been doing before the group formed. Sybil had simply said, "*I found her on the streets.*" This was all well and good, but surely there had been more to it than that. Finn had been on the streets as well before he was picked up by the circus. Matthew ran away from his Orphanage multiple times and spent months on the streets before being forced back. Sawyer had even been on the streets after his parents died. There had to be a reason behind it, but Sybil had always respected Whitney's desire to keep her past hidden. No one knew Whitney's old life but Sybil, and that was how it would always stay.

"Did you work at all over the past ten years, Matthew?" Whitney asked, trying to distract the shifter from his despondent thoughts.

Matthew shrugged. "No. Didn't really need to."

"Why is that?"

"Just lived day by day in different people's houses. Shifted the previous night, picked someone up, and then stayed with them for a few days."

Thursday raised her eyebrows. "You spent ten whole years doing that?"

"No big deal." Thursday wasn't used to Matthew's voice being so plain and indifferent. Usually, he was so animated, it was very … wrong to see him this way. "It's what I'm bred for."

That use of wording. Bred. Like they had been created in a lab by some crazy scientist. Thursday didn't like it because it reminded her too much of Sawyer. Especially now since he was experimenting on humans to give them artificial abilities. He had a real Doctor Frankenstein complex.

"I think you may have dated one of my dancers," Titus said thoughtfully.

Matthew lifted his head only a little, his eyes meeting Titus' across the orange and yellow flames. "Go on then," he said wearily, "I'm ready for it. Shame me all you like. Dating the human filth, as Sawyer would say."

Titus let his head rest against the grass again. "You seem to forget that I was once married to 'the human filth'."

"Yeah, but she was a real cow," Thursday replied.

Titus scrunched his face up, clearly displeased by Thursday's description of Yvanna. Even after all these years, he still couldn't fully stick people insulting his ex-wife. Or an actual wife since they never really got a proper divorce. The days following Yvanna's leaving must have been painful for Titus for many varied reasons, one of those reasons being that Thursday had called the woman a colourful array of names that she refused to apologise for. She never understood his desire to keep Yvanna on a pedestal, after everything the wretched woman had done to him. Thursday had even offered to go and kill Yvanna for him, or even the Duke who whisked her away, but Titus had refused, openly disgusted by the very thought.

Yvanna had committed Titus. If she hadn't thought herself capable of it, then she shouldn't have done it. Thursday didn't care about faithfulness in relationships but being a courting couple and being married were two completely different things. Thursday had the sense to never commit herself, while Yvanna had done the opposite. Yvanna had married Titus and then ran off with a Duke not long after. What had even been the point of leading Titus on like that? Thursday didn't like dishonesty like that. She chose to be an open book, no matter who it hurt or offended. It meant that everyone knew where they stood with her and there would be no misunderstanding her. She only manipulated the truth if she saw it necessary and that was on exceedingly rare occasions.

It was the part of Titus that still loved Yvanna that didn't like anyone insulting her. Even though she was long gone and was now mulch in the earth.

"Yeah, *married* being the keyword here," Matthew answered.

"Believe it or not, Matthew, I don't care what you do with your romantic life," Titus replied. "I didn't care when you were committed to Finn, and I didn't care when you weren't. It's your life, not mine. I don't care how many men and women come into my studio murmuring your name to each other like you're some sort of God of Sex."

"Wait, what?" Whitney interjected. "Even straight men? As in you still use the name Matthew when you're a girl?"

Thursday frowned. "Didn't you know that he doesn't change his name?"

She hadn't realised that this may have been something only Matthew had shared with her. It made sense, though. Matthew had always struggled with his identity because of his ability, and he chose not to change his name even when he was in female form because all it did was confuse him further. It was no secret to any of them that Matthew had always found difficulty in knowing who he was because he was constantly forced to change shape, but Thursday had never considered the idea that she may have been the only one (besides maybe Finn) who he had spoken to about it in depth.

"Why not?" Whitney asked. "You used to change your name all the time back when we were all first joined together. What changed?"

"I shouldn't have to do it," Matthew bit back acidly. "People find it quirky when they find a girl called Matthew anyway."

Matthew clenched his jaw and resumed staring at the fire. Well, that conversation attempt flopped. They were just going to have to leave him alone to brood. If Matthew wanted to sit and mope like a child for the night, then they should just let him. Tomorrow morning, he would have to pick his chin off the ground and become organised. Until then, Thursday was perfectly happy to allow him to act like a spoiled child.

Whitney shrugged her jacket off and threw it over Sybil's sleeping form. She examined her nails and laughed blithely. "My manicure is somehow still intact," she said, more to herself than anyone else.

Whitney had always taken immense pride in her appearance, and it wasn't too hard to tell that she was quite happy that her nails were still in good condition, despite how she tried to hide it.

Thursday snorted. "Well, at least you'll be ready to hand model as soon as we're finished here."

"I paid good money for these," Whitney replied. "It's hard to find a manicure that doesn't get destroyed from fire shooting from the fingertips."

She had a point there for sure.

A rustle in the grass drew Thursday's attention away from Whitney's pink and white nails. Both girls jumped to their feet at the same time, alarmed by the disturbance. "What was that?" Whitney whispered.

"The Grass Gremlins that make all those humans vanish?" Thursday guessed.

Whitney did not appreciate the joke, articulated by the exasperated expression on her face. She turned away from Thursday and ventured into the grass, the tall, billowy strands enveloping her at once like an unwanted hug. Thursday followed her, taking a quick glance back at their camp as if Matthew, Titus, and Sybil were going to suddenly vanish into thin air.

The only way to navigate through the grass was to look up at the sky. The tiny glowing stars in the blanket of black were the only source of light as they drew away from their camp. Thursday could just about make out the blobby form of Whitney a couple of steps ahead. She hoped that the woman was able to keep their cool or else the entire Meadows would go up in flames. The only sound in the still air was Whitney's heavy breathing and the occasional chirp of a cricket, making the rustle even more disconcerting in origin.

Thursday was reminded of when she and Matthew had pushed through the corn fields to retrieve Sybil's money from the slave drivers who had owned Titus. It had been dark like this, too, and the two of them had struggled to stop giggling to themselves as they pushed through the tall stalks of corn. They had wanted to surprise Sybil by returning her money, but it had more been for Titus than their leader. If Titus' captors had Sybil's money it meant in a sense that Titus belonged to her and, where buying him had been necessary to get him off those torturous fields, such an idea was unthinkable. Besides, those greedy rich pounces wouldn't even notice their money was missing, they had so much of it.

There was another rustle to Thursday's right and suddenly a body lunged out at her with a scream, trying to whack her with a stick of some sort. Thursday grabbed the top of the weapon and wrenched it out of their weak hands before it came anywhere near her head. Throwing the weapon away, Thursday grabbed the weakling and ignited her hand, her Glow a lot less flammable than Whitney's fire. "Who are you?" Thursday barked.

"Me?" they hysterically replied. "Who are *you*?!"

Thursday lifted her glowing hand closer to her attacker's face. The Glow revealed a scrawny young woman with a pinched face. There was a gigantic scar across her left eye, leaving her from what Thursday could see blind and only able to see through the one.

"I asked you first," Thursday growled.

"I asked you after!"

Thursday thrust her glowing hand into the woman's face. "I have fire coming out of my hands!" she threatened.

The woman cringed away from Thursday's hand. "My name is Mackenzie!" she snapped. "I've been wandering through these damn grasslands for days! I don't know where I am!"

"You're in the Meadows," Whitney said, appearing by Thursday's side. "Outside of Castlebrooke."

Relief flushed through Mackenzie's face. "Seriously?" she asked, her voice lifting.

"Uh …yeah."

Mackenzie jumped forward and hugged Thursday. "Oh, thank god, thank god, thank god!"

"Lady, quit! Ever heard of personal space?!" Thursday pushed Mackenzie away from her, releasing her from her grasp in the process.

Mackenzie didn't make a run for it. She didn't even try to retrieve her weapon. She stared at Whitney and Thursday like they were her saviours, adoration shining in her chestnut brown eyes. "You swear I'm not near the hill anymore?" she asked.

Thursday cocked her head with curiosity. "United Arms Hill?"

Mackenzie nodded.

"You're far from it."

Mackenzie released a long breath and crouched down on the ground. Her shoulders were shaking. Thursday stepped back with disgust. Was this woman *crying*? "Look, lady, I don't know what your deal is but"-

"Why are you crying?" Whitney asked, sounding just as uncomfortable as Thursday.

"I thought I'd never escape!" Mackenzie cried. "I thought I'd be stuck there forever!"

Thursday's eyebrows drew together. "So, you're a patient?" she asked. "An escaped patient?"

Mackenzie started shaking her head, unaware that Thursday had come from United Arms as well. "No, you must believe me, I'm not! I was kidnapped and brought there against my will!" she insisted.

Thursday straightened and exchanged a look with Whitney. "By who?" she asked.

"I don't know who they are." Mackenzie was still shaking her head like she could somehow shake an explanation out of her ears. "They just took me! They gave me this scar!" She pointed to her damaged eye, which, now that Thursday could get a proper look at it, looked fresh.

Whitney crouched down to Mackenzie's level, keeping a decent distance between them just in case. "Do you, by any chance, know a man named Sawyer?" she asked.

Mackenzie's face lit up like a Christmas tree. "Why? Is he here? I'm trying to get back to him!" she said.

Thursday looked away. Things were starting to make sense. This must have been another one of Sawyer's human subjugates ...

"Who is he to you?" Whitney carefully probed.

"He's my lover, of course!" Mackenzie exclaimed. "He told me to be weary of United Arms and I didn't listen to him!" She moaned dejectedly and covered her eyes. "How could I have been so foolish! I should have listened to him!"

"You said that they stole you, Mackenzie," Thursday patiently reminded her.

"Did I?" Mackenzie removed her hands from her eyes and looked up at Thursday in confusion.

There was something about her gaze that was almost … blank. Almost as if the thin layer of emotion she was presenting to Thursday and Whitney could easily be peeled away to expose nothingness. It reminded Thursday of how Bram looked when he passionately pledged his allegiance to Sawyer. The determination and emotion were there but it almost seemed …fake. Like it had been fabricated instead of developed.

Whitney looked up at Thursday, unsure about what to say to Mackenzie. She was under Sawyer's spell, or hypnosis, or whatever it was that he did to humans to make them so loyal to him, and she didn't understand that it was most likely him who sent her to United Arms for experimentation. In which case, it was highly likely that United Arms was his Castlebrooke base. That made it more plausible that Dr. Weeks was there. Someone needed to oversee Sawyer's work while Sawyer himself was absent.

"Look, Mackenzie, whatever Sawyer has told you is lies. He's the reason you were taken to United Arms. I wouldn't be surprised if he brought you to the damn door himself," Thursday bluntly put.

"You're lying!" Mackenzie barked back, her face turning scarlet with rage. "He wouldn't do that!"

"He's a psychopath! Your malleable human brain was perfect to leave his imprint on!" Thursday snapped. "I'd strongly recommend not returning to him because he is currently in Opara City doing God knows what to the people he's captured there. You'd be walking straight back into the slaughterhouse, my friend!"

"My Sawyer wouldn't do that!" Mackenzie screamed, her voice echoing into the night.

Thursday laughed harshly. "*Your* Sawyer? Do you know how many people there are just like you who all think that Sawyer is theirs? I'd hash my bets on hundreds. Hundreds of people just like you who think they're special, or the apple of his eye, or the one he loves the most when in reality you're just a bunch of soft mortals who are easy to entrance!"

Mackenzie was violently shaking her head in denial, clutching the ground like the soil was on her side. Thursday scoffed and rolled her eyes, unable to handle such a pathetic sight. She didn't blame the humans for falling under Sawyer's spell, but she couldn't help how pitiful she found their actions because of it. How long had Mackenzie been trapped in Sawyer's attic before she became convinced that she needed him so desperately?

Spinning on her heel, Thursday gestured for Whitney to follow her. "Let's go back to camp."

"Don't leave me here!" Mackenzie attached herself to Thursday's leg, clinging to her for dear life. "I don't know how to get home from here!"

"Get off me!" Thursday snapped, trying to shake her off her leg. Mackenzie wouldn't budge. She tightened her grip on Thursday's leg as she shook.

"No! I'll get lost! I can't handle these Meadows alone!"

Thursday had enough. She grabbed Mackenzie by the hair and dragged her up to eye level. "Look, girlie, we're heading to United Arms, so you don't want to follow us, alright?" she snarled.

"You mentioned a camp!" Mackenzie exclaimed. She cried out when Thursday tightened her grip on her hair. "Please, if anything, let me come back there! Please!"

Whitney nudged Thursday's arm. "Just let her follow us. What harm can she do? Look at the state of her."

Thursday clenched her jaw and leaned in close to Mackenzie's face. "If you follow us, do not-if you value your life-bring up

Sawyer. We are not going to stand for your co-dependent praise of him. One word about him and you leave, understood?"

Mackenzie nodded frantically. "Understood!"

Thursday threw Mackenzie to the ground and started marching back to camp. If this woman showed any sign of still being under Sawyer's control, then she was out. Right now, her affection seemed to only be on a mild level, nothing like what Bram had been like. If this changed even the slightest, then Mackenzie would have to find her way back to Castlebrooke. If she refused to leave Thursday would have no problem killing her. The last thing they needed right now was for some idiot human to sit down at their campfire and start singing Sawyer's praises or do Sawyer's bidding. If Mackenzie dared to do such a thing, Thursday wouldn't need to kill her. Matthew would most likely kick her face-first into their campfire.

"Can I ask," Mackenzie's voice floated in from somewhere behind Thursday, "before we return to the camp and I have to be silent about him, why do you hate my Sawyer so much?"

Thursday clenched her jaw. "Call him 'my Sawyer' again and you won't make it to the camp."

"Sorry," Mackenzie replied.

"Sawyer has done us wrong, let's just leave it at that," Whitney curtly answered.

"Is it because of his actions as a member of the Seven?" Mackenzie enquired.

"He told you about that?" Thursday sighed heavily. How many people had Sawyer exposed his identity to? Then again if he was hypnotising them did it matter? There was no way his overzealous lackeys would expose him as Sunday's Child.

"It's how he earned my trust," Mackenzie dreamily explained. "He told me that he only tells the people he trusts the most that he's Sunday's Child." A pause. "You did know he was Sunday's Child, right?" Panic suddenly gripped Mackenzie's tone as the realisation dawned on her that she may have just exposed Sawyer to a bunch of strangers.

Thursday rolled her eyes. "You haven't even asked our names yet, Mackenzie," she said sweetly.

"What's your name, then?"

Thursday spun on her heel, causing Mackenzie to nearly bump into her. "My name is Thursday, now please stop talking before I chop you in the neck to get you to shut up."

When she turned back around and continued picking her way through the grass, Mackenzie asked, "As in Thursday's Child?"

"God, you're a quick one," Thursday sarcastically replied.

Mackenzie fell silent. Thursday didn't care if she feared the Seven or liked the Seven or if Sawyer was the only one of the Seven, she wanted to be associated with. If Mackenzie decided to run away screaming now it would save them the trouble of having to have her obsessed butt around their campfire.

"I'm Whitney," Whitney piped up, amusement in her voice. "In some circles, I'm called Whit, although in keeping with the theme of this conversation I feel inclined to inform you that I'm also Wednesday's Child."

"W-wait, does that mean…"

The warm glow of their campfire came into view and Thursday clamoured out of the grass into the area they had set up for the night. Matthew was still sitting by the fire, rigid as a statue, but Titus was now sitting up. He looked a lot better than he had when Thursday had dragged him out of the wreckage, so that was encouraging. Sybil was still asleep.

Mackenzie stumbled out after her, eye wide with shock and head flipping back and forth between Thursday in front of her and Whitney behind her. Her gaze then bounced between Matthew and Titus, briefly landing on Sybil's sleeping form before jerking back up to Thursday.

"I suppose there's no point in hoping that Whitney and yourself hang out with humans?" she asked.

"You could try, but it would be very stupid," Thursday shrugged.

Mackenzie swallowed hard but did not run like Thursday had hoped. "So, this is the Seven?"

"Who is this?" Titus asked, watching Mackenzie through critical, but undoubtedly drowsy, eyes.

"This is Mackenzie," Whitney answered, returning to where she previously sat in front of the fire. She resumed warming her hands. "We found her in the grass. She escaped from United Arms and got lost."

"United Arms? Did you ask her if she knew if Dr. Weeks was there?" asked Titus.

"Good question." Thursday squatted by the fire and looked up at Mackenzie. "Was there a blonde doctor at the asylum? Big birdlike nose and eyes the colour of pig crap?"

Mackenzie started shaking her head as soon as Thursday started speaking. "I don't remember," she insisted. "One minute I was walking to his house and then the next minute I'm tied to a bed in the asylum getting my eye gouged out."

"Whose house?" Titus frowned.

"Doesn't matter," Whitney quickly brushed over. "Is that all you remember?"

The human woman edged closer to the campfire, encouraged by the fact that none of them had yet lived up to their violent reputations. She nodded. "I don't remember a lot of it. It's all a blur of torture and pain ...I had to get out of there. It was such a rush; I don't even remember how I got out."

By her feet, Sybil stirred. Their leader awoke with a moan and struggled to sit up. Mackenzie jumped back from the fire, nearly falling backwards into the tall grass. Thursday was amused by how on edge Mackenzie was.

Sybil looked completely taken aback by Mackenzie, her tired eyes taking in the display with unease. "Who is this?" she demanded, instantly suspicious.

"Mackenzie," Thursday answered. "She escaped United Arms."

Sybil looked at Thursday with great alarm. "You allowed an escaped mental patient to follow you back to our camp?" she exclaimed.

"I'm not a mental patient, I was kidnapped!" Mackenzie barked, taking immediate offence to Sybil's comment. She broke free from the grass that was trying to pull her into its grip and brushed her orange hair back from her face indignantly.

"By who?" Titus incredulously asked.

"That's what I'm trying to find out," Mackenzie responded. "That's why I need to get back to …" She looked to Thursday, who gave her a warning look, and trailed off pathetically.

Sybil, never having been one to miss anything, instantly noticed the looks exchanged by the two women. "I don't appreciate secrets being kept from me, Thursday," she said tiredly.

"Mackenzie is like Bram," Whitney bluntly said. "She's obsessed with Sawyer and thinks he'll help her if she finds him. Odds are he's most likely the one who put her into the Asylum in the first place. They were experimenting on her, whether to make her obedient or a metahuman, I don't know."

"My Sawyer would never..." Mackenzie trailed off again when she received four sets of reproachful eyes glaring at her.

"Oh, your Sawyer would, trust me," Sybil answered.

"Hold on, isn't he one of you? Why are you all so hostile?" Mackenzie demanded. "Sawyer did nothing but speak highly of every one of you and yet here you are slandering him and dragging his name through the dirt! Is Sawyer the only decent one of you people?"

Titus snorted with amusement. "You've only seen his good side." He looked thoughtful. "Or you simply choose not to accept his bad side. I mean, he admitted you to an asylum, after all."

"You have no proof of that!"

"Can you count, Mackenzie?"

Mackenzie looked down at Matthew, grimacing at him like she feared he was about to jump to his feet and slap her for speaking. Thursday concluded it was probably because she had bigged up the 'don't praise Sawyer at camp' spiel to the point where Mackenzie expected to be harpooned any moment now.

"Of course, I can count," she replied.

"How many of us are here?" Matthew didn't look at Mackenzie, the fire worthier of his attention. "Not including yourself."

"Five," Mackenzie replied.

"How many are there in the Seven?"

Mackenzie stared at Matthew, confused. It was clear that she couldn't tell if he was joking or not. "Seven, obviously."

"How many are missing, then?"

"Two."

"One of them being?"

"Sawyer, of course."

Matthew turned his head slowly and gazed up at Mackenzie with a bored expression on his face. "The other absent one is Finn, our healer, who has been kidnapped by *your Sawyer* just today right before my eyes and is being held prisoner in Opara City just like you were being held prisoner in United Arms. If you had any sense in that puny brain of yours, you'd use this opportunity of escape to run, run fast and far before Sawyer catches up with you. There's your evidence now shut the fuck up before I do it for you."

Matthew looked back to the fire and immediately resumed his staring. It almost looked like he hadn't spoken at all. Mackenzie gawked at him with her one good eye, completely taken aback at being spoken to in such a way.

Titus raised his eyebrows at Mackenzie. "You're lucky you only got a scolding from him," he dutifully pointed out.

Ignoring the annoying human woman, Thursday crawled over to Sybil. "Are you feeling any better?" she asked.

Sybil shrugged. "A bit, I guess." Her eyes were heavy and lined with wrinkles, the past few days having aged her horribly.

"What about your stomach? Does it hurt?" Thursday asked. "There's still no blood or anything, right?"

Thursday hated playing doctor. This was Finn's role, not hers. She didn't do concern or healing, it went completely against her uncaring, detached image. What in the world would happen if people began to believe that she cared about others? Right now, she was just being Finn's understudy during his absence, with no gooey emotions attached. Or so she liked to believe, anyway...

"Yeah, I'm okay. *We're* okay," Sybil assured. She rubbed her eyes with the heels of her hands. "How is everyone else?"

"Titus seems to be healing just fine and Matthew is acting exactly as I figured he would, so nothing out of the ordinary," Thursday explained.

Sybil shivered and pulled Whitney's jacket over her shoulders. Thursday shrugged her plaid jacket off as well and added it on top as an extra layer. She didn't find it that cold a night anyhow, she would cope without it.

"Can we talk about this as civilised people, at least?" Mackenzie asked.

"Talk about what?" Whitney asked back.

"The current situation."

Thursday sighed and heaved herself to her feet. This woman didn't know when to *shut up.* "What current situation? There's *our* situation and *your* situation. Completely different situations. When morning comes, you'll be going on your merry way, and we will be going on ours. And, as my beautiful friend here by the fire put it, if you had any sense in your carrot top head you'd get as far away from Sawyer as possible."

Mackenzie continued to pretend like she had a higher position in this conversation than she did, tilting her chin up pretentiously as she said, "What if I told you I knew a secret way into United Arms?"

All eyes turned to her, including Matthew's. "What?" Titus asked slowly.

"I escaped from United Arms, remember," Mackenzie said. "It's not like I strolled out through the front door. I went out the back way. You do realise that there's an entire underground network to the Asylum, right? Right below our feet." Mackenzie stamped her foot against the ground.

Sybil eyed Mackenzie critically. "How do we know that you're not lying to us?"

"They took my eye," Mackenzie deadpanned, an unmistakable waver to her voice. "Why would I be on their side?"

"Your precious Sawyer," Whitney reminded her.

Mackenzie folded her arms defiantly. "I still believe that he had nothing to do with that, no many how many times you curse at me for it."

Matthew's face twisted, and he opened his mouth to retaliate. Thursday promptly kicked him to shut him up. "Where is this secret entrance?" she asked.

"Round the back of the Asylum, at the bottom of the hill, there's a trap door covered in grass. It's been there since the Asylum was first built, back when the building was a lot larger. It used to be the service entrance," Mackenzie explained. "It's where I came out when I escaped. I can't remember how I got there … but I did. You'd probably find it quite quick if you follow my path. I mowed down a whole lot of grass trying to find an open road."

Something about Mackenzie's story rubbed Thursday the wrong way. Why couldn't she remember how she escaped the asylum? Surely that wasn't something a person could forget. Unless the trauma of her torture had caused short-term memory loss? She had lost an eye at the hands of the asylum doctors, after all. Maybe she went into a dissociative state for a while and did what she had to do to get out before they completely brainwashed her into one of Sawyer's slaves.

If Mackenzie was telling the truth, then they had a way into United Arms without having to go through the front door. That would buy them more time before Weeks was alerted of their presence in the building. Security at the bottom of the hill was a lot looser than the security at the top of the hill, which meant that they would have a much better chance of infiltrating the asylum.

"The only way I would trust it would be if she came with us to prove it's safe," Titus said.

"Agreed," Whitney and Matthew said at once.

Mackenzie's face fell. "I'm not going back there," she said.

"What if we promised to tell you Sawyer's address in Opara City?" Sybil tempted. "Would you come with us then?"

Mackenzie looked to be struggling through an internal battle. Thursday didn't feel the least bit bad for manipulating her emotions this way. It was the only way they were going to be able to get her to cooperate. Besides, she did *want* to find Sawyer, they weren't forcing her into his arms. And whether they did or didn't know his address in Opara City wasn't relevant right now.

"I'm not entering the asylum. No money in the world would

make me go back there," Mackenzie told them. "I'll show you to the door. Nothing more."

Thursday grinned and thrust her hand out towards Mackenzie. "Deal."

CHAPTER TWELVE

IT WAS HER SOUL DAY.

Thursday didn't know if this was what the Soul Day felt like for the others, but for her, it felt like her ability was constantly buzzing. Like there was some sort of electricity in the air, coaxing her Glow to seep out of her fingertips against her will. Almost like ... desperately needing to pee but knowing that there's no toilet nearby. Except instead of her bladder being the problem, it was her hands.

Thursday was lucky in the sense that her ability was not overly dangerous. Sure, if she focused hard enough her Glow could explode objects but even on her Soul Day such a thing took major concentration. She mainly used her Glow to fly or melt things. So, thankfully, on her Soul Day, she wasn't in danger of blowing people up, like Whitney was.

None of them knew how to explain their origin in the first place, never mind the fact that their abilities were stronger on what they decided to name their 'Soul Day.' It was just how things worked out. Sybil had attempted to explain it away with some vague tirade about how it was probably because it was their day of birth and that in some way made their ability stronger, but beyond that they had nothing.

They had ditched their camp mid-morning the next day and started the trek to United Arms Hill. Due to Mackenzie's help, they would most likely reach the Asylum by nightfall. Thursday was glad about this because it meant that she would be able to face Dr. Weeks when she was at her strongest. There was nothing she wanted more than to wipe the smug smirk off that woman's face by showing her what she was truly capable of when she was at her best.

"You certainly left an obvious trail," Sybil commented as they picked through the grass Mackenzie had trampled during her escape.

Thursday was immensely relieved by the fact that Sybil hadn't shown any signs of miscarriage since the accident. It could have been so easy for Sawyer to try to make fate swing that way with his ability, especially since the child wasn't his, but clearly, he did not want to stoop to that level. Or he had another plan entirely, but that was something they'd toil with later.

"Yeah, you're lucky someone from the Asylum didn't follow you," said Titus. "They would have just been able to follow your path."

Mackenzie, who had been in a much more upbeat mood with the prospect of receiving Sawyer's address at the end of all of this, shrugged happily. "I guess I just got lucky."

Now that it was daytime, Thursday could see Mackenzie with more clarity. There was no way she was an admitted patient; she had been telling the truth about that. If she had been a patient from United Arms, then she would have had a strait jacket and regulation hospital trousers on her. Instead, she was wearing what looked like an ordinary top and skirt, covered in dirt and full of holes, most likely from the ordeal of escaping.

"Luck and the Asylum don't coexist together," Thursday replied. She was directly behind Mackenzie as they walked and was talking to the back of her head.

Something that Thursday found odd, however, was her hair. It was clean and almost completely straight. Shouldn't someone who had been subject to such horrendous torture not look like they had just come out of a salon? Maybe she was overanalysing but there was certainly something strange about the fact that

Mackenzie's ginger hair was tidier than Sybil's auburn locks. And Sybil hadn't been the one to lose an eye in United Arms.

There was something about Mackenzie's story of escape that Thursday still couldn't get her head around. United Arms may have been a corrupt establishment, but it was a well-guarded corrupt establishment. Thursday didn't understand how Mackenzie had escaped from the tight security without getting caught. Unless Thursday's escape and the massacre of guards had somehow impacted the security at the Asylum? But Thursday had always been under the impression that they had plenty of backups.

"I suppose I just sort of escaped when the guards were on break or something," Mackenzie answered.

"The guards are on a rotation," Thursday told her. "They don't leave the wards until their replacement shows up."

There was a pause, and Thursday didn't know whether she should poke Mackenzie to check that she was still listening to her. There was nothing Thursday despised more than getting ignored. Eventually, Mackenzie did reply, her voice slightly strained as she said, "You know the Asylum?"

"Know it?" Thursday laughed. "I practically lived there."

"Understatement," Titus muttered under his breath.

Thursday chuckled and pushed up onto her tiptoes to see Titus over the procession of heads. "Speak up, my love, you know I can't hear you when you mutter like that!"

Titus looked over his shoulder at Thursday. He seemed much better as well (albeit very tired) than he had the previous day. His eyes were less vacant, and the colour had returned to his face. "I said under-statement," he reiterated as if talking to a child.

Thursday grinned and winked at him. "Thank you."

Mackenzie was silent throughout Thursday's exchange with Titus. Thursday couldn't gauge what the human was thinking since she could not see her face, all she had to go on was the obvious jitter to her voice as she said, "Well, whoever was guarding my ward must have been untrained. New, even. Whatever the reason, he didn't know anything about a rotation."

Thursday was surprised when Sybil spoke up before she got a chance to. "It said on the United Arms website that no untrained members of staff are allowed on guard duty, especially not those new to the job. The risk would be too high."

Thursday had been planning to say something along the same lines. Sure, United Arms was not professional, by any means, but it was still a building holding many insane patients. Insane patients that they taunted and tortured regularly. They couldn't risk a breakout, mainly because the first targets would be …well …them. So, they never put untrained personnel in charge of patients or subjects. It was a precaution they took very seriously to save their asses.

"I told you; I don't remember a lot about my escape, anyway," Mackenzie insisted. "I don't know why you keep asking me about it."

Matthew weaved around Thursday, and said as he was passing Mackenzie, "It's because we don't trust you."

Mackenzie stopped and watched Matthew as he trekked ahead, Titus and Whitney in tow. Sybil and Thursday stopped at either side of her. "Why?" she asked, confused.

"Don't listen to him, he's in a bad place right now," Sybil reasoned.

"Why is that?" Mackenzie asked curiously.

"Trust me, it's a long story," Thursday explained. "And it won't exactly paint your precious Sawyer in very generous light, either."

Mackenzie narrowed her eyebrows as she watched the three figures get further ahead of them. "Is it because of that Finn man he mentioned last night? What? Are they brothers or something?"

Thursday couldn't help it: she burst out laughing. Out of all the connections to make between Matthew and Finn, *brothers* had been the first thing Mackenzie had thought of? Sybil even looked mildly amused by the assumption, but she was a lot more dignified about it than Thursday was, choosing not to laugh to the point of having a stitch.

"Not exactly," Sybil answered as Thursday rubbed the tears out of her eyes. "But they did have a particular bond with each other, let's just leave it at that."

"And he's under the impression that Sawyer will hurt this Finn man?" Mackenzie asked as they started walking again.

Thursday folded her arms and sighed. "It's no impression. It's a guarantee," she said seriously.

"What makes you think this?"

"Sawyer wants to make himself unbeatable by combining all the abilities of the Seven into one body," Thursday explained. "His own body. As you know you keep up with the politics of the Seven anyways-Finn was"-

"*Is*," Sybil quickly corrected.

Thursday swallowed hard at the realisation that she had referred to Finn in the past tense, like his not being here already meant he was dead. "Sorry, Finn *is* our healer. Sawyer needs his healing ability to…well…heal. If he can heal himself, who can stop him?"

Mackenzie frowned through Thursday's entire explanation like all of it sounded too fanciful for her comprehension. "I thought your healer couldn't help himself, that's why the government has always tried to uncover his identity first? If he died, then the rest of you wouldn't get healing privileges anymore?"

"The government are biased idiots," Thursday muttered, rolling her eyes.

"You're right, though," Sybil said. "Finn can't heal himself and, yes, the government has always targeted him more than the rest of us because if he died then the rest of us could be easily picked off. They've never been able to uncover our identities, though, and they never will."

"What if I exposed you all?" Mackenzie asked, a smug grin growing on her face.

Thursday glared at her. "If you dared expose us the first thing that I would do the minute I'm arrested is tell them that Sawyer is one of us too. If I'm going down, I'll bring that bastard down with me."

The smile immediately dropped off Mackenzie's face.

"If you want us to comfortably let you go once we find this service entrance, Mackenzie, I wouldn't ask questions like that," Sybil advised. "Matthew already doesn't trust you because of your allegiance to Sawyer and I trust him more than I trust you."

"About Matthew," Mackenzie said, quickly trying to deflect the effect of her moronic comment, "isn't he the Shifter? Shouldn't he have, I don't know, morphed into my idea of beauty or whatever his ability does whenever I looked at him?"

"He has self-control, you know," Thursday answered.

"I helped him train himself to control his ability," Sybil elaborated. "He can change back and forward between two bodies in a millisecond, even less than that. It's so quick you don't even notice it. It's only when he chooses to hold an image that you can notice it. Or when he's placed in a room or situation where there are a lot of people who are highly charged with emotions such as love or lust."

"I see," Mackenzie mused.

Thursday lifted her hand above her eyes to block out the suddenly intense burst of sunlight. If she squinted, she could see the United Arms hill in the distance. Her fingertips began to buzz as her heart sped up. When she lifted her other hand, she saw that small lines of Glow were webbing her fingertips, like static electricity.

"What if I tried to run? Would you let me?" Mackenzie asked.

Sybil looked at her like she was insane. "Why would we stop you?"

"Well ...we have a deal and you're ...well..."

"The Seven," Thursday taunted in a deep voice. She wiggled her glowing fingers in Mackenzie's face. Mackenzie cringed away from Thursday's hands but didn't dispute the answer. Thursday leaned back and rolled her eyes. "You pay too much attention to your television screen."

"If you want to go, you can go," said Sybil. "However, suddenly running away would only lead us to believe that you have been trying to trick us, which means that Titus will be on your tail in an instant."

Mackenzie pulled a face. "And he'd kill me," she concluded.

Thursday snorted. "Murder is my thing, darling, not Titus'."

Watching Mackenzie try to absorb this information was like watching a toddler try to put a square block through a circle hole. It was so easy to believe what was said on television these days, even if it was all warped to fit an agenda or suit a narrative.

Thursday chose not to bother keeping up with local news. As much as she enjoyed listening to them report her crimes and discuss her insanity, it had always left a bad taste in her mouth whenever crimes that had nothing to do with them were instantly pinned onto the Seven. Even when rumours spread through the human circles that the Seven had separated, somehow the media still managed to accuse them of destruction.

It was hard for the humans of Castlebrooke to acknowledge their faults. They preferred to constantly blame the invisible metahumans whom they had never even seen let alone spoken to than maybe look in the mirror and realise that maybe they were no better. It was easier to blame someone who could not fight back than to conclude that you could be the problem.

Thursday thought that it spoke volumes that when the Seven separated, the number of Castlebrooke crimes shot through the roof. That just meant the Seven of them were off committing atrocities on their own. Such rubbish.

"If we were really like how we're depicted on television, you'd be dead by now," Thursday said flatly.

Mackenzie sighed. "I suppose you're right."

"It took a lot of bribing from Whitney to convince me not to kill you," Thursday joked.

The look on Mackenzie's face was hilarious. It was like a screw in her jaw had come loose and now it was hanging open, waiting for a fleet of flies to pass by.

"She's joking," Sybil said.

"How do you know? You were sleeping!" Thursday teased.

"Oh, shut up, woman."

Thursday grinned and continued ahead of them. She could only deal with Mackenzie in small doses. The woman was constantly asking questions and, while Thursday supposed it made sense that she was curious about their abilities, she just couldn't be bothered answering her. Thursday had given up trying to defend her innocence to humans long ago. It was clear they were only going to believe what they wanted to believe.

The sun burned in the sky during their journey, a seventh member of the pack constantly beating into Thursday's back.

She hated walking just as much as she despised running and only hoped that she was right in the prediction that they'd reach the hill by nightfall.

It would almost feel like a normal walk if Finn wasn't missing. Even when Sawyer first left the group, they had spent a great deal of time together as a sextuplet. Thursday remembered when they used to go out on walks with Titus every other morning when he was struggling with his weight. Some days were beyond freezing, and Thursday always thought her fingers were going to snap off into tiny icicles, and then other days were like this, so hot that Thursday felt like she was legitimately melting. She still went out on the walks, despite the weather and her distaste for exercise. Titus liked the company.

"What would you be doing right now if all this hadn't started?" Whitney asked mid-afternoon. Thankfully, the sun was beginning to lay off a little and Thursday could remove her hand from above her eyes and not be blinded by a massive golden blot.

"I'm in charge of a dance recital that is supposed to be on tomorrow," Titus sighed. "I doubt I'll make it."

"Ballet?" Sybil asked.

"Yeah. It was only a recital for children, but I take them just as seriously as the adult ones. Especially with ballet," Titus replied. "It's important to nurture the desire to dance when it's young so that it can flourish properly."

"I wanted to be a ballerina," Mackenzie said thoughtfully. "I watched Swan Lake when I was a kid and I fell in love with it. My parents discouraged it. They wanted me to do gymnastics instead. I didn't stick with it. It wasn't the same."

Titus laughed. "If we survive through all of this and you don't turn out to be a mole or double agent, drop by the studio and join a class. Adult classes are on Friday nights," he told her. "If you're still up for it, that is."

Mackenzie looked genuinely taken aback by such an offer. "Thanks," she feebly replied.

"Can I join, Titus?" Thursday asked sweetly, clasping her hands together and rubbing herself against the dancer's arm.

"No," Titus answered.

"D'aw, why not? I fancy myself a rather good ballerina."

"You're not serious about dancing."

"There is that," Thursday conceded.

Thursday could have been hallucinating due to heat stroke, but she could have sworn she saw the corner of Titus' mouth quirk upwards into a smile. Maybe he was delusional because of lack of sleep. Lack of sleep and the heat.

"What would you have been doing then, Thursday?" Whitney prompted.

"Uh … What time is it?" Thursday looked to the sky, giving the impression that she knew how to read the time of day from the sun's position when she honestly had no idea. "I think I'd be in for questioning again. They usually took me in around afternoon-evening time."

"By questioning …do you mean"-

"ZAP!" Whitney jumped in surprise when Thursday yelled, crossing her eyes, and pressing her fingers into her temples to mimic Dr. Weeks' electric shock therapy.

"I remember that part," Mackenzie said quietly.

Thursday rotated her upper half around to look at Mackenzie. "How many volts, do you think?"

Mackenzie shook her head. She suddenly looked very pale. "There's no way to tell. When it was happening, I didn't know if it was possible or not, but it felt like millions. Then his face would flash in between, and I didn't know if it was a saving grace or a bad omen."

Thursday frowned and turned around completely. "Sawyer?"

"Over and over and over," Mackenzie said quietly. "The only time I ever saw him was when they briefly stopped."

Was it possible that Sawyer used fear conditioning to make the humans dependent on him? Never mind keeping them in a basement until they developed Stockholm Syndrome, if someone was tortured enough and led to believe that someone was their only reprieve, of course, they would grow to love and depend on them. How had Thursday not considered this before? She felt so stupid. Of course, Sawyer wouldn't leave a facility like United Arms unused! Who knew how many humans could be under conditioning there?

Sybil wrapped an arm around Mackenzie's shoulders. "Remember, you don't have to go back in. You're only taking us to the door," she assured her.

Mackenzie nodded. Her eye glittered in the evening sunlight. Oh, dear God, she was crying again. Thursday tried not to turn her nose up. She turned back around to Whitney and Titus.

"Hey, Whitney, you haven't said what y"-

Something pushed through Thursday's ribcage and grabbed hold of her heart. She screamed in agony and her Glow exploded from her hands, singeing the grass at either side of her. She was held up by the pain for a long moment, as an invisible hand reached into her chest and was squeezing her heart. Thursday grappled at her throat and tried to breathe, the world around her spinning as she fought to get oxygen into her body.

Then it was gone.

The invisible hand released her, and she fell onto the ground. Thursday gasped, desperately sucking air back into her body. Her heart was beating faster than ever, trying to make up for the lost time. She instantly recognised what had just happened.

Finn.

Thursday threw herself off the ground. Her head spun, and she instantly stumbled back onto her knees.

Confirming her suspicion, everyone but Mackenzie was on the ground, each one of them looking as mortified as Thursday felt. Sybil was clenching her chest and heaving; Whitney had vomited into the grass; and Titus was pounding his chest as he tried to breathe properly again. Matthew was scrambling around on the trampled grass, trying to stand but inevitably falling over again.

"Mat-Mat-Mattie, tak-take a min-min-min-minute!" Thursday choked out.

Matthew crumpled to the ground. Thursday saw his fist go up and down, up, and down, up and down, beating the earth like it was somehow responsible for what had just happened.

Finn was not dead, but something bad had just happened to him. Whatever it was, it was severe enough for the five of them to feel it. The only conclusion Thursday could reach was that Finn had *almost* died and that was what that moment of agony had been. It was different from when Whitney had almost drowned. Almost like their deaths being at the hands of one of their own made the impact so much worse.

Mackenzie dropped to her knees beside Sybil and started rubbing her back. "What just happened?" she cried out.

Thursday braced herself against the ground for a moment, ignoring Mackenzie while she regained her composure. She glanced beneath her arm and noticed that Sybil was crying. Whitney had stopped vomiting and was sitting in the crushed grass, head between her knees, but Thursday could see how tensed her body was. She was fighting it, too. When Titus looked over at Matthew, the sunlight caught his eyes and Thursday saw the beads of saltwater sitting precariously on his lids, as well.

Thursday reached up and touched her face. Her fingertips slid through something wet.

Oh.

She was crying, too.

~T~

Thursday looked at the dingy door with disdain. The Summer day had morphed into a Winter night. It was even starting to rain, which just perfectly matched the wretched mood everyone had been in since the Meadows. Thursday preferred the cold over the blistering heat, even though Sybil still had her jacket. Sybil had tried to give it back, but Thursday refused. She didn't need it, anyway. She hadn't caught a cold since 1923.

It was a wooden trap door right at the bottom of the United Arms Hill. Drenched in the thick cover of black that the night provided, it could be easily hidden in the shadows of the forest.

The asylum itself stood high above them right on top of the hill; an intimidating giant drenched in shadow. It was a presence Thursday had never been able to shake, no matter how hard she tried.

"So, this is the service entrance?" Whitney asked.

Mackenzie stood as far from the door as she could, her arms folded against the cold. She nodded frantically. "Yeah, that's it. That's the door I came out of," she said. The closer they had gotten to the asylum, the greener she had turned in pallor.

Thursday blew a loose strand of hair out of her face just in time for a fat droplet of rain to nail her right in the eye. "Beautiful. Let's do this, then."

Titus thrust his arm out in front of Thursday as she took a step forward. "We need a plan, first."

"Yeah, the plan is to find Dr. Weeks, make Matthew shift, and find out what the eyepatch does," Thursday said.

"I mean for as soon as we enter, genius," said Titus. "For all we know there could be twenty armed guards down there."

"I'll blow them all apart, just like I did when we were rescuing Thursday," Whitney said firmly.

Thursday raised her eyebrows, impressed. "Really?"

Whitney's gaze was sharp as a knife, slicing through Thursday's skin like it was nothing but cotton. "This is necessary. I never want to experience pain like that again. And if that's what we felt, imagine what *he* felt. We need to get Finn out of Opara as quickly as possible. I don't care what I must go through anymore. If they're working for Sawyer, then they're already condemned."

"Only kill if it's directly necessary to the mission," Sybil shouted as the rain grew heavier. "We are not going to live up to our reputations! We do not kill innocent people!"

"Why shouldn't we live up to our reputations?" Matthew challenged. "They're never going to change their minds, Sybil! Don't you see that? They hate us anyway! We might as well just kill every sorry sod in there until we reach Weeks!"

Sybil glowered. "Don't say things that would make Sawyer proud."

Matthew's bottom lip trembled. Whether it be from anger or sadness, Thursday was unable to tell. He didn't say anything back to Sybil. Maybe he knew that anything he said would be construed as a product of his extreme bias towards the immediate rescue of Finn. Thursday certainly didn't believe that he truly wanted to plough through hundreds of innocent people just to reach Dr. Weeks. He didn't have the mind of a cold, heartless killer. He just wanted Finn back with them, safe and unharmed.

"I changed my mind," Mackenzie said.

"What?" Thursday looked sharply at the human woman.

"I …I, uh, thought Sawyer was the only good member of the Seven. I, uh, realised during our journey that maybe the way the

News talks about you is wrong," Mackenzie explained. "You're all just sort of ...normal."

Thursday didn't know what to do with this. By the looks of the other four, they didn't either. Thursday looked away, refusing to look at Mackenzie anymore. She didn't like not knowing what to say to people. Normally, she had plenty to say, but now she had nothing. Never in her life had she ever been confronted by such an admission, especially not by a human. Every human that had ever learned of their identity had to be killed because they saw them for what they had been built up to be. The vermin of Castlebrooke. Never had they ever changed their minds.

"Thanks, I guess," Whitney awkwardly said.

"Thanks for bringing us here, too," Sybil added.

Mackenzie looked at her feet. "Yeah, no problem."

Matthew grabbed the handle on the trap door and pulled it open. Thursday and the others crowded around him and gazed inside. It was completely black. Thursday whistled in appreciation, and it echoed down into the abyss beyond the doors.

"That's deep," Titus commented.

"That's what he said," Matthew quietly said under his breath.

Thursday glanced at her friend and smiled. "So, who's going in first?"

"Whitney should," Sybil ordered. "She would need to be at the front in case there are any guards at the bottom. You think you'll be able to get angry enough to unlock your inferno?"

Whitney laughed hollowly. "Oh, trust me, there will be no issue."

Thursday stepped back to give Whitney room to step through the door. There must have been stairs somewhere in that thick black space as her foot connected with something and she was able to descend. Titus followed her and then Sybil. Then Matthew. Thursday took up the rear, in case someone saw them going in and decided to follow them.

The rain had gotten unbearably heavy. Thursday could just about make out Mackenzie standing in the treeline, watching them go. "You better get going if you don't want to get caught," she advised.

Mackenzie nodded. "Yeah, okay."

Thursday turned around and stepped down into the unknown. It was as she was shutting the door that she realised something. Her stomach bottomed out as it hit her like a freight train.

Mackenzie didn't ask for Sawyer's address.

"Wait!" Mackenzie suddenly shouted from above her. "Don't go in! It's a trap!"

Thursday's heart lurched into her throat, and she spun around, trying to throw the trap door open again before it was too late. Two arms immediately wrapped around Thursday's middle and pulled her down the stairs. Her hand was forced from the door handle, and she was dragged down into the void.

The trap door snapped shut behind her, locking out Mackenzie's voice as she continued to scream into the unforgiving night.

CHAPTER THIRTEEN

THURSDAY YELLED AS SHE WAS THROWN DOWN THE REMAINING STAIRS. She hit the concrete floor below with a smack, Glow exploding uncontrollably from her hands as a sharp pain shot through her neck. Fucking Mackenzie. Thursday knew there was something weird about that woman, why had she been so stupid? Matthew had been right the entire time; they shouldn't have trusted her!

A light exploded above her head. It took her a moment to realise that the gates of heaven hadn't opened before her, and it was just an artificial light.

"Oh my god, Thursday!" Sybil's voice was echoed and when Thursday's eyes adjusted to the sudden burst of light, she realised they were in a massive concrete bunker that was, presumably, beneath the asylum. "Are you alright?"

"Who threw me?" Thursday roared angrily, throwing herself to her feet and spinning around in search of the perpetrator.

A boot connected between her shoulder blades and kicked her forward. She landed face-first against the ground, her nose taking the brunt of the impact. Sybil screamed in horror but was drowned out by Thursday's scream. Hers was more out of rage than pain. She flipped onto her back to see who the hell had the nerve to touch her this way.

A man Thursday didn't recognise loomed over her with a satisfied smirk on his face. He wasn't wearing a United Arms uniform, which led her to believe that he was another one of Sawyer's projects working from the Castlebrooke base.

Thursday bolted off the ground and attached herself to the freak, digging her nails into the man's face and scratching wherever her hands could find purchase. She wrapped her legs around him and squeezed as tight as she could so that he couldn't unseat her easily.

"Thursday, grab his hair!" Titus shouted from somewhere Thursday couldn't see.

Thursday grabbed a handful of her attacker's hair and held his head steady, knowing exactly what Titus was about to do.

When Titus' foot connected with the man's face, Thursday kept a firm grip on his hair to keep his head up. He tried to unseat her by trying to throw himself against a wall. Titus predicted this, grabbing a fistful of his shirt, and kneeing him in the gut. None of their attacks seemed to be making much of an impression on their attacker. He was even beginning to *laugh* at them.

"Get out of the way!" Sybil barked.

Thursday jumped from the man's back at Sybil's word, Titus also lunging out of the way.

Sybil thrust her hand out and threw it in the direction of the wall. The smile fell from the man's smug face as his body was thrown against the wall so hard that his head cracked open on impact. It seemed that Sawyer enhanced the humans to be strong, but he did not try to make them unbreakable. Thursday doubted that he cared all that much about losing any of his artificial metahumans.

As the man slid to the ground and began to bleed on the floor, Thursday got an opportunity to fully digest the situation. Whitney was lying unconscious on the ground. That explained why the attack hadn't been swiftly ended with streams of fire. She didn't seem to be severely hurt but there was a lump on her head. She'd been struck as soon as she got off the ladder.

The only object in the concrete room was the ladder in which they had descended from the trapdoor. Thursday threw herself at it and made quick work of ascending back up to the door in question. She pushed up on it, but it didn't give. "Mackenzie!" she screamed. "Mackenzie, you pathetic excuse for a being! Unlock this door now!"

No one answered her. The only sound beyond the locked door was the rhythmic beating of the rain against the wood. Thursday yelled in frustration and threw herself off the steps, choosing to use her Glow to fly back down to the floor. "I will kill her," she announced as soon as her feet hit the floor. "I will find out where she lives and kill her in her sleep."

"We were idiots," Matthew said plainly. "We should have known better than to let her trick us."

The more Thursday pondered on Mackenzie's betrayal and their stupidity in the matter, the angrier she got. "I'm going to blast that door open," she growled, spinning on her heel, and pushing her Glow towards the ground to thrust herself back into the air.

"You can't!" Sybil shouted.

Thursday looked over her shoulder at their leader as she hovered in mid-air. "What do you mean, I *can't*?" she spat.

Sybil closed her eyes regretfully. She pointed to the only other door in the room. There was a piece of paper attached to it.

Thursday shook the Glow from her hands and landed back on the floor. She marched up to the door and snatched the page off.

It was a note.

Try anything, and the healer will die.

I'll be around to see you when we come to pick up Jacob's body.

~Dr. Weeks

Thursday stared at the words intensely, as if they were somehow going to rearrange themselves into a better message. When they stayed the same, she ripped the page apart. "They're watching us?" she screamed, throwing the tiny pieces of paper into the air. "How? I'll break every one of their damn cameras!"

"You do anything that endangers Finn, and I will take you down myself, Thursday," Sybil said measuredly.

Thursday glared at Sybil. "I would have expected Matthew to say something like that," she sneered.

"I mean it, Thursday." A pause. "Maybe it's a bluff," Sybil reasoned.

"It's not exactly a trivial bluff," Titus sighed. "The consequences if they are telling the truth could be catastrophic."

"So, you're just going to lie down and take this, then?" Thursday yelled.

"What else is there?" Sybil demanded. "We blast open the door? Finn is dead. You damage their cameras? Finn is dead. You do *anything* that they don't like? Finn is dead. Do you *want* to be responsible for him being dead?"

"Maybe that's just the consequence of him getting caught in the first place!" Thursday didn't know what she was talking about. She was just so *angry*. Her mouth was going way ahead of her brain, and she couldn't control it. There was still logic to her statement, though. They couldn't simply do *nothing*. They'd be playing right into Sawyer's grasp if they did nothing!

Matthew lunged to his feet and squared up to Thursday. "Keep talking, Thursday, see where it gets you," he growled.

"Or what? You'll hit me?" Thursday snapped. "Go ahead, hit me! Or do you have to be a girl before you can bring yourself to hit a woman?"

"I will hit you no matter what I look like if you do anything stupid," Matthew snarled.

"Hey, you two, calm down a minute," Titus said, trying to step in.

Thursday grabbed Matthew by the shirt and threw him against the nearest wall. "Finn wouldn't want us trapped in here like sitting ducks! If we don't get out of here, Sawyer is going to find us! Finn wouldn't want us to be quibbling over whether we should be risking his life, and you know it!"

"Don't try to tell me what he would or wouldn't want, Thursday!" Matthew snapped out of Thursday's grip and spun them, so he was now pushing her against the wall. He had a much stronger grip than her and despite the fact she knew he wasn't exerting his full strength on her; she still couldn't snap out as easily. "I know full well what he would want!"

"Yeah, for us to escape!"

"Finn tries to be a damn martyr, of course, he'd want us to damn well escape!"

Thursday felt her hands beginning to glow again. She tried to smother her outrage, but she was struggling. Everything had just turned so pear-shaped so fast. They had gone from having a decent plan and way forward to being completely trapped with no aid.

"Matthew, I'm going to teach you a philosophy I think it's about time you learned," Thursday said carefully, her voice aggressive but controlled.

Matthew glared at her but did not speak. His hands were trembling as they dug into her shoulders. Thursday made sure to hold eye contact with him as she spoke her next few words.

"One life does not equate to five."

Matthew's eyebrows bowed upwards, and his jaw clenched. Thursday watched him wearily, her chest heaving as her rage began to ebb. She wasn't trying to hurt Matthew, but he had to know the truth of the situation. Both she and Whitney had told him that there was a possibility that Finn was going to get caught up in the crossfire back at camp. This was exactly the sort of thing that they meant. Of course, Thursday had known that Matthew probably wouldn't have accepted such a thing even if Sawyer had sent them a personal note detailing such a prospect to them himself.

Matthew lifted his fist and for one slightly jarring moment, Thursday thought that he was going to hit her. Matthew, her closest friend; the person she had trusted the most through her entire existence; who she had run through the corn fields with to steal back Sybil's money; the only one who would play noughts and crosses with her; who she had found hiding in an apple tree beside an old orphanage in Castlebrooke, sitting on the highest branch trying to hide from human view …was about to hit her.

Of course, Thursday wasn't angry at Matthew. He had been driven to this point. They had all been driven to this point. By Sawyer. They were being forced to choose between two horrible resolutions, all to satisfy Sawyer. He didn't consider how they would feel about it or what emotional strain this would cause them. Sawyer only cared about himself and how he felt and about the perverse connection he felt between them that he called love.

The wall by her head cracked. Thursday turned and looked at Matthew's fist as it dug into the concrete. She returned her gaze to his face. Tears freely fell from his eyes and slid to the ground, his fist dragging down the wall with him.

"I'm sorry," he whispered hoarsely.

Thursday frowned and wrapped her arms around his head. "This isn't your fault, idiot," she muttered between her teeth.

"I don't want to lose him," Matthew cried, voicing for the first-time what Thursday knew he had been thinking the entire time.

"I know." Thursday clenched her teeth tight, feeling her mask slip. She pushed her dark hair back behind her ear as if trying to put it back on. "We knew that this was going to happen eventually."

"Like this, though?" Titus said despondently.

Thursday pressed her face into Matthew's hair and closed her eyes. They'd always known that they would eventually overstay their welcome. Even immortals had a time limit. Thursday had always thought she would die grandly, in a blaze of fire and a rain of bullets, cackling with joy the entire way out. Thursday had never imagined that any of them would meet their end in an underground prison, upon Sawyer's order.

If they killed Finn-if *Sawyer dared* to kill Finn-then Thursday would rip open the ground and bring hell to earth to avenge him.

Thursday reluctantly detached herself from Matthew and moved to the door that the note had been pinned to. She flicked her hands and ignited her Glow, lifting them to the door and putting her energy into increasing the intensity of the Glow.

It was difficult, due to the bump to the head she had received after being thrown down the stairs, but she was aided by her Soul Day strength.

The door flew open, and Thursday jumped. Had she done that?

As soon as Thursday's gaze landed on Dr. Weeks, her body acted before her brain even fully comprehended the situation. She lunged at the woman and grabbed her by the lapels of her coat, dragging her into the room and throwing her against the wall.

"Where is he?" she screamed at her.

Someone-Thursday presumed a bodyguard Weeks had brought with her-was dragging her from the woman. Dr. Weeks sighed and straightened her coat as Thursday was pulled away. "That's not a very nice welcome, Thursday."

Titus grabbed Dr. Weeks by the shoulder and floored her with a single punch. The guard released Thursday when he saw this and ran for the dancer. Titus jumped out of the man's way, weaving around behind him, and giving him an extra push by kicking his ass forward. The guard couldn't stop and stumbled head-first into the same wall that Sybil had tossed the human subjugate against.

"Stop this right now or your precious healer won't live through the night!" Dr. Weeks barked. Her voice was harsh and nasally as her nose gushed blood all over her hand. Thursday took cruel pleasure in the fact that Titus had flattened the gigantic tumour the doctor had called a nose.

Matthew was next to his feet, jumping over Whitney's unconscious body and dragging Dr. Weeks off the ground. "Where is he?" he hissed. "What has Sawyer done with him? Tell me!"

Thursday did a double take. It wasn't Matthew holding Dr Weeks, it was Sawyer.

Even Dr. Weeks herself looked overwhelmed by the sudden change. It was clear that she had underestimated how intense being confronted by one's ideal picture of beauty was, just like many others before her had done. Even though she had probably seen Sawyer regularly, Matthew's ability always took the vision of beauty and improved them so that not a single flaw existed. For example, both of Sawyer's eyes were wide open and the birthmark stood out on the right eye, clear as day. No need for an eyepatch.

The *eyepatch*!

"Sybil!" Thursday shouted. "The eyepatch!"

Sybil dug her hand into her pocket and produced the eyepatch, quickly chucking it to Thursday. Thursday caught it clumsily and dragged Matthew away from Dr. Weeks to put it on. She grabbed a handful of his long dark hair and pulled his head back, not even bothering to check if it was the right way around before slapping it over his marked eye.

Matthew stepped back from Thursday and Weeks, the patch covering what would have been his emerald, green eye if he had been in normal form. Dr. Weeks had started backing away. Thursday snorted. The woman must have known that there was nothing she could do to prevent them from discovering what the purpose of the eyepatch was now.

"What's happening?" Titus asked.

"Letters are appearing on the screen. It's spelling something out," Matthew answered, frowning.

"What's it spelling out?" Sybil pressed.

Matthew was still frowning, clearly waiting for the screen to stop spelling. Then, suddenly, his hand snapped up and he ripped the eyepatch off. As the patch left his eye, he flickered back into his ordinary form. He looked mortified; his usually unblemished skin having turned a sickly pale colour.

"What did it say?" Thursday exclaimed.

Matthew held the patch away from his body like it was radioactive. He was shaking his head in denial and had begun sweating profusely.

"Matthew, talk to us!" Sybil exclaimed. "What did it say?"

Matthew looked up at them, face painted with fear. "Gotcha."

As soon as the word left his mouth, the door slammed shut.

Thursday spun around. Dr. Weeks had locked them back in. She threw herself at the door and started pounding it with her fists. "Get back in here, Weeks!" she roared. Her voice had gone shrill with panic. "*Weeks!*"

There was a loud bang from behind her and Matthew roared in pain. Thursday looked back behind her and watched with horror as Sawyer's eyepatch landed on the ground in a shower of sparks. It was releasing a thick, green gas that was quickly filling the room.

"Hold your breath!" Thursday shouted before slapping her hand over her mouth and nose. The others did the same, Titus rushing to Sybil and helping her take her jacket off, so she could cover her mouth with it.

Thursday turned on the door and lashed out on it. She couldn't scream for Dr. Weeks to come back. Ultimately, she knew that this was a losing battle, but that did not mean that she was going to go out without a fight. She threw her free hand out and let the Glow return, but her brain was already beginning to spin from the gas, and she couldn't concentrate on getting it to grow strong enough to blast the door open.

This gas was not meant to kill them, that much was obvious, but Thursday found it more disconcerting that they would be unconscious for who knew how long. This had been Sawyer's intention from the beginning. As soon as they located Dr. Weeks and used her to put the eyepatch on Matthew, the patch was designed to combust and knock them out. Thursday could only assume so that Sawyer could come pick them up.

Thursday's beating against the door grew weaker and weaker. She couldn't breathe. She *needed* to breathe. Her lungs felt like they were shrivelling up inside her body and if she didn't gasp for breath soon, she was going to pass out. It was impossible to die or even pass out from self-suffocation but that hardly mattered. Either way, she was done for.

Thursday turned around and the ground spun beneath her feet. She stumbled into Matthew, who clumsily caught her as he sank to the floor in submission. Thursday dragged him against her, using her last moment of conscious thought to show her friend that they were still good, despite it all. Maybe it was also for a bit of comfort, but she would never admit that to anyone.

Thursday's eyes fluttered heavily and the last thing she saw before they shut was the door to the cell reopening.

CHAPTER FOURTEEN

THURSDAY WOKE UP VERY SUDDENLY. She fell off whatever she was sitting on with a yelp, her exclamation punctuated by a rattle of chains. She looked around frantically, trying to figure out where she was, but her brain was too fuzzy to fully understand what was going on. It must have been the gas still in her system, but she could have sworn they were in a Church.

She had been sitting on a chair that was part of a front row of many others. Thursday struggled back up onto her seat and glanced down the row. To her left, Whitney and Titus sat, chained up as well. To her right, Sybil, and Matthew. It seemed she had been the last to wake up.

"What's going on?" Thursday blurted out. The room was compact, but her voice still echoed around the walls like an annoying twin repeating her.

Sybil didn't answer, all she did was nod her head towards the top of the room.

Thursday looked to where Sybil had gestured. An altar? Yeah, that was an altar. There was a crucifix up there and everything. How had they gone from a cold, concrete cell to a Church? Titus was the only Christian one here, for Goodness sake! Why were there flowers everywhere, too? What in the name of insanity was happening here? Something was not right here.

"Welcome home!" A voice suddenly boomed, causing the five of them to jump in their seats.

Thursday jumped to her feet instantly at the sight of Sawyer walking up the aisle between the rows of chairs. He was dressed up in a fancy black suit like he was about to attend an especially important meeting. "What is this about, Sawyer?" she shouted. She tried to get closer to him, but her chains tightened around her wrists and ankles, preventing her from taking more than five steps away from her seat.

Sawyer took a step up onto the altar at the top of the room, ignoring Thursday's question completely. The madman was wearing his usual uncomfortably wide smirk. He no longer wore an eyepatch and was opening and closing his marked eye with no issue. The entire thing had been a ruse from start to finish.

"Answer her!" Sybil barked. "Or I'll throw you right off that altar!"

"You won't do that," Sawyer laughed.

"Didn't we have this conversation at the hospital?" Sybil growled. She was already standing up, preparing to throw Sawyer against another wall if the need presented itself.

Sawyer sighed dreamily; his eyes misty as he watched Sybil stand. He shook his head, having the gall to look *amused* at their distress, and walked around the altar. Sybil's hand shot into the air, her chains complaining but not tightening enough to restrain her. Thursday hoped she threw him against something sharp.

Sawyer reached behind the altar and grabbed something, pulling it up from behind the stone where it had been out of sight.

No. Not something.

Someone.

"Finn!" Matthew was off his seat so fast he tripped over his chains as they tightened. He staggered up again and started pulling against them as hard as he possibly could. "Finn! You bastard, what have you done?!"

Finn pushed Sawyer away from him and stumbled down the steps of the altar and fell in front of Matthew. They hugged each other, holding on so tight Thursday wondered if they could even breathe. They were talking to each other, but Thursday couldn't hear what they were saying. It didn't matter.

Thursday had tortured many people in her past, but she had never seen such damage before. The healer had to lean against Matthew, he was so weak. There were stitches all over his face and arms, so many places where he had been opened and probed and then stitched shut again.

But his *hand*...

There were patches of red from where the skin had been stained with blood, but most of the appendage had turned a painful purple, so dark it almost looked completely black. And there, on the fourth finger, was a golden ring, emblazed with sparkling red jewels. A wedding band. Except the piece of jewellery had buried itself into Finn's finger so that, Thursday guessed, it could not be removed.

"How does it feel, Matthew?" Sawyer asked, a sick grin on his face. "He married me first."

"I'll kill you!" Matthew screamed.

"Sawyer, I'm warning you!" Sybil yelled.

Sawyer smiled at Sybil. "I mean, you could hurt me. But if you do, I have men outside this Church with orders to come in and shoot Finn on sight if anything happens to me."

Thursday clenched her fists. It had been so easy to have the moral high ground when they had been given a vague threat and she wasn't looking right into Finn's eyes. "What do you want?" she asked.

Sawyer pointed at a pillow that was sitting on top of the altar. He picked it up and stepped down to show them what was on it.

Thursday felt sick.

There were five more rings.

"You're still on that stupid notion of marrying us all?" Thursday spat at him. "How pathetic."

Sawyer sighed at the pillow and shrugged. "You have a weird way of expressing your love, Thursday."

Thursday was horrified by his implication. "You think that I"-

"I *know* you do," Sawyer interrupted. "Finn knows. I taught him. Don't you understand, Finn?"

Matthew wasn't letting go of Finn any time soon, so the healer had to speak over Matthew's shoulder instead. "Don't bother trying, Thursday. I don't know what happened to him since he left us but he's even more unhinged than before. He believes that we all love him just like he loves us."

"Marriage is only marriage if there is consent, Sawyer," Titus growled. "You won't find any consent in this room."

Sawyer picked up one of the rings. "The rings are the consent!" he excitedly explained. "They're a symbol of your consent! And once we're all joined together in matrimony, I'll bring us together body and soul!"

"Otherwise known as killing us," Whitney threw back.

"You won't die, you'll all be here." Sawyer placed his hand flat on his stomach.

Thursday pulled a face. "Your guts?"

"My *being*." Sawyer closed his eyes and inhaled, relishing the very thought.

Thursday leaned back, her skin crawling at the very idea of being anywhere near him ever again. How did she ever touch this man in any manner that wasn't a punch to the face? Sawyer's insanity had reached a branch even Thursday couldn't reach, and she and Sawyer used to pride themselves on understanding one another's crazy. She didn't know what happened to him when he left them but whatever it had been, it had turned him into something she didn't even recognise.

"Sybil already bears the fruits of my labour, see!" Sawyer gently put the pillow down and hurried over to Sybil. He was pointing at her baby bump.

"Stay away from me, Sawyer," Sybil said in a faint voice, holding her hands up to keep him at a distance.

"The baby isn't yours," Thursday dutifully pointed out. "Didn't Bram get word to you?"

Sawyer laughed. "Of course, the baby isn't mine, Thursday," he said. "Sybil and I have not had a physical relationship in decades."

Thursday didn't understand. Neither did the others, by the looks of it.

"What the hell do you mean by fruits of your labour, then?" Titus demanded.

Sawyer's smile disintegrated a little. "Didn't she ever tell you?"

"Tell us what?" Whitney snapped.

Sybil was beginning to look extremely uncomfortable. Thursday looked between her and Sawyer, trying to figure out what secret the two of them had been keeping from the rest of them.

"I experimented on Sybil during our relationship to make her capable of conceiving a child," Sawyer took pleasure in explaining. "Coupled with the tests that I conducted on myself to make myself fertile, I worked extremely hard to make our relationship work in every conceivable way. Right down to having a child. Except I never got to see if what I had done worked before we broke up…"

Finn finally sat back from Matthew's embrace, although their hands remained intertwined. "Did she consent to these experiments?"

Sawyer looked peevish for a moment. "Consent is a barrier in terms of experimentation. No one knows the true benefits they will have until it's all over"-

"So that's a no," Matthew interrupted.

Thursday stared at Sawyer, waiting for him to announce that it was a joke. He didn't. He simply continued to beam at them, waiting for them to shower him with compliments and praise. He ...he ...he ...*experimented* on Sybil right under their very noses? He hurt her against her will while the rest of them remained oblivious and treated him like the family they believed he was.

"Sybil, you should have told me," Thursday growled. She was pulling against her chains again, trying to get to Sawyer so that she could rip him open and decorate the flowers with his blood.

"I didn't want to," Sybil firmly replied. She drew herself up to her full height and indignantly held up her chin. "I knew you'd react exactly like this."

"But Sybil-" Whitney began.

"I am not a child!" Sybil snapped back. "This was my problem and I handled it myself."

Sawyer gestured to Sybil's baby bump with both his hands. "And look!" he declared. "It worked! You're pregnant! Who's the lucky man?"

Sybil eyed Sawyer tiredly. "That's none of your concern."

There was a sparkle of malice in Sawyer's eyes that Thursday didn't like. She pulled harder against her chains, but they refused to release her. "Oh, it's very much my concern. I need to know who I must deal with."

"You won't need to deal with anyone."

"Why is that?"

Sybil squeezed her eyes tight. "He's already dead," she said quietly. "He died a month after I conceived."

There was silence in the Church. Thursday stopped her tugging and stood there uselessly for a moment.

It wasn't that Sybil hadn't wanted to speak about the father of her child this whole time, she *couldn't*.

Sybil had always had this impression that her problems were hers. She never shared anything. Thursday felt awful. She should have pushed Sybil harder back at Del Monte Forest Manor. She should have made her say something, *anything* about the father that could have lessened the burden she was carrying.

Then there was laughter.

Sawyer was *laughing*.

"Ah, well, that's good, then!" he chuckled. "One less job for me!"

"You sick bastard," Whitney snarled.

Thursday wanted to call Sawyer every colourful name she had gathered in her long and tiring life. She wanted to rip the chair straight out of the floor and throw it at him. She wanted to strangle him with the very chains that bound her into place. How *dare* he do this to Sybil? How *dare* he do this and still claim that he loved her?

Finn suddenly stood up and crossed the distance to Sawyer in two long strides. Taking advantage as the only one not chained up, he punched Sawyer across the jaw with his good hand so forcefully that Sawyer's head jerked in the opposite direction.

Sawyer rolled his head around on his neck, a dopey grin on his face as blood began to seep out of his lip. "I thought you were a pacifist?" he chuckled.

Finn shook his hand. He had hit Sawyer so hard that his knuckles were already starting to discolour. "I made an exception," he muttered.

This answer made Sawyer laugh. Then, like a switch flipped, he turned and punched the healer right back. Except Sawyer had years of experience with violence and easily floored Finn with a single hit. The hit didn't knock him out, but it had disorientated him because he had to brace himself against the floor. Thursday concluded that Sawyer had probably enhanced his strength in the same way that he had enhanced Bram's.

"Don't hit me again, darling, please and thank you," Sawyer told Finn in a patronising voice.

"Touch another one of my family again and I will rain down on you like fucking Ezekiel 24.17," Thursday growled.

Sawyer held his hands up. "I do not intend to harm," he insisted. This statement was ironic because Finn had more stitches than skin by Sawyer's hand.

Sawyer spun around, hair flying around his shoulders like a woman in a shampoo commercial. Retrieving his pillow, he returned to them and asked, "Who's first?"

"How about Bas?" Matthew challenged. "You promised he'd be a member of the Seven, after all. Oh, wait, you can't. You killed him!"

Sawyer looked completely lost for a moment. Thursday wanted to say that she was disgusted that he couldn't remember who Bas was, but she had been guilty of the same thing in the past. They had all lived so long, lovers came and went. Names and faces and stories are all so different and so unique. Sometimes they all mixed into a medley, and it grew hard to separate and connect everything. It was one of the few things about her immortality that Thursday could say that she deeply despised. If she could, she would remember every human who had affected her life.

Sawyer's eyes lit up. "Oh, Bas! I remember him. Yes, he was a clingy one for sure. He wanted me to break up with you, Sybil, can you imagine?"

"Your people murdered him," Sybil deadpanned.

"Yeah, but he was a human, so where was the loss, really?" Sawyer answered.

"Why did you tell him he could be an eighth member of the Seven?" Matthew asked. "Why did you lead him on like that?

Why did you abuse his trust to then strap him to a table and take his arm from him? Only to later throw him away like a used rag?"

Sawyer groaned, clearly irritated with this conversation. "I couldn't mind control Bas. It was annoying. Every once and a while, a human comes along who has a mind too strong to control. There's no point having a human around who isn't willing to throw themselves in front of a bullet to protect you."

Thursday raised her eyebrows with amusement. "A human bettered you?"

"A human did not better me," Sawyer said indignantly. "A human was simply a nuisance and honestly the planet is better off without him."

"Don't you feel the slightest bit guilty for taking so many lives? Does it not prey on your conscience at all?" Titus asked.

Sawyer shrugged. "Death is a natural part of human life. So, what if I quickened the process for some of them? They're all heading in that direction anyway." He pointed over to Thursday. "Thursday understands."

"Don't throw me in with you, we're completely different," Thursday answered. "I must be given a reason to hurt a human, you just mow through whoever gets in your way. It's why you killed all those people at the bar. It's rather ironic since you depend so heavily on humans to do your bidding. Where would you be without Dr. Weeks, Sawyer? Would you have somewhere to experiment on humans? What about those United Arms soldiers she let you control? What about Bram? Or even better, Mackenzie? We wouldn't even be here if it hadn't been for Mackenzie! Admit it, you desperately need humans because you aren't strong enough to do the dirty work yourself!"

Sawyer's dark, beady eyes were unreadable. Thursday knew she had struck a nerve. Sawyer's prejudices against the humans of Castlebrooke were ancient and deep-rooted. The insinuation that he depended on them did not go down well with him. Thursday didn't care. It was what he needed to hear. She was sick of listening to his tired 'humans are impure' spiel when everyone in his service was, in fact, a human.

"I make them better," Sawyer eventually said.

"But deep in their genetics, they're still human," Thursday responded. "No amount of shock therapy; scalpels and stitches are going to change that. You can't change a human any more than you can change one of us."

Sawyer's lip curled with distaste. Finally, his joyous attitude was beginning to fall away.

He snatched one of the rings off the velvet pillow and marched over to Thursday with a determined look on his face. She braced herself for a fight, winding her chain around her wrist in preparation, but he simply grabbed her left hand.

She knew what he wanted to do.

The ring Sawyer had prepared for her was intricate, the band made up of pure golden strands winding together like vines. Then, embedded at the top, was a jewel the same shade of purple as Thursday's Glow. It was a gorgeous, well-made piece of jewellery, but even from where she stood Thursday could see the holes where the rods were going to shoot out to embed in her flesh.

Malice hidden beneath beauty.

"Don't do it!" Titus shouted.

"Sawyer, those rings won't change anything!" Sybil tried to reason.

"The second you hurt her, Sawyer, I'm warning you...!" Matthew threatened.

Thursday smiled bitterly at Sawyer. "Aren't you supposed to have vows prepared?" she asked.

Sawyer looked at her, a confused glint in his eyes. He couldn't tell if she was being serious or not. Amongst the confusion, Thursday saw a glimmer of hope. Like he really believed that maybe she believed in his cause as well. That their craziness had finally clicked together and there was a possibility that they could join forces and enlist the others to their side.

Pathetic.

Thursday used the moment of pause to act. She threw the chain around Sawyer's neck and pulled as hard as she could.

Sawyer's hands flew to grab the chains, dropping the ring in the process. It chinked against the stone floor and rolled away beneath the chairs. He began to make loud noises that vibrated off the cavernous walls of the tiny room, like a chorus of choking frogs. He wanted to be heard.

"Sybil put yourself between Finn and the door!" she barked.

Sybil did so just in time. The doors to the Church exploded open and five United Arms men came charging in. She easily disarmed them with a wave of her hand and threw them flying back out the front door, which she then slammed shut and locked.

Thursday was pulling the chains with all her strength. She could feel Sawyer weakening against her and she grinned maliciously. She could do it. She could end him right now and they would be free of his filth forever-

The hand thrust itself into her chest again. Thursday yelled in agony, forced to let go of the chain due to the intensity of the pain. As soon as the chain fell from Sawyer's neck, the hand drew away and disappeared once again. The Seven weren't supposed to kill one of their own.

Sawyer fell to the ground, gasping for breath and rubbing the marks on his neck. Thursday glowered at him, her chest heaving with emotion. She kicked him over onto the ground with a satisfying grunt.

Whitney had started melting everyone's chains. She started with herself and then worked her way up the row. The first thing Thursday did once freed was run to the top of the altar and kick the pillow that housed the rings. The jewellery went flying in all directions across the Church, one ironically soaring at Sawyer and pinging right off his head.

"Do you have anything to say for yourself?" Sybil asked the man lying on the ground.

"You haven't won, you know," Sawyer answered, rolling onto his front, and sitting up on his knees. His suit was now dusty from the ground, the pristine black now covered in large patches of white.

"Neither have you, that's good enough for me," Sybil answered.

"I have plenty more men who will break that door down in due course."

"We'll be long gone by then," Titus assured.

Matthew was examining Finn's hand, clearly trying to figure out a way to remove Sawyer's ring. Thursday went over and had a look too. The rods attached to the interior of the ring seemed to have embedded themselves through the flesh and most likely attached themselves to the bone of Finn's finger. These rings were not designed to come off easily.

"Don't bother," Sawyer said, quirking an eyebrow at them and smirking. "It's not going to come off. Not without cutting your finger off first, anyway."

Finn sighed. The sound was weighted down with exhaustion. Judging by the black bags beneath his eyes, he had not slept since he had been taken prisoner by Sawyer. To be fair, one of them was also deeply bruised from Sawyer's assault so that could also be a factor.

"Looks like I'm amputating my finger, then," Finn muttered. He held his hand out and looked at the red ring like it was going to bite him. Harder than it already had.

Thursday grinned and patted his back. "Don't worry. We'll drug you up good and hard before we do it."

"Come on, we need to find a way out before more of Sawyer's men return," Sybil said.

"Come, you worthless excuse of a man," Whitney growled, hauling Sawyer to his feet. "You're coming with us. No more laboratories or experiments for you."

Sawyer smirked at Whitney as she threw him into a chair. "What are you going to do with me, then?" he asked, deeply interested in what their answer would be.

"Probably lock you up somewhere," Sybil said. "Not somewhere official, you'd just manipulate your way out. No, I think we should keep you somewhere where we can keep an eye on you."

Thursday's eyebrows bowed downwards as she tried to imagine such a place. "Where would that be?" she asked.

Sybil shrugged with one arm, brushing her hair back from her face as she answered, "Well if you're all willing, we could find a place of our own and live together again. Keep the maniac locked in the basement where we all know to keep watch."

"Just like old times," Sawyer said sarcastically.

Sybil slapped him for speaking. She turned to the others. "What do you think?"

"I'm up for it," Matthew said, being the first to offer his thoughts on the idea and causing Sybil to smile. "I always have been up for it."

"Me too," Whitney agreed. "I mean, I never really thought about it until we were all together again." She pulled a face. "I did miss you losers."

Titus rubbed the back of his neck sheepishly and nodded. "Yeah, I can't say I don't feel the same," he said, smiling as well.

Finn laughed breathily and shook his head. "I can't believe I'm saying this but, yeah, me too. I want to do this." As he spoke, his arm came out and wound around Matthew's shoulders. Matthew was so happy it looked like he could sprout wings and soar straight through the roof.

All eyes turned to Thursday.

Thursday didn't know what to do with such a suggestion. She was completely at a loss for words again. She hadn't been miserable during the decade the Seven had been separated, nor had she ever taken the time to mourn the loss of the times they had had together. However, it did always feel like something had been missing all those years. Not getting to laugh about stupid stuff with Matthew; not getting to argue with Whitney and Titus; not getting to tease Finn and not getting to question Sybil's authority regularly... It had all added up. There were times when she had been tempted to find them again, but she had always dismissed it because then it would seem like she missed them. Thursday had a reputation to uphold. She did not *miss* people.

Thursday grinned uncontrollably. "Think you can get rid of me that easily?" she chuckled. "No, I'm like a bad rash. I disappear for a bit, but I always come back."

Sybil exhaled with relief. Sawyer didn't look too amused by their decision, but he seemed to have decided not to voice his disappointment. "That's settled then! First things first, we got to find a way out."

Finn broke away from Matthew and jumped onto the altar. "I think there's a door back h"-

Thursday didn't even see it. It came so fast that it was practically invisible. It cut through the air like a knife, the only indication of its journey being a high-pitched '*whizz*!' She didn't absorb any of this. The only thing she saw was it reaching its destination.

The bullet embedded itself into the back of Finn's head so fast that nobody could have stopped it.

Thursday threw herself at Finn as he fell, like if she somehow stopped him from hitting the floor then she would be able to save him. It was too late. She knew as soon as her arms wound around his body, and it dragged her down to the floor. Her ears were ringing, and she could hear muffled screaming in the background. All she could see was Finn's head, weeping blood onto the stone floor of the Church.

Someone pushed her away. She fell backwards, hitting her head on the altar in the process. She stared with wide eyes at Matthew as he turned the body around as if Finn was only sleeping and all they had to do was wake him up. No. Finn's eyes were locked open. The brilliant blue that had always been determined to heal and repair, to learn and learn and learn some more, completely emotionless.

Dead.

Thursday couldn't breathe. She looked around desperately for some way to solve this. It couldn't be right. This was a mistake. As she sat against the altar watching Matthew scream and clutch the body, she felt something tearing away inside her. Then, very suddenly, it felt like someone had ripped an entire chunk out of her being. Thursday covered her mouth with her hand. She still couldn't hear, Matthew's heartbroken screams still muffled in her disbelieving ears. She felt empty inside. A part of her had left; was gone; not coming back.

They'd...lost him.

Finn was dead.

Thursday rose off the altar. Sybil was sobbing, and Titus was screaming at Sawyer, obviously thinking that the man had made some sort of secret order when they weren't focused on him. Whitney was on the floor of the Church, ice clawing its way up her arms and neck as she cried into the stone floor. Even Sawyer looked horrified, his dark eyes wide and disbelieving as his face twisted in anger.

All the voices were nothing but mournful murmurs through her ears. All Thursday could hear was the angered thump of her dejected heart pounding in her chest. Tears were soaking her face, sliding down her cheeks and covering her clothes.

Thursday looked up at the balcony above the door. Standing there, gun in hand, was Dr. Weeks. The woman was panting, like she had run there upon hearing that they'd captured Sawyer. Their eyes met, and Weeks lowered her arm.

With a scream of anguish, Thursday threw her hands down towards the ground, her Glow exploding and thrusting her up into the air. She soared across the top of the Church and landed on the balcony in seconds.

Dr. Weeks raised her gun. Thursday kicked it out of her hands. She tried to run but Thursday grabbed her and, without mercy, threw her off the balcony. Thursday did not hear the impact of the woman's body hitting the floor. She slid down onto the floor of the balcony and covered her already damaged ears like she could blot this entire world out and return to the one they had described moments before Finn was shot.

There was an explosion beneath her. Thursday knew more of Sawyer's men had poured in. She didn't need to look to know they'd be captured again. Emotion had always fared well in their favour when it came to controlling their abilities, but not this kind of emotion. Not when one of their own had just been shot in cold blood *mid-sentence*. Thursday bit her knuckle and squeezed her eyes shut, causing more tears to spurt out of her eyes.

Finn hadn't even seen it coming.

Thursday didn't want to think about them dragging Sybil away in floods of tears; of them detaching Whitney from the floor as her ice melded her to the stone; of them hauling Titus, kicking and screaming, away from Sawyer and out the doors. Most of all, Thursday did not want to think about them forcing Matthew to let go of Finn's body and pulling him away, where he would most likely never see him again.

It didn't take them long to find Thursday. The doors to the balcony exploded open, men pouring into the tiny space just to apprehend her. She didn't protest as they grabbed her. She felt too numb for that.

So, this was what it truly felt like to lose one of their own. First, there was misery. Then anger. Then…numbness.

A cloth was pressed against Thursday's mouth, and she submitted to the darkness it offered her.

It was all over.

EPILOGUE

Thursday paced her padded cell, unable to stay still. The only source of light was coming from the small, barred window at the top of her door. It could have been days; weeks; minutes; seconds, she didn't know how long it had been since she had regained consciousness in the room. She recognized it well: It was her old cell in United Arms. Sawyer clearly thought it was a novelty to put her back there. As much as she joked about returning to her cell in the past, now it sickened her. Everything sickened her. A large part of her humour left the minute Dr. Weeks shot Finn.

She missed her family. She didn't care about admitting it now. She had grown so used to their company and now they weren't there anymore. She didn't even know if they were okay. She didn't know anything. She didn't know who was hurt or who wasn't. All she knew was what she felt and what she felt had not been good. Not at all.

The air was so thick, she could barely breathe. She was used to getting out of the cell regularly for questioning. She was beginning to feel claustrophobic. She wanted to scream and tear out her hair.

Thursday couldn't stop shivering in the cold cell. She felt like she was going to pass out from fatigue at any moment, her desperation for answers being the only thing that was keeping her upright.

Eventually, she had to sit down, her legs no longer able to hold her up. The floor was grubby, and she winced as she sat down. She felt like she was stewing in her filth, just waiting for someone to come along and tell her that it was her turn. She knew it was coming. She was number four, after all. It was only a matter of time, now.

Thursday was aching everywhere, and she just wanted to fall asleep. She drowsily lifted her damaged hand and held it up against the light piercing through the bars. It trembled violently, and it took a great amount of effort to keep the blackened appendage uplifted.

The purple jewel on top of her ring winked at her, like the piece of jewellery was taunting her.

Thursday decided to close her eyes, only for a couple of minutes. A couple of minutes wouldn't do her any harm …

~T~

She was asleep for a couple of hours before someone woke her up.

Someone was stroking her head gently and, in her sleepy haze, she thought it had to be one of her family. It was only a minute later that everything came rushing back to her. She forced her eyes open again with a confused frown.

Her heart dropped into her stomach.

Sawyer was sitting in front of her, flanked by a group of armed men. He was smiling proudly at her, the birthmark in his eye standing out more malevolently than usual. He reached out and brushed his hand down her face, a golden glow exuding from his fingers as he healed a self-inflicted wound across her face.

Thursday stared at him, refusing to speak or express her disgust. So, he managed to take Finn's power despite his death. Thursday wanted to be sick. Sawyer sighed and leaned back on his heels.

"It's your turn," he told her.

Thursday squeezed her eyes shut and shuddered.

It was Sunday.

About the Author

Erin Curran is an unapologetically queer, neurodivergent writer from Northern Ireland. Having fostered a passion for creative writing at a young age, Erin is rarely seen without two things: a cup of tea and a pen. She won the English Millennium Cup in High School and went on to have her now self-published novel, The Seven, longlisted for a GALA award in 2020. Her goal as an author is to contribute to normalising LGBTQIA+ characters and stories, bringing them into the mainstream where they belong. When not writing, Erin is either reading; drawing; video editing or listening to Queen. Not necessarily in that order.

Printed in Great Britain
by Amazon

53227298R00225